PIECES OF BLUE

Also by Holly Goldberg Sloan

The Elephant in the Room

To Night Owl from Dogfish

Short

Counting by 7s

Appleblossom the Possum

Just Call My Name

I'll Be There

PIECES
of Blue

HOLLY GOLDBERG SLOAN

FLATIRON
BOOKS
NEW YORK

PIECES OF BLUE. Copyright © 2023 by Holly Goldberg Sloan. All rights reserved. Printed in the United States of America. For information, address Flatiron Books, 120 Broadway, New York, NY 10271.

www.flatironbooks.com

Designed by Donna Sinisgalli Noetzel

The Library of Congress Cataloging-in-Publication Data

Names: Sloan, Holly Goldberg, 1958– author.
Title: Pieces of blue / Holly Goldberg Sloan.
Description: First edition. | New York : Flatiron Books, 2023.
Identifiers: LCCN 2022048748 | ISBN 9781250847300 (hardcover) | ISBN 9781250847324 (ebook)
Subjects: LCGFT: Domestic fiction. | Novels.
Classification: LCC PS3619.L6273 P54 2023 | DDC 813/.6—dc23/eng/20221209
LC record available at https://lccn.loc.gov/2022048748

Our books may be purchased in bulk for promotional, educational, or business use. Please contact your local bookseller or the Macmillan Corporate and Premium Sales Department at 1-800-221-7945, extension 5442, or by email at MacmillanSpecialMarkets@macmillan.com.

First Edition: 2023

10 9 8 7 6 5 4 3 2 1

To my girls,

Samy Hemond Sloan and

Ali Hoffman Sloan

PIECES OF BLUE

1

The family stepped through the double-glass doors into the open-air concourse of the Daniel K. Inouye International Airport, and the clouds overhead exploded with rain. The dripping palm fronds bobbed in the humid breeze as the foursome walked under the portico to the baggage collection area. Lindsey put her arm around Sena, her younger daughter. The little girl's expression was tense, and the look on Lindsey's face was equally strained. Lindsey took in a deep breath, telling her kids, "It's raining, just like at home."

Olivia, the oldest, corrected her mother. "Hawai'i is home now."

At the baggage carousel, friends and family carrying colorful leis greeted the arriving passengers. Soon more than half of the people on their flight had wreaths of flowers hanging around their necks. Lindsey impulsively reached for her wallet. "Come on, kids!" She headed toward an older man in a brightly printed shirt seated on a three-legged stool. Behind him was a glass-doored refrigerator filled with garlands of plumeria, tuberose, carnations, orchids, and maile leaves.

Lindsey could hear the suitcases starting down the chute as she lifted her phone and took her first photo in Hawai'i. Her children, draped in their newly purchased wreaths of expensive, fuchsia-colored orchids, were all smiling. She hadn't seen that in a long time. Then Sena's smile dissolved. "Mama, you don't have a flower necklace."

"I don't need one, sweetheart."

Sena lifted her lei over her head. "Here, we can take turns."

Carlos seemed eager to get rid of his orchids. "No. Really. Have mine."

Sena stepped back. "Don't fight."

Olivia answered as if taking a bite out of her sister. "Who's fighting?"

And suddenly the spell was broken. Fatigue, disappointment, and heartbreak were back.

Lindsey started toward the baggage carousel, angry at herself for spending nearly one hundred dollars on the flowery strings. It felt like a real tourist move. They were going to be living here now.

She turned around, hoping to reset, only to see the kids were gone. For the briefest moment her adrenaline surged, then she spun in the other direction and discovered her children talking to the flower salesman. They appeared to be cutting some kind of deal. In seconds her daughters and son were back at her side, their expensive orchid leis gone. Around the kids' necks were bright blue carnations. A fourth string of the dyed flowers was in Sena's outstretched hands.

"We traded, Mama. So you got one, too."

Lindsey kissed the top of Sena's head and slipped the electric blue lei around her neck, always startled at how easy it was as a parent to go from fiery frustration to affection. She worked hard to keep it together as she mumbled, "Thank you, sweetheart," and then pulled her kids together in a hug so tight that Olivia yelped.

"Mom, you're hurting my ear."

Their bags dribbled out as if they had been separated in the cargo hold to cause maximum irritation. Olivia's suitcase was the very last one to hit the carousel. In the twenty-six months since their family tragedy, they had whittled down their possessions until each had only a carry-on, a backpack, and a Costco Kirkland Traveler's Choice, a thirty-inch piece of luggage with spinner wheels. Starting over, Lindsey kept repeating, meant making hard choices and leaving the material past behind.

Carlos took charge of commandeering a cart for the luggage. Sena insisted on still pulling her carry-on. It wasn't until they were in the small bus heading to the cheapest car rental agency available online—the one two miles from the airport's central ring—that Lindsey realized her youngest child had been quiet for thirty minutes. Sena alternated from being the most talkative of the three kids to the mute observer, and both states came with red flags. But at least Olivia, fourteen going on twenty-four, looked steady as she scrolled through pictures on her phone. The girls, separated in age by seven years, were so different.

Lindsey could gaze at each of her children and see something of herself, but only if she did so with a penetrating stare. Teenage Olivia had a long neck and an oval face that might appear severe but at the right angle could be as classic as a Renaissance marble sculpture. She had straight brown hair and muddy eyes that in low light seemed flecked with gold. Seven-year-old Sena had a round face and a head of curls inherited from her father's side of the equation. Carlos, only two years younger than Olivia, completed the exercise in the variable nature of genetics. He had copper-colored hair, blue eyes, and skin so pale his medical chart read "ultra-Caucasian." He reacted so badly to the sun that the pediatrician had warned moving from the Pacific Northwest to Hawai'i was a health risk. But by then Lindsey's decision had been made.

The E-Z Car Rental Agency didn't live up to its name. The office was a narrow trailer on cinder blocks, and there was no parking lot filled with shiny waiting cars. This place had a cramped driveway with several beat-up vehicles wedged into a short alley. A hose dripped into a black puddle of sludge, and the smell of diesel fuel hung in the air. After electronically signing what felt like a mortgage application, Lindsey and the kids were finally directed outside to a white four-door Ford Crown Victoria. The sedan didn't look like any rental car she'd ever seen and had to be at least ten years old. Lucy, the smiling woman with the clipboard who appeared to be E-Z's only employee, explained that Lindsey's reservation promised no specific vehicle.

Carlos elbowed his big sister. "I think it used to be a police car."

Olivia shook her head. "No way."

Carlos held his ground. "Well, it looks just like a police car. You know they sell them when they're done."

Lucy then asked a question Lindsey got all the time. "Are these all your kids?"

Lindsey was from Wales. Strangers often assumed that because of her accent, and how different her children all looked, Lindsey was a nanny.

"Yes. They're mine." She flashed a weak smile and wished she weren't so tired. A good mother would have sounded more enthusiastic.

She took the keys after being informed by the cheerful but increasingly firm Lucy that the Crown Victoria was the only available car on the lot. Lindsey felt certain the Ford would get terrible mileage and drive like a tank, but it was only temporary, so she and the kids dumped everything in, grateful that it had a big trunk. Lindsey settled behind the wheel, her phone in one hand and a printout of a map with directions in the other as a backup. "We've got about an hour-and-a-half drive. Honolulu is a major city. It's a big place. We're moving to a remote location."

Olivia shot her a withering look. "You've told us that maybe one hundred times. Plus, we have Google Maps open on our phones."

"Except me," Sena piped up. "I don't have a phone."

Lindsey didn't respond. But Olivia did. "You're seven. No seven-year-old has a phone."

"Wrong, Olivia. Lots of *six*-year-olds have phones. At least at Ross-Stanton."

The name of their former private school hung in the air, a reminder of all the changes in their lives.

Carlos, ever the diplomat, called out, "Mom, can we just go? It's hot in here."

Lindsey pressed down hard on the gas. Too hard. The Crown Victoria lurched forward, and before Lindsey could turn the steering wheel the car slammed into a row of garbage cans lined up like bowling pins against a cement wall. The left side of the front bumper and the hood sustained significant damage.

Back in the E-Z office, there were new forms to be filled out. Lucy was icy as she intoned, "*This* is why I said it was a good idea to take the extra insurance." Olivia slumped down into one of the blue plastic chairs by the door, and Carlos took a seat at her side. Only Sena stayed at the counter with Lindsey as Lucy organized the accident paperwork.

The little girl whispered to her mother, "You break it, you buy it. Remember that sign in the antique market in Lake Oswego?" Lindsey nodded. She had no idea where this conversation was going. Sena leaned closer. "Maybe the best thing would be to just buy the car."

Lindsey hoped she sounded patient. "Honey, why don't you go wait with your brother and sister?"

Sena didn't move. "We have to buy a car at some point. Maybe they could sell us this one since you smashed it. Plus, our bags are already in the trunk."

Lucy looked up from her computer screen. "You're not just visiting?"

Lindsey shook her head. "We're moving here. From Oregon. It's a long story."

"You aren't British tourists?"

"I'm Welsh, actually. Originally. I'm a US citizen now. We're going to be residents of Hawai'i. I bought property near Lā'ie."

Lindsey was unaware that she pronounced the town wrong, but Lucy's formality instantly disappeared. "So, you're going to live in the country. Your kid's right. You should buy a car. Rentals are for tourists. Way too expensive."

The Crown Victoria got eleven miles to the gallon and had dings on all four doors as well as sizable creases in both the front and rear bumpers, not including the new damage Lindsey had just done. Yet it still felt like they won a prize when the powers that be at E-Z (Lucy's aunt Coco, who lived in Makakilo) agreed to the sale. In the time it took to complete the purchase paperwork, the sky had cleared and there wasn't a single cloud overhead when they finally drove away from the rental agency. The Crown Vicky, as Carlos called the sedan, belonged to them.

Lindsey wished she could put blinders on her three kids as they stared wide-eyed out the car's open windows when they merged onto the H-1.

"I didn't know there would be so many tall buildings," Carlos said. "And these kinds of wide freeways."

"There won't be where we're living," Lindsey replied. She didn't admit she was equally surprised by what she could see. The enormous, sprawling metropolis of Honolulu was built on a wide, deep-water bay with the volcanic tuff cone known as Diamond Head on the eastern edge. Early British explorers had believed that the crystals found there were diamonds, and the name they gave the place stuck. The largest city in Hawai'i was anchored by this half-a-million-year-old land mass, which at all angles presented itself as a wonder. Nearly one thousand hotels, from the highest-end resorts to residential motels, crowded together, angling for a glimpse of the bay's famous beaches. Forty thousand tourists from around the world descended on the place each day. But Lindsey had no intention of starting her family's next chapter in the big city. The highrises, shopping plazas, and mostly man-made beaches weren't why they had moved to this island.

It was late afternoon and traffic was heavy as they headed inland, leaving the buzzing city behind. Soon they passed Wheeler Army Airfield. All the windows on the Crown Victoria were down and the warm wind whipped their hair and riffled their T-shirts. Sena shrieked at a man on a motorcycle driving in the adjacent lane, "This is our new car!"

Olivia, usually too old to join anything that she didn't start, yelled, "We own our own motel!"

Lindsey, laughing hard, shouted, "We have no idea what we're doing!"

The motorcycle driver gave them a thumbs-up, and as he sped off, they all cheered.

Further north, the businesses and houses of Wahiawā disappeared and were replaced by green fields and a wide stretch of land with asparagus and papaya groves. On acres of red soil that once grew sugar cane, coffee plants hugged the ground. There were rolling hills of farmland wondrously framed by the sharp angles of the volcanic Koʻolau Mountains on the right and the arresting emerald-green Waiʻanae Range on the left. Nothing felt further from Portland, Oregon.

The Crown Victoria chugged along, guzzling gas, until they reached the crest of the highway that cut across the island. Revealed below was the bluest-blue Pacific Ocean, off the North Shore of Oʻahu, spread out in breathtaking splendor. The sight made them all giddy. The angle of the afternoon sun caused large portions of the endless indigo expanse to shimmer as if millions of jewels were floating on the surface. There were no skyscrapers below, no cruise ships, nothing but verdant land meeting the deep blue sea.

Olivia's mouth dropped open. "That's *our* ocean?"

"And it's not cold, right, Mom?" asked Sena. "It's warm like a bath?"

Lindsey worked to keep her eyes on the road. The sight of the water was hypnotic. She managed, "Yes, sweetheart, it's warm. All year long. And it's our ocean."

Carlos murmured, "Dad would've loved it."

The mention of their father could darken any conversation. Lindsey needed to keep the mood positive. "Dad and I were here together before any of you were born. And we were so happy."

Of course, they had heard this fact many times, but Lindsey's proclamation sounded suddenly very important. She looked up into the rearview mirror to see Sena reach over and take Carlos's hand.

Under other circumstances she knew her son would have freed himself from his little sister's grasp, but today he held her small fingers as they all did their best to believe that part of Paul Hill, husband, father, protector, provider, dreamer, coder, surfer, and dead man, was on this ride beside them.

2

They drove along Kamehameha Highway almost an hour past the small town of Hale'iwa, no longer on the North Shore but in the Ko'olauloa District. There were times when the ocean was visible, but more often it was obscured by a curtain of green landscape, overgrown and wild. Lindsey, staring at her phone screen's approaching blue dot, slowed down. Carlos shouted, "There it is!"

An old wooden sign on the right side of the two-lane road read: MAU LOA MOTEL. An arrow pointed left toward the dense thicket of tropical trees and plants, which stood between the blacktop and the unseen water. Lindsey put on the brakes. They were only going thirty miles an hour, but the Crown Victoria's tires squealed, sending puffs of burnt rubber into the air. Everything about the car was dramatic. They all held their breath as Lindsey swung left and headed down a single lane. It wasn't paved; there were cement runners designed to be the width of a car axle. The tires, in theory, were supposed to stay on the two parallel paths, but Lindsey hit the entrance at an angle, sending gravel flying into the air as the tangle of greenery scratched against the wide Ford.

Sena scrunched up her nose. "This is sort of creepy."

Lindsey kept her foot evenly on the gas. "We just need to have the plants cut back."

Bougainvillea threaded through massive leafy trees. Coral creeper vines wrapped around ferns. Tropical flowers popped against the choking vegetation. Olivia rolled up her window after a branch

whipped inside and slapped her across the cheek. "Well, it's dangerous. And what do we do if we meet up with another car?"

Lindsey had no idea. She went off the cement treads again as
she steered the Crown Victoria around a wide curve, and the jungle
suddenly gave way to a manicured area where dozens of palm trees
bent in gravity-defying arcs. Parked under them was a rusty, once-
turquoise 1940 Chevrolet panel truck without tires. Leaning against
the decaying vehicle was a sign that read:

PRIVATE ROAD

IF YOU AREN'T SUPPOSED

TO BE HERE

DON'T BE HERE!

KAPU!

Sena looked at her mother with alarm. "That's the motto of our
new motel?"

Lindsey continued steering around the wide bend. "We're supposed to be here, so it's okay."

Carlos asked, "What's *kapu* mean?"

No one knew. Suddenly the ocean reappeared, an enormous
plain of green-blue. In the foreground was a grassy area with
eight plantation-style wooden cottages all built off the ground
on uprights. Each one of the small structures was tilting. It was
impossible to tell what color they had been originally, but they
were now a washed-out gray-green with flakes of honey-colored
window trim.

To one side of the eight cottages was a two-story structure, also in
the plantation style, with a wraparound veranda. Painted above the
front door in large, faded red letters was the word OFFICE. A mud-
splattered pickup truck was parked close by. Next to it was a battered
motorcycle. A dozen chickens, with a single rooster at their side,
darted from underneath one of the cottages onto the lawn, where they
pecked at grass blades, seemingly oblivious to the one-eyed brindle cat
crouched under the canopy of an African tulip tree, ready to spring.

The place was beautiful, fragile, and lost in time. This was the Mau Loa Motel.

Lindsey put on the brakes and slowed to a stop.

No one moved inside the Crown Victoria.

Sena saw only the chickens and imagined making the feathered creatures her best friends. Carlos saw only the waves launching toward the shoreline in perfect sets and imagined becoming a lifeguard. Olivia saw only a tall, lanky teenage boy coming out of the office and slumping down into a wicker rocking chair on the veranda and imagined having her first real boyfriend. And Lindsey saw only eight rundown cottages surrounded by an overgrown jungle and imagined working eighteen-hour days for the rest of her life.

The Crown Victoria edged off the cement runners onto a parking area made of gray pumice that crunched under the car tires like potato chips. Lindsey cut the engine and hoped she sounded upbeat. "Well, this is it!"

Carlos kept his eyes on the ocean. "Can we go swimming?"

Olivia took charge. "Of course not. We've got to meet the Kalama family." She was still staring at the teenage boy on the office porch. Carlos didn't put up a fight, but no one moved to get out of the Crown Victoria, which was starting to feel like a safe haven.

Sena piped up. "Are those our chickens? Or do they go with the Kalamas?"

"I'm not sure," Lindsey answered.

Rangi Kalama, eighty-four years old but with the gait of a man ten years younger, emerged from the office and headed toward them, shouting, "I heard you bought yourselves a car."

They spilled out of the dented Ford, and Rangi bowed his head in a formal greeting. "Welcome. We've been waiting for you."

The screen door slapped shut as Pearl Kalama appeared. She was also in her eighties, rounder than her husband, with white hair that trailed in a thick braid down her back. Lindsey could see that she walked with a pronounced limp.

Pearl called out, "You're finally here!"

The teenage boy on the veranda got up with a sour look and walked behind the building. He emerged with a fat-tire bike and a backpack. Olivia kept her eyes on him. The boy barely looked in her direction before slinging the backpack over his shoulder and pedaling off, disappearing down a path that appeared to run parallel to the driveway. Pearl Kalama started to call after him, but changed her mind and redirected her attention to Lindsey and the kids, making a clicking sound with her tongue. "Three children. Like you said. Good ages." She added, "We thought you'd be here earlier."

Lindsey tried not to sound defensive. "Buying the car took some time."

Sena turned to Rangi. "It's not a police car."

Rangi smiled. "You have on leis. Very good. We have more for you. My wife made them."

The Kalamas escorted Lindsey and the kids across the gravel to the grass. Pearl's right index finger sliced the air as she spoke. "Rangi and I have lived here for almost sixty years. Can you believe it? But that's over. This is yours now. We moved out all our stuff last week. We've been sleeping at my sister's."

Lindsey was struck by Pearl's emotionless tone. It was impossible to tell if she was happy or sad to be leaving.

Rangi started up the porch steps. "Anyone need to go *shishi*?"

Pearl said, "He means use the bathroom."

They all did. But they shook their heads.

Rangi headed into the office with Pearl at his heels. Lindsey and the kids followed up the uneven wooden steps and through the screen door into what was both the Mau Loa reception area and the Kalamas' home. It had been so bright outside that their eyes took a moment to adjust. Lindsey saw that aged fishing nets had been attached to the ceiling, holding shells, driftwood, old Japanese green glass buoys, and other dried-up "treasures" from the sea. Tiny Christmas lights were threaded through the webbing, and the whole effect was simultaneously amazing and unsettling, at least to Lindsey. Olivia and Carlos gazed up in wonder, but it was Sena who pointed to the ceiling and asked what Lindsey had been thinking. "How do you clean that stuff?"

Rangi Kalama opened his mouth to answer, but Pearl beat him to it. "You don't." She put her hand down on a large desk as if she were touching a beloved pet. It was made of dark mahogany, its legs shaped like swirling fish with dull inlaid jade eyes.

Pearl exhaled. "We're leaving this. It came over originally with my parents. We think they framed the place around the furniture because it's bigger than the door. We would have had to cut open the wall to get it out."

Rangi added, "Which is why we didn't take it."

There was a flash of sadness on Pearl's face. Lindsey wasn't sure what to say, so she settled on a simple, "Thank you. We'll take good care of the desk."

Sena stepped forward. "What about the chickens? Do they stay?"

Rangi looked amused. "Oh, they come with the property. So do a pair of owls. We see them mostly just after sunset. There are many owls up at Ka'ena Point. You'll need to go check them out. *Pueo.* They're hard workers. Owls keep down the rodents."

Pearl leaned close to Sena. "Pueo is our *'aumākua.*"

Sena nodded but looked confused. The old man turned away from the unmovable desk to head up the stairs. They all followed.

"We left you with the basics. The three bedrooms have fresh sheets and towels. We put two beds in one room for the girls." The kids peered into open doorways. They were all small spaces, but every window had a postcard view. Wallpaper, once possibly gold, now the color of dried Dijon mustard, held the barest outlines of cherry trees. At some point varnish had been applied, and the sealer was mottled with age, giving the surface a three-dimensional quality.

They only had time for a quick glimpse before they were back on the tour, descending to the kitchen, where Pearl opened an old, avocado-colored refrigerator and removed four leis wrapped in moist paper towels. The garlands were nothing like the ones in the Honolulu airport salesman's cooler. These were made of fresh plumeria. Knotted blue string held the flowers together. Pearl slipped a lei around each of their necks, murmuring something they couldn't understand as she buzzed both sides of their cheeks. They all said thank you, but it was Sena who turned her face upward and, standing on tiptoe, gave the old woman a kiss. Lindsey and the other two kids exchanged a look. Sena was always the slowest to warm up to anyone.

Next, they got a quick view of what Rangi called the "utility room." It was just off the kitchen and the size of a bedroom, but inside were three dryers and three other machines that were unrecognizable. "What do these do?" Carlos asked.

"Those are washing machines," Pearl answered.

Lindsey stepped closer. They didn't look like any washing machines she'd ever seen before.

"Run on gas. Same with the dryers. If you lose power, you can still do the laundry," Rangi added brightly.

Lindsey nodded, but she didn't feel reassured. "Are they hard to service?"

"I do it myself. I'm leaving you the manuals. You can write away for replacement parts."

Carlos smiled at Rangi. "I tried to build a go-cart and it had a gas engine. Maybe I can learn how to do it."

Rangi was encouraging. "Son, I bet you can. Let's go take a look at one of the cottages."

The cottage closest to the office had a bed covered with a floral Hawaiian quilt and vintage rattan furniture that curved in the pretzel style Lindsey knew was from the 1940s. Everything was clean and well maintained, but Lindsey felt a growing sense of unease. What would she do when something broke or needed repair? How much would she need to replace? Rangi pointed to a wooden shed barely visible behind three trees covered in large white flowers all pointing down at the ground. "We left you all our tools in the shed. We've got no need for them now."

Lindsey fixated on the flowering trees, not the mostly obscured storage structure. "What kind of plants are those—with the flowers?"

"*Nānāhonua.* Angel's trumpets," Pearl answered.

"They're beautiful."

"Poisonous. All the parts, not just the flowers."

"They have a narcotic inside," added Rangi.

Lindsey tried not to seem alarmed. She knew her way around the plant world, yet she still was taken aback as Pearl added in an even tone, "Daisies are poisonous to kids. People just don't talk about it. *Nānāhonua* are so much prettier."

Rangi and Pearl grabbed sinamay fiber tote bags off the porch and headed across the lawn, a thick, dirty-green carpet that to Lindsey resembled spiky blades more than grass. The wind had picked up and was blowing strong. Was a storm coming? As though reading her mind, Pearl said, "Afternoon breeze. Like this pretty much every day. Mostly from the northeast." She pointed back toward the office. "I made a pot of chicken long rice and left it on the stove. Just heat it up. There's red punch to drink in the fridge."

Rangi opened the door to the pickup truck and grabbed a thin notebook from the front seat. "We tried to put everything we could think of about the place in here." He gave the cover a pat as if it were an old friend. "Of course, a lot of stuff is just in our heads, but if you have questions, you've got my cell number. We don't leave the island until the day after tomorrow."

Lindsey was unable to hide her surprise. "You're going on a trip?"

Rangi smiled wide and his whole face lifted. He looked suddenly a lot younger. "We're off to Nevada. Plan on being gone for at least six months."

Sena chirped, "Have a good time."

But Lindsey couldn't keep the anxiety out of her voice. "Oh. Wow. I was thinking you'd be around. I mean, to sort of walk me through things. Just in the beginning. I've never run a motel before and—"

She didn't get a chance to finish her sentence because both Pearl and Rangi were on the move. With the gravel crunching under his feet, Rangi scooped up the one-eyed cat sulking in a patch of weeds. He put the animal into a molded plastic pet carrier on the front seat of the pickup. "Aka stayed until the last minute because he's a good hunter. We took our cockatoo to Pearl's sister's last week."

"We could help with the cockatoo if you need it," Sena said eagerly. "While you're gone to Nevada."

Rangi looked as if he was trying not to laugh. "He's a great bird. Only doesn't take to strangers."

Pearl gave a single nod of agreement. "He's a biter. But thank you." She headed for the motorcycle, and Rangi got into the pickup. "Okay then," he said, leaning out the window. "We want to be on the other side of the island before it gets dark. The old gal shouldn't be on two wheels after the sun goes down."

Pearl pulled on a silver helmet and slung her good leg across the motorcycle. Rangi turned over the Toyota's ignition and the truck engine sputtered to life. After several coughs it evened out into a mechanical gurgle. Lindsey and the three kids watched as Pearl flipped down the red rocker kill switch and turned a key on the motorcycle. Did she shout "good luck" as she took off on the souped-up dirt bike? She definitely shouted something.

Rangi followed his wife, giving a final wave as the two vehicles rounded the sweeping curve and disappeared from view. A cloud of dust, lit by the low angle of the late-afternoon sun, fluttered up into the sky as the sound of the engines receded. The wind coming off the ocean quickly blew the dust away, and all signs of Rangi and Pearl Kalama were gone.

The Hill family was alone at the Mau Loa Motel.

3

The sky was inky black when Sena pushed back her mildewy-smelling sheet and slid out of bed. She moved silently to the door. Everyone else was asleep and it was still dark outside, but Sena wasn't up early to look at the scenery. She was in search of the chickens.

It didn't take long to find them. They were huddled together underneath the office. The day before, Sena had seen a rainbow inside the rooster's black plume. When he turned his body, bright green and purple appeared in the dark shimmer of his feathers.

Now, Sena watched in the shadows as the rooster flapped his wings, arched his neck, and immediately began to crow. Loud and proud, he announced the coming of the new day. In the distance, the sun turned the black sky to the slightest hint of purple. There was so much to be seen in the unseen of this place. Sena decided the rooster was magic. And so was this island. She sat down and watched as the birds began picking at the ground, eating ants and worms and beetles. The more Sena looked at the birds, the easier it became to tell them apart.

She would give them names.

She would take care of them.

One minute Carlos was on the rocks looking into the sparkling blue water, and the next thing he knew an enormous wave knocked him senseless, sucking him right into the surf. He battled to move his arms, but they remained immobilized at his side. His feet thrashed, but he continued to be pushed down to the ocean floor. Carlos opened his mouth to scream, and water rushed in, filling his lungs. Then a yellow rope appeared right at his side. He wrapped an arm around the line and felt someone pulling as he moved up through the churning water straight toward the light. He clung hard to the rescue cord, spinning without control until he rose up through the crashing waves and broke the surface. His head craned back and he gulped for air, shouting, "I made it!" His eyes opened to see the dimly lit room and a tangled bedsheet wrapped around his right arm. Close by, a rooster was crowing.

For more than two years Carlos had been dreaming about drowning, and for the first time someone had finally saved him. It felt like a big deal. Things were turning around because his second fear, after being swallowed whole by the ocean, had been the very real possibility that his mother would move his family to Wales. It was cold and it rained all day there, and if they were just going to be sad in a wet place, they could have stayed in Oregon. They had been to the UK to visit his gran when his father was still alive. There was no grandpa because his mom had lost her dad when she was really little. Younger than Sena. The grandpa that Carlos never met had been in a car accident, and his mom said it was hard to remember him because there weren't that many pictures and also no one back then had a phone that could make videos. Carlos wanted to know more about the guy; he'd worked for a dairy, which was why the people he met there called his grandfather, with a lot of affection, Dave the Milk. His gran's little house was in the middle of nowhere and she didn't have video games or good cell service. She was a nice person, but she smelled like a basement and one of her eyes was always oozing. She wasn't crying; she just had a runny eye, like some little kids have a runny nose all the time. Gran couldn't help it, but that eye really bugged Carlos.

Maybe his mom had left Wales because she was worried she'd get a runny eye. Her explanation was that she had just "wanted more" out of life. By moving to America, she definitely got more; they all did.

For a while his family really had a lot of everything. Then they lost it. Now, after so much waiting, his father's life insurance money had come through. Carlos had already decided that he was going to get a big insurance policy when he grew up, just like his dad had done. Because insurance was what had changed their lives for the better after everything went bad. He was really glad his mom had bought a motel, even if it was sort of falling apart. He used to love staying in hotels, and now they were doing that permanently, because they owned one. Carlos sat up and listened to the waves. The last place they'd lived was in an apartment in Portland so close to the freeway that he had tried to convince himself the roar of the traffic was an ocean. Then after a while he didn't hear the sound anymore. He wondered if that would happen here. Would the waves grow silent?

He hoped not.

He was going to make a point of listening.

Olivia had discovered from Pearl that the boy on the porch was named Koa. He sometimes did work at the motel. Koa had always believed that one day his family would own the place, which was a fantasy for sure. At least that's what Pearl had said when her mom was looking in the cottage with Mr. Kalama. Things were really expensive in the islands and Pearl explained that Koa's family didn't look like they were making much money. Koa lived near Kahuku and his mother worked in a shrimp truck on Kam Highway, which was how they referred to the Kamehameha. Olivia couldn't remember what she'd said about Koa's father except that he worked for the state of Hawai'i. Koa went to Kahuku High School, where she would be going.

Olivia was very nervous about starting a new school in a new place. Just thinking about it made her feel sweaty. So many things had gone wrong in the last few years, and she was having trouble not seeing everything as a trap. But she knew she needed to stop thinking that way. What if this guy Koa was the key to her future? She'd felt a connection when she first saw him. Olivia was in bed half awake and half asleep as she imagined Koa would take her under his wing, first as a friend, and then as more. They would finish high school and after graduation go together to the University of Hawai'i, where one day they would realize they were meant for each other. They'd get married and her mom would give them the motel and he would have everything he'd always wanted.

So their lives would be perfect.

But that was probably a long shot.

Lindsey's eyes opened and focused on a tiny lime-green lizard just inches from her face. The gecko had bulging, turquoise-rimmed eyes and what looked like a splash of red hot sauce on its spine. Lindsey jerked back, and the gecko disappeared into a crack in the wall.

It had been very late when she'd finally drifted off to sleep. She had spent hours sitting at the enormous wooden desk downstairs, staring at the net-covered ceiling above, questioning every decision she'd ever made in her life. For the first time, she longed to be back in her childhood room, scrunched up under a soft quilt. The upstairs of that old Welsh house always smelled of bacon grease, chimney smoke, and mold. Back then, it had felt like a stone bunker pressing in on her from all sides. Now, she yearned to feel so protected and safe. The gaps in the wood of her new home were making it difficult for her to breathe, even though the air was warm and scented with saltwater spray and sweet plumeria. She tried to think of an inspirational quote, a line of something to clear her head. Words formed: *You must put your life into good hands—your own.*

It only made her feel worse.

Her hands didn't feel capable.

And then in a flash she hit on a different truth: This was all Paul's fault. He should be next to her doing the work of running this place. The ridiculousness of that thought rebounded. If he were still alive, she wouldn't be here. They'd be home in Portland. Couldn't the company have gone bankrupt without taking the founder down with it? Lindsey suddenly realized that she heard the waves and nothing else.

Where were the animals?

She often thought of her children this way. Maybe it was her upbringing, with all the dogs and cats and sheep. Parenting involved so much herding, and after Paul died, the kids were more compliant but less manageable, which seemed a contradiction yet was the truth. She pulled on her running shoes without taking the time to untie the laces and properly get her feet inside. Dozens of grisly possibilities crossed her mind, first and foremost being the kids had all died swimming in the ocean. Her husband had, so it didn't seem that far-fetched.

A few anxious minutes later, Lindsey found her children sitting together on the beach. They had a box of cereal from the kitchen and were sharing handfuls of soggy Cheerios. Sena had already assembled a collection of shells and feathers (mostly from the chickens). Carlos was staring off into the distance at a surf point where small bodies bobbed in the water, waiting for the right wave. Olivia was half-heartedly doing some kind of deep breathing exercise.

"Sorry, guys, I slept in."

"You never do that. You must have needed it," Olivia answered in her authoritative voice.

"Who could sleep with that rooster making so much noise?" Carlos answered.

Sena's brow furrowed. "It wasn't that loud. You'll get used to it." She held up a chicken feather. "I'm starting three new collections. Feathers, shells, and sea glass. But I only have one piece of sea glass so far. Don't worry, it's not sharp."

Lindsey looked at Carlos. He seemed pink. "Do you guys have on sunscreen?"

No one answered.

Lindsey didn't feel like walking back to the office to get lotion, so she moved to block the sun from Carlos. Then she reached into the Cheerios box. "It's hard to know where we begin."

Olivia saw her opening. "We should head to the market and get food and then go shopping. I feel like we have all the wrong clothes."

"I meant with the motel. My schedule has us up and running in two months."

Sena held one of the chicken feathers close to her chest. "Don't worry, Mommy. We're all going to help you."

Carlos pulled his gaze from the surfers. "Yeah. We're going to do chores and stuff. I looked in that shed. They left all kinds of tools and even a big sword."

Lindsey was alarmed. "Don't touch anything like that without asking me first."

Olivia no longer pretended to do deep breathing. "We're going to have workers—right? People who make the beds and stuff? Is there a cart with shampoo and soaps? I can help stock that with new products. Interesting, organic stuff."

Sena was matter-of-fact. "I looked around. I didn't see any carts."

"There are baskets with wheels in the shed. But nothing in them." Carlos appeared to enjoy being an expert since he so rarely got the chance.

Lindsey had discovered from reading Rangi and Pearl's notebook that for the last six months, once they decided to sell, the Kalamas had completely stopped renting the motel cottages. They no longer had a gardener or a handyman or a cleaning person. They'd even let their business license expire. No wonder the driveway was so over-grown. Lindsey hadn't asked to see financial records when she made her offer on the motel, and they hadn't provided anything. Her face grew hot as she squinted into the hard light. "We've just got to keep a stiff upper lip. Keep calm and carry on."

Olivia sighed. "You sound more Welsh over here."

"Or keep calm and corgi on," added Sena. "Do corgis like chickens? We could get a corgi from a rescue place. Mom, where do you think the chickens' eggs are at?"

Carlos sparked to the idea. "Maybe we could sell eggs to make extra money. Free-range organic."

Sena dropped the chicken feather she was holding and watched it zigzag down to the wet sand. "All of us are free-range organic now. Maybe that should be the motel's new motto."

A group of sandpipers skittered down the beach at the surf's edge, and they all fell silent as they watched. Two gulls passed overhead. A bristle-thighed curlew, with a long, downcurved bill, walked out into the water. The bird's thin, blue-gray legs were in sharp contrast to its cinnamon-feathered rump as it moved with purpose in search of food. It was motivating.

Lindsey got to her feet. "Come on, lovebirds. Let's find ourselves a real breakfast."

Sena turned to her mother. "Dad liked to make us breakfast when we were really little."

"He got too busy with work to do that very much, but he always loved cooking for you guys in the morning."

They all stood up and headed away from the blue-blue ocean, with Sena dragging her feet as if she were walking through snow, not sand.

Over the first week, a routine developed. Sena got up early to watch the sunrise and monitor the chickens. No one else left their bed until midmorning. Carlos spent a lot of time in the toolshed. Olivia seemed to be permanently reading the same book. Just keeping everyone fed, in clean clothing, and wearing sunscreen felt to Lindsey like a full day's accomplishment. They spent their afternoons down at the water. The Kalamas had left a box of leaky masks with snorkels and a collection of swim fins. Carlos, always wearing a long-sleeved T-shirt, spent hours in the surf. He reported daily seeing turtles, small sharks, parrotfish, perch, triggerfish, butterfly fish, mullets, and eels. Sena dug holes and collected rocks, shells, and feathers, whispering to her new treasures as if they were old friends. Olivia worked on her tan while she dozed. And Lindsey made motel to-do lists and strode the shoreline. She deputized Olivia to keep an eye on her brother and sister when she left the property, sometimes finding herself gone for over an hour.

In Portland after Paul died, Lindsey had started walking. Not strolling in Macleay Park smelling muddy pine needles, but trudging for miles in the rain on broken sidewalks, preferably moving uphill on a steep angle in the whispering cold. She chose routes that were strenuous and required real effort. Lindsey wore a digital wristband to measure her steps and had formed a strange attachment to the device, needing to hit the magical number of ten thousand in order to consider her day any kind of victory. But walking became an addiction and the ten thousand became twelve thousand. And then fourteen thousand a day and climbing. She understood physically what happened with each step. Her blood flow and circulation increased, which calmed her nervous system. Her bone density improved, and research suggested that her eyesight benefited as well. But it was her heart that she hoped to heal. Not her actual, beating organ, but her emotional state. In the first dozen months after Paul died her concentration was shot. Her brain was in a fog. Her focus was gone. It had only recently started to return.

Here, Lindsey had the beach as her footpath and she didn't wear shoes. She stopped listening to music or podcasts or audiobooks while she dug her toes into the wet sand, walking always right on the water's edge. She gave herself an assignment: not to consider the practical realities of motel ownership, or to think about how to handle her children and their loss, but to become a detective of her own life. She was going to investigate her relationship with Paul and how things had fallen apart.

At night she lay in bed with aching ankles. But the heels of her feet were becoming soft and smooth from the friction of the sand against her skin. Lindsey had a timetable for the motel's grand reopening, having given herself ten weeks to get her business operational, but actually staying on schedule wasn't looking good.

Intention and execution didn't always walk hand in hand in her world.

4

———

ortunately, Lindsey had put the kids' educational plan in place before they left Portland. Olivia and Carlos would both be attending classes in the small town of Kahuku, where the high school butted up against the middle school, forming one large campus. Olivia was to be joining the ninth-grade class, Carlos the seventh. Sena would go to the elementary school just up the road.

The cost of property in Hawai'i had escalated substantially in recent years, driving out locals. An increasingly large number of the area's homes had owners who didn't even live in the islands, and the residences were used as vacation rentals. The ranks of children in the community had thinned, but Kahuku had managed to hold on to a good portion of working families and had kept its schools intact.

Sena seemed excited, sitting up straighter in her seat as her head swiveled to take in the sights and sounds as they drove up to the green buildings of Kahuku Elementary. The school was perched on the hillside in front of a tropical rainforest, where large trees with leafy canopies fluttered in the sea breeze. In front was a sloping grassy area, which included a playing field that looked like a park. But what caught the eye wasn't the surrounding natural beauty but rather the windmills. Standing forty stories tall, the enormous structures had wingspans like jetliners. And they were, to Lindsey's eyes, shockingly close to the school. The wind blowing off the water turned the blades, slicing the air as they cast fitful shadows below. A mechanical hum lay on top of the noise from the traffic and the more distant ocean waves.

Carlos stared up at the turbines. "Do you think one of those blades has ever fallen off?"

Lindsey wondered the same thing but shook her head. "Of course not."

Olivia typed something into her phone. "Wrong. One broke apart in Maui."

Sena stared hard at her sister. "Did anyone die?"

"No. But there's always a first time for everything."

"Was that necessary?" Lindsey whispered to Olivia, who only shrugged.

Lindsey parked the Crown Victoria in the small lot on the side of the building. She opened the door, informing her two oldest kids, "We won't be long."

"We don't actually know how long we'll be," Sena clarified.

Olivia and Carlos seemed relieved to be getting rid of them. Olivia stuck her legs out the window of the Crown Victoria to work on her tan, which was turning into an obsession. Carlos took the opportunity to lie down in the backseat. Any anxiety he might have had about school didn't keep him from falling asleep in under a minute.

As Lindsey and Sena walked toward the building, three of the island's many feral chickens darted around a corner and disappeared into a row of shrubs. Sena started after them, but Lindsey stopped her.

"Honey, you don't want to get dirty."

The look on Sena's face seemed to suggest otherwise. Lindsey held open the front door and they entered the school to find a smiling woman in the front office seated behind a counter. She wore a red T-shirt that said KAHUKU ELEMENTARY. They were barely through the door when she called out, "Good morning. You must be Lindsey and Sena."

Lindsey stepped forward. "Yes—I phoned last week. This is my daughter Sena Hill. We just moved to the island and she'll be going into second grade."

The woman grabbed a clipboard and a pile of already assembled paperwork. "We are very happy to have you here, Sena. I'm the school's office manager. You can call me Mrs. Bengay. I've got enrollment and medical forms ready for you to fill out."

"This was a sugar plantation a long time ago," Sena observed.

Fran Bengay nodded. "Yes, originally. The school started in the 1890s for the families of local workers, but the building we're in right now was constructed in 1988."

"I'm ready for school, Mrs. Bengay." Sena's voice was filled with resolve.

The woman smiled. "That's the right attitude. You're coming in just over a month into our school year. I know it's hard to be the new kid in class."

"Because you were once a new kid who moved here?" Sena asked.

"Well, no, I actually never had that experience."

"So you've seen that it's hard from other kids, or are you just guessing?"

Lindsey didn't wait for the answer. "Sena, she's just saying that new things can be stressful."

Sena looked from the school administrator to her mother. "That's not what she said."

Lindsey tried to keep a smile on her face. "Well, that's what she meant."

Sena leaned close and whispered to her mother, "It's not nice to put words in other people's mouths." She then moved to one of the chairs that were in a row up against the far wall. She took a seat, adding, "Mrs. Bengay, I don't have *ukus*."

The office manager looked taken aback but responded, "That's good to hear, Sena."

Lindsey waited for an explanation. When none came, she asked, "What's *ukus*?"

"Head lice," Mrs. Bengay answered. "We had a small outbreak at the start of the school year. It's all under control now."

Back in Portland, Sena had checked the Kahuku Elementary

website every day. There had been an *ukus* outbreak in September, just days after school had started.

"I had them before in Portland." Sena smiled at Mrs. Bengay. "We got a head lice comb at CVS. And that smelly shampoo. It works."

When they got up to leave, twenty minutes later, Fran Bengay said cheerfully, "*A hui hou.*"

Sena answered, "I will try to be *pono*."

Lindsey had no idea what either of them meant.

Olivia saw Sena come out of the school building and was filled with equal parts relief and dread. The car was hot and uncomfortable, but going to a new high school for the first time was next-level stress. Before her father had started his own company, she'd attended school only blocks from their house. The kids all knew each other, and the pecking order of who was good at sports, who might one day be a doctor, and who was a bully didn't need explanation. Then, after her family suddenly had a lot of money, Olivia and her siblings were moved to private school. That transition was both exciting and stressful. But after two years, things went bad and her family couldn't afford the tuition. Then they moved. Three times. She stopped seeing her friends because she didn't want to explain what was happening to her father's company. It wasn't as if she even really knew. No one sat her down and said, "Your dad is brilliant but not a businessperson." Olivia went from having a circle of close classmates to hanging out by herself. She wasn't by nature a loner, but she'd become one.

Olivia watched as her mother and sister emerged from the main building, squinting into the bright sunlight. Her mother appeared pale and disoriented as she reached into her bag, searching no doubt for her sunglasses, which were one of the things her mom was always losing. Because of that she had a half dozen pairs—all dorky-looking. Olivia felt a stab of emotion. Where would they be without Mom? What if she had died, not Dad? Her stomach lurched. Losing her mother would be the end of everything. She was the glue. Olivia hated to admit to anyone, most of all herself, that she would be utterly lost without this freckled Welsh woman with long toes and a high-pitched laugh.

Olivia flung an arm into the backseat and slapped her brother on the leg. "Here they come. We're next on the chopping block."

She was silent as Lindsey strained to navigate the big sedan out of the parking space. Three kids were a lot. Plus, there was now the run-down motel to worry about and so much to do to get it ready for guests. The idea of the business was both thrilling and awful to Olivia. There would be strangers on the property, coming and going. If there were kids her age, that would be one thing. But Olivia suddenly imagined disgruntled guests who showed up in the office at all hours. They might leave super-gross garbage in the cottages and steal the bathmats and washcloths. Who wanted to deal with that? But hopefully it would be her mother's problem. She was the one who had come up with the whole plan to run a motel.

Lindsey parked under the shade of a big, leafy tree at the high school, and Sena announced, "I'm staying in the car. I want to look at my new stuff."

Mrs. Bengay had given Sena a math book. Olivia was glad Sena wasn't going in. She didn't need a little kid trailing behind her when she made her first entrance.

"Good idea. Right, Mom?"

Lindsey looked unsure, but then answered, "The windows are all down. Hopefully we won't be long. You come inside if you need us."

"I won't need you."

Olivia wished she could bottle whatever Sena had running through her veins. Her little sister had a shocking sense of confidence.

Olivia felt okay until they reached the front doors of the school complex. But once they were inside, she could see that she'd picked the wrong outfit. She was wearing the wrong shoes. Even her hair seemed to be parted in the wrong place. It was cold in the building. Olivia wished she had on a hooded sweatshirt, long pants, and wool socks. Maybe even a winter scarf. She felt the tip of her nose tingle.

Maybe this was an educational tactic. No one could fall asleep at this temperature. A few kids looked her way, but mostly she felt invisible.

In the front office, her mother was directed to fill out forms with information for the school's computer system, and she and her brother were taken to see a counselor. Carlos, at her side, saw something posted on a bulletin board and elbowed her ribs. "Lunch is a pork chop *patty*, whipped potato, and edamame." She couldn't tell whether he considered this good or bad. The way she saw it, either something was a pork chop or a patty. How could it be both? With the idea of a hybrid pork product clouding her brain, she was disappointed to see that the school counselor didn't have his own office. There were at least a dozen students milling about, and it was obvious that they were watching and listening as she was steered into a chair to meet Mr. Ed Lam. Did she hear someone say "We got a new haole"? She definitely heard somebody whispering.

Olivia hoped she appeared calm, but her skin felt prickly, as if she'd just run through a field of stinging nettles. She'd never actually done that, but she decided this was what it must feel like. Then she heard a voice saying, "Olivia, tell me a little about yourself."

All she could think about was the pork chop, ground up, bone and all, and formed, unwillingly, into a patty. She opened her mouth to answer and nothing came out. Was it too much to say she was fourteen years old and normal except for the tragic loss of a parent, most of her family's money, security, friends, a hometown, and a large measure of her self-esteem?

Olivia felt her breathing turn shallow.

She was having trouble taking in air.

She forced her lungs to expand and then coughed, which made things worse. She swallowed. Then inhaled and exhaled in a rapid, uncontrolled way. She knew that aquatic animals took many more breaths than land creatures. That made sense because she was drowning. Suddenly she felt pain in her chest. Was she having a heart attack?

She shut her eyes and struggled for control. She could do this. She marshaled her will, managed to regain her oxygen supply, and spoke. But her voice had a heavy Welsh accent as she said, "I'm fourteen and my father died two years ago whilst surfing in Oregon."

The room stilled as everyone turned to look at her, including her brother. Olivia blinked several times. She hadn't intended the accent; it just came out. Now what was she supposed to do? Laugh it off? Or was she stuck being Welsh for the next four years?

The solution she settled on was to say not a single word for the rest of her time with the counselor, Ed Lam. Carlos could do the heavy lifting. One swift kick to his calf muscle got him going. "Well, Mr. Lam, we just moved here from Portland," Carlos began. "My sister and I spend a lot of time on computers, because our dad was into that. We went to coding camp for two summers. It wasn't sleepaway. I was super into Legos when I was little, but these days I like robotics. Also, I want to study Japanese. We have a little sister who is seven years old and she likes animals in a very major way. Olivia spends a lot of time alone lately, but she always had friends, so I bet she'll make friends here, too. She used to tell people she wanted to be an astronaut when she grew up, but she doesn't say that anymore. Maybe only the super-rich get to be astronauts nowadays. She watched reality TV shows like *The Real Housewives*, but after the last two years she says seeing rich people throwing fake parties makes her sick to her stomach."

Under ordinary circumstances Olivia would have been horrified by all of this intimate sharing; now she was only relieved someone else had Ed Lam's attention. The counselor got to his feet. "We need to figure out schedules and which classes will be able to fit you in. So today is just an introduction. Let's take a look around the school. What do you say?"

It felt to Olivia like the other people in the room were pretending to go back to their business but were still watching. She managed a crooked half smile and gave Carlos a pinch. He got up, wedging himself between the counselor and his sister. "That sounds good."

As they walked out of the office, Mr. Lam recited a list of facts, most of which Olivia barely heard. There were almost nineteen hundred students between the middle school and the high school, and more than half the kids wore bright crimson shirts proclaiming support for the schools' teams, the Red Raiders. In the halls and the classrooms nearly all of the kids Olivia saw were mixed. They were beautiful and confident, literally hugging each other every few steps as they laughed their way down the corridors. She had never felt so pale, pasty, and persona non grata.

After a brief tour, Mr. Lam escorted them to the middle school, where her brother was introduced as "a new boy from the mainland." The principal was warm and friendly. "We are very happy to have you joining us, Carlos."

Her younger sibling gave the woman a winning smile and announced, "If it's okay, I like to be called Carl."

"Of course. I'll let the teachers know."

Olivia looked at her brother. *Carl?* Why was he suddenly Carl? But she didn't say anything because she wasn't sure if her brain was still wired in such a way as to make her sound Welsh.

Finally, back outside again, Olivia resisted the urge to run to the Crown Victoria. She felt close to what she imagined it was like to spot a lifeboat after going overboard in the ocean. She opened the passenger-side front door to see Sena with two chickens in the backseat. Thankfully her mother showed up and chased out the birds. Olivia climbed in the front, dropped her head against the seat, and closed her eyes. She heard Carlos (or was he Carl?) get in the back. Her mother asked, "So how was it? What did you guys think?"

"It was pretty good. Olivia didn't say much."

Olivia opened her eyes. "I don't think the school is a good fit for me." She was relieved to hear no accent.

"You don't have a choice," her mother replied. "It's the local high school. That's where the kids here go."

"I'm fine with online learning."

"Well, I'm not." Lindsey's voice was firm.

Carlos leaned forward to get closer to his mother. "Mom, I'm okay with the middle school, so don't worry about me. Can we drive to Hale'iwa and get those good fish sandwiches?"

"Hale'iwa is too far to go for fish sandwiches. And Mom, he told people to call him Carl."

Lindsey turned around to meet her son's gaze. "What's wrong with Carlos?"

"I'm still Carlos. I'm just shortening it for school. Getting rid of two letters. What's the big deal? Plus, Dad loved the Beach Boys."

"What do the Beach Boys have to do with changing your name?" Lindsey asked.

Sena looked up from her book. "There are beach girls—right?"

Carlos was patient with his little sister. "The Beach Boys were a band. One of the guys was named Carl. It was a million years ago, but now we live on a beach, so it makes sense. Plus, I've got red hair, and I'm not Hispanic, and the name doesn't really fit me."

"We picked the name because we loved Carlos Santana."

"Who's he again?" Sena kept her eyes on her math book.

"A wonderful musician."

"And I'm shortening it to another musician. So that's cool."

Olivia was ready to join the fight. "It's by definition cultural appropriation to use a name not from your own culture. Plus, it's just so random."

"What's cultural probation?" Sena wanted to know.

"Appropriation," Olivia corrected. "It's taking something without asking permission."

"You don't have to ask permission when you name something you love." Sena closed her book. She was good at getting the last word.

But Carlos wasn't done. "I don't want to talk about my name. I'm starving. Can we just go get the good fish sandwiches?"

Lindsey put the car in reverse and backed out of the parking spot. "No to the fish sandwiches. We have to prioritize. We have to get vaccinations. They didn't receive your health records."

In the backseat the sound of a seatbelt unclicking was followed by Sena's voice. "What do you mean, vaccinations? Do you mean *shots*? I had all my shots!"

Lindsey didn't answer, but Carlos spoke. "I gotta eat something. My stomach is getting achy."

"You need proof of tetanus-diphtheria."

"I had that!" Sena yelled. "Mom, you need to find the records. I'm *not* getting any more shots!"

Lindsey tried to stay calm. "There are things that we don't have a choice in."

She put the car in drive and stepped on the gas. The Crown Victoria lurched forward in its unpredictable way, and out of nowhere, or at least that's how it seemed to everyone in the car, a teenage boy, moving fast, streaked across Lindsey's peripheral vision. She slammed on the brakes and in the same instant they heard the thud. A skateboard sailed up into the air and landed on the asphalt as a five-foot-ten body bounced across the hood of the vehicle.

Inexplicably, the figure landed on his feet on the other side of the car. Everyone screamed. Except the boy. He stared, wide-eyed, right at them.

"*Ohmygod!*" Lindsey flung open the car door. "Are you all right?"

Olivia froze. She recognized him. It was Koa. Olivia sputtered, "Mom, he used to work at the motel. He's friends with the Kalamas."

Lindsey didn't hear. She was already standing, horrified, in front of the boy. But Koa seemed only embarrassed. "Sorry, lady. I didn't see you."

"No. My God, *I'm* sorry! Are you okay?"

All three kids were out of the car now. Olivia asked, "Do you need to go to the doctor?"

Koa looked at her. He was so calm. "I'm good."

He headed across the asphalt to retrieve his skateboard, looking back over his shoulder at the car. There was a big crease in the hood. "Hey—sorry about the ding."

Carlos called out, "The car has a ton of dents already. My mom hit a bunch of garbage cans the first day we got it."

Olivia mumbled, "Zip it, *Carl*."

They all got back in the Crown Victoria. Sena's steady voice declared, "Learn. Achieve. Succeed." She pulled on a red Kahuku Elementary T-shirt over what she was already wearing. She pushed her arms through the sleeves but her head stayed hidden inside, under the logo LEARN-ACHIEVE-SUCCEED. She then announced, "I'm a turtle."

Carlos whispered to his mom, "Can we please go to Hale'iwa and get fish sandwiches now?"

Olivia snapped, "Hey—we were just in a car accident!"

Lindsey looked from Koa, who was nearly out of view, back to the kids. "I'm going inside to report what just happened."

Olivia shook her head. "No. Mom, really. Don't do that!"

But Lindsey was already backing up into a parking place. And in seconds she was heading to the front doors of the high school.

The people in the office didn't seem concerned—at least once they heard that Koa had walked away from the incident apparently unharmed. Lindsey wondered if kids got hit all the time in the parking lot. Or maybe it was an island thing, the ability to stay so calm. The woman at the front desk gave her the telephone number for his family and assured Lindsey that they'd be following up with Koa. And then it was on to the next thing, which turned out to be a pep rally in the gym and a broken water faucet in one of the science labs.

As Lindsey stepped out of the high school office, her left eye began to twitch. This had only happened once before, right after Paul died, and it had lasted for over a month. Now it was back. With her eye in some kind of muscle spasm, her jaw tensed up. And then a surge of pain shot down her spine. Was her back about to go out?

She'd hit a kid with her car, but she was the one who was feeling run over. She was not a good driver. She doubted she ever would be. Maybe it was a childhood spent around vehicles moving on the opposite side of the road. Something in her DNA seemed to have her always looking the wrong way. Her father had died when his truck hit a patch of ice and went off the road. She had long ago decided that cars were a kind of enemy. The irony was not lost on her that she would be completely dependent on one here.

Lindsey headed out the school door consumed with the idea that she needed Paul. She had to have help, at the very least an extra driver to share the shopping, the cooking, the unpacking, and the organizing. There were no checks and balances to her life because every damn thing was on her. And it was all new. Every person, place, and thing was unfamiliar.

But hadn't that been the point? The fantasy? The reason to escape to what she had imagined to be a warm island paradise? Wasn't she fleeing the ghosts of so many shared memories? Lindsey stopped walking, bit the inside of her right cheek, and used every ounce of determination not to burst into tears. This was a technique she'd mastered where she allowed physical pain to override emotional suffering. It worked. The idea of Paul disappeared. She realized it was bloody lucky she hadn't killed that sweet boy on the skateboard. She needed to muster some gratitude to the universe.

She would call Koa's parents as soon as she got home.

Maybe drop off something at the house.

Or have something delivered.

What was better—food or flowers? What was the right thing to do when you drove your oversized Ford into a teenager on a skateboard?

She got back to the Crown Victoria to find her kids eating french fries. A food truck had appeared down the street and Carlos had been sent on a reconnaissance mission. She was shocked that they were, like the people in the school office, ready to move on to the next thing. Lindsey started the engine and turned onto the main road, where traffic was moving at a crawl.

It was good you really couldn't go faster than forty miles an hour on Kam Highway.

5

———

That weekend, it felt as if they lived in the Crown Victoria. The car picked up enough of the area's oxisol to have a permanent coat of the rusty orange soil over its lower half. Even the daily downpours couldn't wash off the color. Lindsey was bothered at first, but then stopped seeing it. Sena was happy about the dirty layer. "We look like we're locals now."

Lindsey and the kids had been shifting gears from tourists to residents. They were all mesmerized by the fact that the road to the northwest traveled past many of the most famous surf breaks in the world. Waimea Bay, Sunset Beach, and Chun's Reef were the home of the big waves, and nearly always clogged with people. Cars, mopeds, and bicycles, many with surfboards attached, wove in and out of the hive of activity, the sheer volume of traffic forcing everyone to slow down. The highway was one lane in each direction with barely any shoulder, and the locals had held firm on no expansion.

Lindsey was thrilled that the area had managed to fight off major developers. There were no high-rise construction sites and no nightlife to speak of. This stretch of coastline had only one major hotel, the fifty-year-old Turtle Bay Resort. It had rental rooms, as well as condos and time-shares, but was set back from the road on a small curl of a cove. There wasn't much visible beyond the resort's golf course but the distant top floor of the main hotel complex. According to the locals, Turtle Bay sold expensive food and twenty-dollar drinks that were spiked with alcohol for adults and simple syrup for children. The hotel was always undergoing some kind of renovation, with owners entering and exiting like a revolving door. Lindsey decided it wasn't a good idea to let her kids see the property. They asked on occasion, but she hadn't given in. Turtle Bay was the kind of place they'd have gone to when they had a lot of money. Those days were over and never coming back.

Her motel, the Mau Loa, was close to the small town of Lā'ie, which had a single traffic light. And even that wasn't needed, but had been put in as part of a negotiation for the construction of the small commercial zone sixty years ago. The area had a grocery store, a movie theater that was permanently closed, three fast-food places, a hardware store, a gas station, and a post office. These businesses catered to the Mormon students and staff at Brigham Young University's satellite campus on the same side of the roadway, which most islanders simply drove past without much interest. Hawaiians, Lindsey was coming to realize, were all about respect. You gave it, you got it. The island's aloha spirit was based on positivity toward others. There were layers Lindsey didn't understand, but she was figuring out that the concepts of honor and courtesy ruled above all else.

The stretch of coastal road north of the Mau Loa included acres of shrimp farms, which served food from trucks, permanently secured onto foundations, to busloads of tourists, who took day trips from Honolulu to view the big waves, down a paper plate of garlic shrimp, and maybe get a photograph of a beached sea turtle. Each of the dozen trucks was said to have its own cooking style, but in reality, they all served a version of the same thing: shrimp in garlic and butter with a scoop of white rice and macaroni salad on the side. Lindsey steered the Crown Victoria right past the busloads of tourists. They invoked an involuntary response to flee. She knew this wasn't a good reaction for someone who was supposed to be soon running a motel.

It was very windy on Monday when Lindsey drove back to Kahuku for the official start of her kids' education in Hawai'i. Olivia woke up claiming she was sick, but Lindsey knew she was faking it. Kahuku Elementary was the first stop. Sena, carrying two bags of supplies and wearing her red school T-shirt with her favorite stretchy pink pants, insisted on going in alone. Olivia made Carl/Carlos accompany her into the high school building, even though his classes were in the middle school. Once they had disappeared inside, Lindsey sat in the parked car and allowed herself to remember her own childhood. Her educational experiences hadn't been particularly joyous, and yet she would have given anything to be back in the always-cold bus, heading off to school in her stiff uniform.

She sat daydreaming, rewriting her childhood isolation and boredom into a reminiscence of cozy comfort. She didn't know what the truth was anymore. She realized that as she changed, so, too, did her reactions to past events. She wondered if her mum had pushed her to leave behind her friends and go to the gifted school when she was eleven, or if she had been the driving force behind that decision. Thinking about the past made her reconnect to a powerful restlessness, a permanent itch that no one in her family or commu- nity could scratch. Maybe that was the real reason she'd been able to leave the United Kingdom.

Maybe that same impulse was why she was now here. The world's most isolated center of human population was located in the Ha- waiian Islands. People were 2,390 miles from the US mainland and nearly 4,000 miles from Japan, smack in the middle of the planet's largest ocean. There was nowhere to run, although plenty of places to hide if you knew the islands well enough.

Lindsey turned the key in the ignition and reversed cautiously out of the parking space. On the way home a single thought formed: She had to stop blaming people, most especially Paul, when things were difficult. She had been given so many advantages in life. Maybe she'd squandered some of them, but if three great kids and six acres of land with the best sunsets in the world was where it all had led, then so be it. She had to make it work.

Back at the motel, Lindsey sat down on the front steps of the office to wait. Everyone had been in rare agreement about what the most important step in motel ownership should be: They needed internet. For days they'd been walking out to the two-lane highway, which was the only place where they got service. Lindsey had ordered a satellite dish, and the installation day had been changed three times. But today had been guaranteed.

She shut her eyes and listened to the stillness. She heard the waves, then the rustle of chickens somewhere close by. There was a high-pitched buzz that was either an insect or the beginning of an auditory problem. The more she focused on the sound, the more she heard it as musical. She opened her eyes and saw the source of the symphony. It was a banza katydid, the exact vibrant green of the leaf that it chewed on, inches away on one of the plants that framed the porch. Just the hint of a smile crossed her face as she imagined the bug singing to her.

Over the last two years, she'd so rarely been alone. That was mostly by design. Raising three kids by herself after a major tragedy demanded putting one foot in front of the other. Every day. Curling up in a ball in a dark room was almost never an option when three sets of eyes were looking for assurance that things were going to work out.

The sun felt hot on her sandaled feet. She rested her head on her knees and shut her eyes again. An image of her husband appeared. He was young, handsome, so assured. She and Paul had met at a brunch in Portland on a roof deck over a garage. She was dating a guy named Drew, who was there with her that afternoon. But she could clearly picture Paul the first time she'd seen him: tall, fit, with curly hair and a profile that would look good on a coin. She couldn't visualize anymore what he'd been wearing, but could easily remember her younger self in sneakers and jeans with a watering-can charm necklace her grandmother had given her that she later lost on a camping trip. It rested between her collarbones on her always pink skin. Her hair was in a ponytail, but a third of it had escaped the scrunchie. Paul said later that, backlit by the sun, her head looked like it had a golden halo.

She didn't know if it was the margarita or the fact that her sort-of boyfriend Drew was glued to a football game that caused her to

spend over an hour with Paul. He told her he worked in computers, but then tried hard to show her that he wasn't a tech nerd.
He picked up a guitar resting against a potted plant and played
"Tomorrow Never Knows." She was a Beatles fan. Of course she
knew the words. It was a studio song, recorded with sampling and
electronic manipulation. Maybe he was testing her. It wasn't a ro-
mantic gesture. It felt like a challenge, but he made her laugh, not
a nervous giggle or a forced howl but something more real and
unconscious. He had confidence. She found that appealing. She
explained she'd left Wales and moved to America for grad school in
biology, which seemed to intrigue him. But while Lindsey enjoyed
science, she told him, she didn't fancy the idea of medicine. She had
continued on her educational journey, getting a second master's in
ecology. She was considering teaching at the college level when she
was finished.

He said, "Immigrants are the best of us."

"Really? You think that?"

"They're willing to leave so much behind to realize a dream."

They didn't exchange contact information and she didn't say
good-bye to him when she and Drew later left. Paul told her the
next day that it took two calls to mutual friends to find her number.
She suggested getting together for breakfast, but he said dinner and
then picked a Thai place that everyone was talking about, down by
the river. They decided to meet in the middle of the week, which
made it seem less like a date and reinforced the idea that while she
was seeing someone, they weren't doing anything wrong.

At least not yet.

But before they met, she took her best sweater to the dry clean-
ers and had her hair blown out, which was something she rarely
did. They didn't kiss or hold hands or do anything physical for four
weeks. Instead, they had a long lunch on the first weekend after the
Thai dinner and then saw a movie a few days later. He got stuck in
a traffic jam on the freeway coming home from work and they were
on the phone for three straight hours. And that didn't seem strange.

They slipped into talking every day. He was suddenly becoming her closest confidant. They were telling each other stories, revealing who they were, and, in the process, they were writing their own possible future. She got out of the relationship with Drew without much drama. They let the past fade into the rearview mirror.

She strained to think if she'd seen things in the beginning that could have warned her that Paul could be stubborn, too competitive, and secretive. Her mother had a theory that when you entered into a relationship you needed to identify what attracted you most to the other person. What quality in your beloved's character did you like best? The second part of her theory stated that if you ever turned against this trait, the relationship was finished.

What Lindsey loved most about Paul was how clever he was.

She admired his mind.

And that was what did them in when everything turned bad.

She had been on the motel steps for half an hour when a white cargo van appeared. The guy behind the wheel looked like he was in high school, but what was more unsettling was how much he knew about her before she was able to even introduce herself. It felt as if everyone she met was related to the Kalamas or had at one time known someone who worked at the motel or stayed there. The new owner from the mainland was fertile ground for gossip and intrigue. Two things were made very clear in almost every conversation she had: Although her family lived on the island and people were friendly and welcoming, Lindsey and her children were outsiders and they always would be. They could die in this state and still be *haole*. They most certainly would never be *kama'āina*, children of the land. Because they weren't born on the islands, they wouldn't even be Hawai'i people. The most they could hope for was to one day be seen as locals, and from the look in people's eyes, that would take years. And years.

The Viasat technician explained that he had taken out the old equipment installed by a company called Exede. He began detailing all of the advantages of Viasat's "high-speed satellite internet service, with streaming video, internet radio, and the easy sharing of digital information."

Lindsey nodded but really had only one question: "Will what you install work in all the cottages when I get TVs?"

"If you set it up that way. The Kalamas only had TV for the office. And no internet anywhere."

Lindsey could feel her left eye, which had been the one continuously twitching for two days, calm down. "Really? So, you think I don't need people in the cottages to have television sets?"

"You mean your guests?"

"Guests. Right."

"Everyone watches stuff on their phones. Or computers. Just make the signal strong enough. But that's your call, lady. I'm only the install guy."

She immediately felt bad. Her confidence level rose and fell so erratically these days. She'd had trouble deciding whether to put almond milk or cream in her tea that morning. She wondered if this was another part of grief. But she had also been a victim of deception. She didn't realize what was really going on with Paul at work until after he died. That might be why her sadness was laced with anger. Was she reckless now? Broken? Damaged goods? Or was her condition a by-product of her family's sudden surge and then loss of wealth? The balance she and Paul shared had shifted once he became the head of a corporation. He never explicitly said he was also in charge at home, but he'd certainly acted that way. There were days when it felt as if *she* worked for *him*. Her solution was to be more forceful with the people who worked for *her*. She wanted her old self back. The woman who was open to the world and optimistic about the future.

The gray satellite dish didn't take long to install, and Lindsey was immediately unhappy. The new equipment was an eyesore, and even if it wasn't very large, one electronic device changed the vibe of the whole place. She had to do some cajoling, but she got the technician back up on the roof and had him use hunks of moss and fern fronds to camouflage the technology.

The guy was in a hurry when he got off his ladder. He took her cellphone, set up a password for the system, and had her online in less than two minutes. It felt like some kind of miracle. She signed the work order and he was back in his van heading toward the highway before Lindsey could even offer him a glass of water.

Having the internet removed all of her excuses for not moving forward at a quicker pace. She was in her second week of motel ownership and every day she added more items to do, without crossing off anything on her enormous list. But internet meant that with the tap of a few keys, she could see local roofers, plumbers, painters, and electricians. Maybe it was better when she was isolated from the world. As she tried to formulate a plan, Lindsey's academic side was at war with her practical decision-making. Her mind easily drifted to the consideration of the psychology of color and the biological effects of natural light versus artificial illumination. But there were so many essential things to do. She had to set up a banking relationship, get a business license, and make some kind of motel website. The more pressing reality was she didn't think it was possible to rent the units in their current state. A single disgruntled internet review would derail the whole venture.

The most tangible evidence Lindsey could find that the Kalamas had actually run a business was the guest books they'd left. Three of the drawers in the massive office desk held stacks of blue notebooks with records of transactions that had all been arranged by telephone or through the mail. It was alarming to discover there wasn't even a set cottage rate. What people were charged per night shifted from customer to customer for no apparent reason. The small notes written next to names showed that most visitors came with regularity. They were friends of friends, relatives of locals, and often residents of the other islands.

From what she could see, the motel had never advertised in any form. Now, if someone called the listed motel number, they heard a recorded message saying the line was no longer in service. Lindsey found a box of mailed inquiries for future bookings (all unopened) in the closet on the office's main floor. How was she supposed to handle those requests? The guest records needed to be made into a database. But was that the best place to start? Maybe she could pay Olivia to figure it out.

Lindsey had to seriously consider a plan for how she might survive in two months if she wasn't generating motel income. She didn't have much money left over after the motel purchase. She would need to get a loan from a bank or else use her credit card to take advances after her savings ran out.

She grabbed a notepad and headed to the first cottage. The front door of every unit opened into a room used for both sleeping and dining. There was no air-conditioning anywhere on the property. An old black ceiling fan, arguably the nicest single thing inside the structures, hung from the high point of each exposed-beam pitched roof, making a heartbeat-sounding swirl as it churned the humid air. The wooden fan blades were cracked and speckled. The hardware had been painted many, many times, yet rust spots still pushed through the cast-iron brackets. Lindsey looked up and wondered if the blades could possibly come loose and decapitate a guest. She had to stop herself from seeing potential danger at every turn.

Below the fan was a bed, which in actuality was two single beds pushed together, with no attempt made to deal with the crevice. There were wooden nightstands, but only one reading lamp on the left. A round bamboo table with two matching chairs completed the room. Each unit had a bathroom, which consisted of a pastel pedestal sink (a different color in each cottage), a tiled shower stall, and a toilet. A sign in the bathroom read: DO *NOT* USE A HAIR DRYER. *MAHALO!* The floors were wide-board pine, painted white, pockmarked and uneven, but with an unexpected high-gloss shine. In the far corner of the room was a kitchenette—a metal sink, a two-burner electric stovetop, and a square wooden chopping block counter with a minibar-sized refrigerator positioned underneath. There was no oven, no dishwasher, no disposal, but an astonishing number of tiny ants. And that was without any food in sight. In the blue binder, Rangi had left a note explaining that having a toaster in the kitchenette would draw too much electricity for the electrical system to handle. Having three gas-powered washing machines suddenly made sense.

The cottages were outdated, but could be seen (if the light was right and the observer was at a reasonable distance) as an organic part of the landscape. There was something undeniably lovely about the proportions of the furniture to the size of the rooms, and the simplicity of the architecture and the design. They seemed to belong to the red earth in a way she understood she never would.

Lindsey's offer for the property came with a legal commitment not to demolish any of the structures. It was the reason her bid was accepted. There had been other buyers who would have paid a lot more money, but she was the only one who gave the owners what they wanted: a binding assurance that the original motel would remain intact. She had purchased sight unseen a place with staggeringly picturesque beauty, sagging beds, corroded pipes, slow drains, and dripping faucets. Half of the old-fashioned, two-prong electrical outlets didn't work, and the metal trim on the kitchen counters and cupboard handles were dark with rust. The screens that once covered the windows were mostly gone and the glass in the wooden frames had seen so many decades of saltwater spray that they were cloudy, even when just cleaned. The bungalows seemed to sweat in the middle of the day when the tropical sun was overhead, and geckos ran along the length of the ceiling beams, catching gnats and the tiny, irritating black flies. Tropical air had turned the faded rice paper on the cottage walls lumpy, giving it texture and complexity.

Nothing, she suspected, would be in compliance with current building codes. Had inspectors looked the other way for years? The structures seemed to be alive, as if they had long ago grown roots in the red dirt, holding on to what was theirs. With the thin, gauzy window curtains swaying in the breeze from the ceiling fan, the cottages looked to Lindsey like aged dancers. They knew the steps by heart, even if time wasn't on their side. Because of one family, the tiny houses had survived the development that had changed so much on the island of Oʻahu.

And that was the best thing about the motel cottages.

They were, against all odds, still standing.

6

Lindsey took a seat on the old rattan porch swing. She had spent the better part of the day assessing every cottage, having formulated a new plan to open them one at a time. She would start with the structure farthest from the office, which would give her family and her first guests the most privacy. She opened her notepad, but instead of adding to her work list, she started to draw one of the palm trees, which was growing at a strange angle, reaching away from the water, seemingly defying gravity. Her job as a chauffeur, short-order cook, maid, tutor, and adolescent therapist would begin again in minutes, when she'd need to leave to pick up the kids. She was thankful to have these last precious few moments to herself.

It didn't last. She looked up to hear the sound of an approaching car. On the second day at the property, she and Carlos had thrown a tarp over the old wooden motel sign. The occasional vehicle that still came down the road did nothing but scatter the chickens and force someone, usually Lindsey, to explain the motel closure.

A new silver Jeep Wrangler rounded the wide curve and Lindsey got to her feet. She saw a Black man behind the wheel. He lifted his sunglasses and with a measure of control swung the Jeep onto the lava chips, where he cut the engine. For a brief moment Lindsey wondered if he was some kind of state official. Everyone wanted to know her plans for reopening and she couldn't help but think that not all of the people who asked wished her well. The best thing to do in these situations was say as little as possible.

The windows were down on the Jeep, so Lindsey knew the man

could hear her. Her voice was steady but, she hoped, off-putting as she called out, "The motel is closed for renovation." So far she hadn't renovated anything, unless throwing away garbage bags full of mildewed sheets counted as a capital improvement.

The man opened the car door and stepped out. He was over six foot two and in very good shape, with facial hair that could have been a style or might have been the result of not shaving for a week. Lindsey guessed they were close in age. He wore hiking shorts and a tank top, and while he was dressed as casually as a local, on him it somehow felt more pulled together. His clothing was crisp in a climate that turned most things soft. Mentally, Lindsey noted the curves of his muscular calves. He was a walker or a runner. An athlete of some kind. She felt her face redden.

"I'm Chris Young." He smiled at her and Lindsey felt immediately disarmed.

"How can I help you, Chris Young?"

The man turned to look out at the ocean. "It's unbelievably beautiful here."

Lindsey accepted the compliment as if it had been about her, not the landscape and the cottages. Her voice came out higher in pitch than usual. "Thank you."

She glanced down at the gravel and noticed that this man named Chris Young had what Carlos would call "shoe game." He was wearing three-color sneakers that she knew her son would envy.

"I've been coming to this motel for eleven years. It doesn't seem possible it's closed. Rangi told me they were selling. So, you're the new owner?"

"Yup. Just this last month."

"And you're not open yet?"

"We've got lots to do before we're back in business." Lindsey's slight smile was because she was thinking of her on-site staff. Olivia. Carlos. Sena. And the chickens.

He nodded. "I figured, but I had to give it a shot. Sorry to bother you."

He turned back to the Jeep and opened the door.

"No bother at all. Sorry I couldn't be more helpful."

"You're from Australia?"

"Wales."

"I'm not great at identifying accents."

Lindsey put her hand over her brow to shield her eyes from the sun. She wanted to get a better look at him. "And you're from . . . ?"

"Philadelphia."

Lindsey realized he was the first adult she'd spoken to since phoning Koa Kahale's parents two days ago to say she was sorry about the accident. His mother had ended up apologizing to her, which was the exact opposite of what would have happened with a parent back in Portland. The cable guy today didn't count because he looked eighteen and she knew she'd never see him again. This conversation with Chris, though, she would remember. A switch had been flipped and something that previously had been turned off was now flickering. Maybe there was a spark still accessible in her emotional circuitry.

Lindsey watched as Chris got behind the steering wheel. She felt a growing unease. He pressed a button on the dashboard and the motor started up. She was irrationally seized with the desire to stop him—to prolong this conversation. Before he put the car in reverse she managed to call out, "Hey—so how did you find this place the first time you came here?"

He took a moment, then answered, "My wife. She was great at locating things off the beaten track."

He'd used the past tense. Lindsey blurted out, "So you're divorced?"

"Widowed."

"Hey—me too." She realized she was smiling and then instantly felt ashamed. She added, "It's an awful word."

"Agreed. Too much like a spider. It's a small club at our age—no?"

Lindsey nodded. "Was your wife in an accident?"

He didn't answer right away. He'd gone somewhere else. She could feel it. Then he said, "We stayed in the cabin with the red sink."

Lindsey exhaled. She shouldn't have asked about his wife. She was around kids too much of the time, and they came out with all kinds of inappropriate questions.

But when he spoke next, he explained, "My wife passed away three years ago. Lung cancer. She wasn't even a smoker. So just bad luck. Or the wrong genes." He looked back over at the ocean. "I put her ashes out there. I've come to the island the last two Octobers to see how she's doing."

Lindsey hadn't been able to spread Paul's ashes, but he, too, was in the ocean. If they had found his body, she'd have brought his remains to this island. Her voice wasn't much more than a whisper. "Did you guys have kids?"

Chris shook his head and then put the Jeep into reverse. "I'll be on my way."

Lindsey wanted to be helpful. "There's the resort at Turtle Bay, which isn't far down the road. I hear it's nice."

Chris half smiled. "I'm not the resort type. But I'll see what I can find." He picked up his phone and then asked, "You didn't happen to put in Wi-Fi, did you? It was one of the charms of the Mau Loa that I could unplug. But now that I'm looking for a place to stay it would help."

Maybe he could see the thirty-inch disk covered with greenery on the far side of the office. "That's all I've accomplished so far. Mau Loa Motel is the network. The password is ABrilliantIdea. All together—one word. Caps on *A*, *B*, and *I*."

Chris nodded. "Thanks. Appreciate it. And buying this place—it *was* a brilliant idea."

She laughed nervously. "Well, I'm not so sure about that."

Before she could say anything more, her cellphone alarm sounded.

"Oh my gosh. That's so annoying." She reached to silence her ringtone, which Sena had set to "old car horn." "My daughter did that."

"How old is she?"

"Seven."

"This will be a great place for you to raise her."

Lindsey nodded, not mentioning Olivia or Carlos. That felt wrong, but she didn't volunteer more. "I've got to go pick her up."

"I won't keep you."

She realized she hadn't even told him her name. She felt an ache inside, the bruise of a missed opportunity. She was so out of practice talking to men. And this was a man who was single. And handsome. Lindsey was coming to realize that you could change where you lived, but it was much harder to change how you lived.

He had said he came to the motel for the last two Octobers.

Maybe he'd be back the next fall.

Where would her life be in twelve months?

She heard his words, "I won't keep you," as she turned toward the office to retrieve the keys to the Crown Victoria.

7

Driving down the highway heading to the kids' school, she turned her thoughts back to Paul. She hadn't just fallen for his mind; she loved his physicality. He was tall, with wide shoulders and strong arms. She would stare at his dark hair while he slept and admire the way it fell in curls. She wished she could know his dreams, but he claimed he was one of the rare people who never remembered them.

They had moved in together after six months. Her lease was up, and his roommates were slobs and he wanted out. Getting their own place was something he had pushed to make happen. From the beginning they liked to keep budgets, and they were good at staying on them. They researched online for deals on everything from wine to major appliances. The furniture for their new place came mostly from yard sales and Craigslist. Their idea of a vacation was to head up into the Cascades to camp with a small flask of bourbon, a few joints, a couple of good books, and freeze-dried dinner packets from REI. It all worked because Lindsey thought *they* worked.

Exactly a year from the day they met, they were married. Lindsey's mom flew over from Wales and brought her aunt Kate and her permanently envious older sister, Margaret. Lindsey designed the wedding invitation and Paul printed it in the kitchen.

For the ceremony, Paul had on a new tan suit. Lindsey wore her grandmother's dress. She had no father to walk her down the aisle, but she wouldn't have wanted that, anyway. She wasn't going to be passed from one man to the next. A collection of friends' children served as flower girls, ring bearers, and even the musical entertainment. It seemed very special—until Paul pointed out, "Everyone *thinks* their wedding is original, but all of these events follow the *same* script for the *same* one-act play. It's just the casting, props, and set design that change. A wedding ceremony is all just a question of production values."

She decided he was right. Traditions and customs varied, but vows, flowers, and words of commitment were essentially following the same conventions. Lindsey and Paul's show was modest and not even up to community theater standards. That wasn't so much an anti-materialistic choice as the reality of their lives. They were saving to buy their first house. Lindsey had some student loan debt, but even if they'd had a lot of money, they didn't believe in showing off or being wasteful. They were glad they lived in Portland, where buying a house was still within reach.

Her mum cried throughout the whole ceremony. Maybe she'd always believed Lindsey would come home to Wales. As soon as she and Paul kissed, it started to rain. Not a drizzle, but hard. Everyone ran for cover, and Lindsey's mother slipped, spraining her ankle. Paul told his new wife he believed the weather was his parents, doing their part from the sky. They were six feet under, but he would never get over thinking they were just around the corner, ready to spoil his plans. That was the legacy of growing up with two drunks.

Olivia was born on their one-year wedding anniversary. Lindsey juggled teaching part-time with motherhood, feeling guilty that she wasn't giving either her best. But that was the conundrum of a career and parenthood. There were never enough hours in the day to find a moment to just relax and feel triumphant.

Carlos came along two years and three months after Olivia's arrival. Once they were both out of diapers and in preschool, Lindsey went back to teaching full-time at the community college. A slip-up with her diaphragm brought Sena, five and a half years later. Lindsey wondered if her ambivalence about having a third child had gotten into her amniotic fluid. Her youngest daughter from the start wasn't like the other two. In Hinduism, Sena was the name given to Indra's wife, who was represented as a thunderbolt. As an infant, Sena cried hard for most of her colicky first six months. She talked shockingly early and never stopped being more expressive than the other two kids. Olivia was always in charge and Carlos strived to please, but Sena was her own person, never fitting the role of family baby. She was too strong for that. Lindsey's mum, visiting from Wales, said at the end of her first week with her second granddaughter, "Sena should have been a character in *Game of Thrones*. She was born to have dragons."

Sena could see her mom at a distance waiting in the Crown Victoria, but still took her time saying good-bye to every remaining classmate, one by one. Both their first and last names. Sena then bowed to Mrs. Bengay, who waited with the students, and finally headed to the dirty white car and got inside. Sena's voice was anxious as she turned to her mother. "Go."

"It looks like you made lots of new friends."

"Mark Twain said an expert is the newest person in town. They don't know me. When they do, it could be different."

Lindsey smiled at her daughter. "I doubt it."

Sena stared out the window, thinking about the events of the day. There was a kid in her class named Belly who was very, very good at math. She was very, very good at math, too. This boy named Belly didn't even have a big belly, so his name confused her.

She didn't want to go to a class with older kids for math. She wanted to stay in the second grade with the rest of the group. She had to be very careful to not be competitive with Belly and show off because then she'd get moved to a math class with older kids. She'd been through that before.

Sena made herself a promise not to jump out of her chair in class when she knew an answer, no matter what Belly did. She might even purposely get some of the problems wrong on the homework sheets. Maybe every fifth one. Most of all, she had to keep calm.

Once they got back to the motel, Sena planned to put away her school supplies and crawl under the house, where she could be with the chickens. They roosted there when they were too hot and wanted out of the afternoon sun. At school she had been told that Hawai'i's chickens were descended from red junglefowl, brought by Polynesian settlers to the islands eight hundred years earlier. So they weren't recent invaders. Sena decided this gave them a lot of rights. The birds didn't like to be separated. That's why she wanted to take chickens home when she found them out in the world. They felt better being in a group.

Plus, the cleverest chicken was impossible to spot when they were all clustered together.

Olivia waited in what she hoped was a strategic location, away from the school buses and the activity of the front doors.

She wished she'd told her brother to meet her so she wouldn't have to stand alone. But he was breaking free from what had been a kind of magical spell where she was always the boss. Since they arrived on the island he didn't seem nearly as interested in following her directives. And her little sister, as always, was a wild card. Sena might end up in prison. Or in the White House. Or both. The little kid was both fascinating and terrifying.

When people had heard Olivia was moving to Hawai'i, they were filled with envy. That felt good, especially after two years of kids whispering behind her back as if they wanted to throw her a big pity party. As far as a lot of the rain-soaked Oregonian ninth-graders were concerned, living on a tropical island without a father was a real fantasy. But they didn't know that having two parents was better than one, at least in her case. And they hadn't seen the Mau Loa, which was nothing like Olivia had envisioned when her mom said she'd bought a motel right on the beach. Plus, they had no idea how much anxiety there was in being thrown into a high school filled with hundreds of kids who had known each other since they were all in diapers.

Olivia had liked a boy in eighth grade who was a hacker. They'd been friends for years. She really had no interest in breaking into closed systems, but Evan Auerbach was consumed with electronic misadventure, and in an attempt to appear to be the kind of girl he'd like, she'd hung out in hacker chat rooms and learned a thing or two about password encryption and cyber footprints. She started playing a lot of video games and talking like a computer geek. She and Evan had spent one fantastic night jumping security firewalls and infiltrating their middle school website. She was Salt-N-Straw, which was the name of an ice cream place she liked in Portland. He was SuperSlice. Once they got into the school district's system, they signed their hacker names to a banner pop-up on the main page saying homework should be abolished and every school day should begin at 11 A.M.

The morning after their amazing online rampage Olivia worried she'd be hauled away by the police. But no one at school said anything about the cyber breach, and she never told a single person what she and Evan had done. Only a week after their crime spree he started hanging out for real, not online, with Chloe Fairbairn, and Olivia knew he was lost to her. Chloe had a big brother named Miles who was a major gamer, and her interest in video knockdowns was real.

Evan had told her about a private school on Oʻahu called Punahou. Barack Obama had gone there. Olivia did a quick search on her phone and found the website. A fantasy began to form where she attended the beautiful campus in Honolulu. It was too far to travel, so she'd have to find people to take her in. She imagined living with another student's family, a guy who looked just like the former president when he was sixteen. She knew she could write a killer essay about overcoming problems, which apparently was what schools were all looking for. Punahou had an entrance test, but that was okay because she did well on those things, especially the math sections. Both of her parents were science types. Her dad, Mr. Computer Genius, sent her to camp to learn to write code when she was nine years old. It was part of their bond. All of that would go into her Punahou essay. But she was on the opposite side of the island from the fancy private school and there was no money for something like that. Maybe they offered scholarships. She could take a crack at redesigning the Punahou website, which could give her another angle to try.

Olivia suddenly remembered that today the cable guy was supposed to finally come to the motel and hook up the internet. She would be able to go online whenever she wanted, not just when she had enough energy to walk out to the main road and squat down in what felt like a jungle to get a signal.

A voice, deep, with an aggressive edge, interrupted her rumination. "This is my spot."

The boy wasn't very tall, but he was fairly wide—thick and sturdy like a barrel with a mop of dark hair. Olivia opened her mouth to speak and felt relieved that she didn't sound as if she were from Wales. "Are you talking to me?"

"Yeah. This is my spot."

"You can't find someplace else to stand?"

"You're the new girl who bought the Kalamas' motel."

"I didn't buy it, my mom did."

"Most *haoles* who bought a motel would go to private school."

Olivia met his gaze. She knew what a *haole* was. Was he a mind reader? Her face reddened. She hoped to cover her embarrassment with sarcasm. "So, you've met a lot of white kids from Oregon who moved here after their moms bought motels?"

"Yeah. And they all go to private school because they have a lot of attitude. They don't fit in."

Olivia's eyes narrowed. "Your spot is under a tree, so I guess you *really* fit right in."

"I never said I did."

Olivia turned her back. She was done. He wasn't.

"My name's Haku. You're Olivia."

She didn't answer. How dare some kid tell her she didn't fit in? She might be new to this school and not understand local customs or history or clothing style or slang or social hierarchy, but she'd faced her share of crap and she wasn't going to be pushed around. She started across the concrete courtyard to the parking lot with her head held high, not even saying sorry when she bumped into a girl carrying a heavy load of books.

Nobody gave Olivia Hill shit and got away with it.

Carlos stood on the grass by the middle school waiting for the Crown Victoria. He could have gone to look for Olivia, but lately he found it better to leave her alone. She had a way of spreading her annoyance with life. He didn't have the negative gene. His focus was on survival. It wasn't until he lost his dad that he realized it was possible for things in his life to get really messed up. But even that tragedy didn't fundamentally change who he was. He missed his father, maybe more than anyone else in his family did, but he could admit that sometimes the guy had scared him. Not when he yelled, which he didn't do very much. It was more nerve-racking when his dad was really excited. He sometimes drove too fast or tried too hard to get Carlos to kick the soccer ball right or catch a baseball even though it was dark outside. He was intense. And in the last few years of his life, he'd gotten even more so. That's what Carlos realized once he was gone. His father had taken up a lot of space in every room he entered.

His mom was harder to figure out. In the name of peace and quiet she seemed to bend to his father's ideas. His dad once told him that his mom was "the very earth beneath their feet." What did that even mean? Maybe his dad walked all over her. He hoped not. A strange thing had happened when his father left them forever under a blanket of cold water: Carlos decided he could be whoever he wanted to be. He didn't have to play baseball or run track or pretend he liked coding camp. He didn't even have to answer to the name of a guitar player who his father had so often reminded him pioneered a blend of Latin American jazz with rock and roll. It was all his choice now.

Carlos removed the tube of sunscreen his mother had placed in his backpack and squirted a blob into his hands. The sun was so hot in Hawai'i. He was certain that his pink skin was burning even when he was standing in the shadows slathered with liquid protection. His freckles were multiplying and turning into a kind of tan as they joined together. He couldn't decide if that was good or bad. Carlos looked up to see his older sister approaching. When Olivia was close enough, he called out, "Hey." She didn't answer but seemed in her own way happy to see him as he asked, "How'd it go?"

"I survived. What about you?"

Before Carlos could answer, a car with three surfboards on a roof rack drove by. A man behind the wheel wore a butter-yellow cowboy hat. His head bobbed to the beat of music. Two twelve-year-old girls in the backseat leaned out the window. One of them shouted, "See you tomorrow, Carl!" He raised his hand and waved back. Olivia gave him the side eye.

"So, this Carl thing is for real?"

He shrugged.

Olivia sighed. "I guess you really have to learn to surf now."

"We could learn together, Liv."

"The water scares me—since Dad . . ."

She didn't finish. Carlos repeated to himself the words the therapist had told him to remember when the wall of grief hit one of his family members: *You can be there in silence. You don't have to solve the unsolvable.*

He reached over and grabbed her backpack. She half-heartedly tried to take it away from him, but he stopped her. "No, I gotta build muscles. I'm a weakling compared to the rest of the guys in my class."

He then handed his sister his tube of sunscreen.

It was at least some kind of protection.

8

Up until Chris Young showed up, it hadn't occurred to Lindsey that single, age-appropriate, attractive men might appear out of nowhere as guests. Before, she was thinking only about escaping Portland to a place where no one knew Paul Hill or the story of his spectacular rise and fall. She wanted every view to hold no memories and for every person to be a stranger. But now she focused on her life as an innkeeper in a new way. She would certainly be meeting all kinds of people. The visitor had given her emotional motivation, which turned out to be more effective than her financial imperative.

The next day she applied for her motel license. She researched cloud-based motel management systems and was surprised there were so many to choose from. Paul would have figured out the best one in an hour. For all she knew, he might have worked on writing the code that was used by some of the programs on the market.

The kids needed to help get the place ready, and the easiest thing to begin with was painting the cottages. Carlos lobbied for bright blue as a nod to the ocean. Olivia had the idea that everything should be green to blend in with the plants. Hiding was her current frame of mind.

Sena had a different idea. She explained, "Each of the main eight islands in Hawai'i had its own official color that comes from plants and flowers, except for Ni'ihau, which used the white pūpū shell."

"Are you studying that in school—the eight islands?" Lindsey asked.

"There are actually more than one hundred and thirty-seven islands."

Carlos and Olivia exchanged looks but didn't say anything. They'd learned that being impressed by their little sister was best left unacknowledged. Lindsey continued her inquiry. "What's the color of our island?"

"O'ahu is yellow. For the 'ilima plant. But I think of yellow for chickens."

Carlos directed his question to his little sister. "The sinks in the cottages are all different colors. So is that because of the islands?"

Sena looked confused. "I wasn't around when they built this place."

"Sweetheart, do you know the other island colors?" Lindsey asked.

"It's on a worksheet. Moloka'i is green. It's the kukui nut flower."

This made Olivia laugh. "It figures I'd like the kooky nut."

"It's kukui. Not kooky." Sena corrected. "Maui is pink. For a rose. The Big Island's color is red."

"For what?" asked Carlos.

"I forget. Kaua'i is purple for the mokihana berry. Lāna'i is orange, and Kaho'olawe is gray, but it's really sort of silver."

And with that, their plan was in place. The newly painted motel would match the Hawaiian islands, bright and optimistic.

They didn't sand or scrap or do prep work. They took hoses and tried to wash the exterior cottage walls, which dried quickly in the sunlight. Lindsey knew that wasn't the way it should be done, but they were all excited and she considered the painting just a test. If the colors looked good, she would hire professionals when she had income. The paint cans, rollers, trays, and tarps had all been assembled and the work was set to begin. Sena had picked a brilliant lemon yellow and was already at work when Oliva strode over. "I saw online that we should paint from the top to the bottom."

"Mom won't let me use a ladder." Sena was already running the roller on the lowest board of her chosen cottage.

"If we have a plan, it will go faster and be more efficient." Olivia sounded like she ran a construction company.

Carlos, several yards away at his cottage, called out, "I don't think there's a right way and a wrong way."

"Well, there is," Olivia answered.

"Maybe there is a right way for some people. But it's not a rule." Sena kept painting the bottom board, adding, "Rules are about safety."

"Safety is why you can't use the ladder. I'm talking about process." Olivia's voice was tight with irritation.

Lindsey headed for the kids. "We don't want to make this a fight. It's a group project."

"Most of those are pretty messed up," Carlos called back.

Olivia bristled. "I'm just trying to help."

"Of course you are, sweetheart."

Lindsey put her hand on her oldest child's shoulder as Sena continued recklessly pushing her roller. She had already come to the end of the lowest board and turned the corner to keep going. Olivia was wide-eyed. "Oh my God, Sena, you need to finish one side before you start on another! What are you doing?"

Sena kept moving. "There are many ways to peel an orange. I like to do it in one piece starting from the bottom."

Carlos looked up from his zigzag painting approach. "I wonder what Dad would have said was best."

"He would have hired someone," Olivia answered.

And on that they all agreed.

The kids' personalities accurately dictated their painting style. Olivia, who was about order and direction, got the most done by the time they were ready to call it quits. Carlos pushed his roller in all directions but got two sides mostly finished. And Sena, not able to use the ladder, had circled her structure, coiling her way upward, leaving a blank space over her head and a trough of paint on the ground below. Lindsey knew it was magical thinking to believe the timbers felt the renewal and straightened, but she couldn't let go of the idea that the cottages looked less crooked, and certainly more cheerful, with their new overlay.

Lindsey called to the kids, "We're going out tonight."

Carlos looked confused. "Really? Are you sure"?

"Come on, aren't you sick of spaghetti?"

"Totally. But we don't have money for restaurant food."

"You all worked hard and we're getting the motel in shape. We need to celebrate."

For the last two years they'd only gone to budget restaurants, and only on special occasions; when they did go, they'd always split orders and leave with take-away containers. Not just because Sena (the world's pickiest eater) never finished: They loaded up what was left in the breadbaskets and walked away with the small, gold-topped butter containers if any were still on the table.

Food was expensive on the island. Lindsey split an order of garlic chicken and chopped steak with gravy among herself and Olivia and Carlos. Sena got salad and peanut butter rolls. They lingered at the picnic table outside and Lindsey let the kids buy ice cream from the market next door. Working together in the hot sun, even if they weren't following Olivia's constant directives, made Lindsey feel they were united in a new way.

When it came to finding places to eat, Lindsey was making an effort to get her kids to try food they'd never tasted before. Sena took an instant liking to poi, which was made from taro root. Carlos fell hard for kalua pig, which was similar to southern pulled pork, but without the barbeque sauce. Olivia gravitated to passion fruit, known as *lilikoi*. Lindsey went for clear mung bean noodles and many of the Asian-introduced dishes that had become part of Hawaiian dining. But it was shave ice, mispronounced by most tourists as "shaved ice," that they all agreed upon. On the mainland there were snowcones. They felt shave ice was so much better since the ice wasn't crushed but instead shaved from blocks. The kids' favorite syrup flavors were a mix of guava, mango, and kiwi. Lindsey liked peach and lemon-lime. Shave ice was sold in small shops along the road, and it didn't take much for the kids to get Lindsey to park the Crown Victoria for a chance at the treat.

Back home the harmony collapsed. The supermarket stayed open until midnight, and Sena insisted on rice cakes for her lunch the next day. Lindsey had tried to convince her younger daughter that they could easily swing by on the way to school, but Sena wasn't going for it. She wanted the rice cakes and she wouldn't back down.

Carlos interrupted their bickering to say, "Sena, the happiest day of my life is going to be when I get my driver's license because you and I would be back with the rice cakes by now."

Lindsey was exhausted when she got into the Crown Victoria. That night there was almost no moon. The island could be very dark, even with a sky littered with stars. Lindsey steered the large Ford cautiously down the drive out toward the main road. The overgrown plants sounded as if they were scratching to get inside the car. Sena, ever alert, looked onto the empty Kam Highway and spotted something in the distance.

"Mama, look! A car broke down. Maybe they need help."

Lindsey had no intention of approaching a parked vehicle at night, but then she realized the shape of the car with the flashing lights looked familiar. "Is that a Jeep?"

Sena nodded, adding, "Those are mostly rentals."

Lindsey didn't pause to ask how Sena knew such a thing. There had to be many Jeeps, and there was no reason to believe that this one didn't have a serial killer behind the wheel. But she put on her blinker and turned right, which was not in the direction of Foodland. "We'll drive by and take a quick look to make sure everything's okay. We're not getting out of the car." Lindsey hit the automatic lock, which activated all four doors.

The taillights of the Jeep continued to turn off and on. Lindsey felt her heart rate increase as her car's high beams revealed a single occupant behind the wheel. From the back of his head, she thought she knew who it was. Lindsey removed her boxy black eyeglasses and ran one of her hands through her hair as she pulled up alongside the Jeep. She hit the power button and the window on Sena's side slid down.

Chris Young turned in surprise. "Hey there."

Before Lindsey could answer, Sena boldly called out, "Are you having engine trouble?"

Lindsey tried to hush her. "It's okay. I know him, Sena."

"Knowing him doesn't have anything to do with his car breaking down."

Chris smiled in the shadows. "My car's okay. Thank you." He pointed up to the night sky. "Delphinus—the Latin version of the Greek word for dolphin."

"You were looking at the stars?" Sena was interested.

"I was driving home from dinner and I had to pull over. The constellations here are so incredible."

Sena leaned closer to the windshield in order to see more.

"You two are out late." He smiled.

"We're just going to the market."

Sena added, "For rice cakes."

Chris nodded. "I like peanut butter on my rice cakes."

This seemed to make Sena happy. "Me too."

"When you're back home, check out the stars. There's not even a quarter moon, so there's a lot to see."

Lindsey answered, "We will." She leaned awkwardly toward the Jeep, pressing her shoulder into her daughter. "Really nice to see you again."

He half smiled, and Lindsey surprised herself by saying, "Hey, stop by the motel if you want—I'm there most mornings after I take the kids to school. You can swim. Or just hang out."

"Really?"

"Yeah. For sure."

"Okay. Thanks. I'll do that."

"Okay then."

Sena pulled back from the windshield. "We gotta go, Mom."

Lindsey gave Chris a wave and put on her blinker. No traffic was coming in either direction, so she made a sweeping U-turn, stepping on the gas in a way that felt powerful and in charge.

Sena looked over at her mother. "Who was that guy?"

"A new friend I met last week. He used to stay at the motel."

"So, I guess you're happy we went out for the rice cakes."

"I would say yes."

"Good."

Sena handed her mother the eyeglasses that were on the seat. "You're supposed to wear these when you drive."

9

The following morning, Lindsey put on a skirt with a button-up blouse instead of her usual shorts and oversized T-shirt. After she dropped the kids at school, she found her eyeliner pencil and for the first time since arriving in Hawaiʻi made an attempt to apply makeup, placing a smudge of brown around her lashes. She borrowed Oliviaʻs shiny rose lip gloss, coppery eye shadow, and clotted brown mascara. The eye shadow was too much and she wiped it off, along with more than half of the eyeliner. Giving up on the makeup, she slipped gold hoops into her ears and slathered her legs with Tahitian vanilla body lotion. When she was finished, she walked to the bevel-edged, full-length mirror at the top of the stairs. Clusters of gray spots clouded the glass, but she could see that she was moving closer to the time when her neck would become like the top of an old sock with worn elastic. It was just beginning to expand in ways that indicated trouble. She turned her head to the side and realized that her jawline had the first hint of a wobble. Her eyelids weighed heavier than she remembered; her lips appeared to be smaller and not as full as they once were.

Everything else seemed to be expanding, but her lips were in retreat.

The mirror revealed patches of inflamed, red skin on her nose and cheeks, and she noticed an indentation above her right eye on her forehead where she'd been hit by a falling tree branch when she was younger. Suddenly that long-ago accident was a prominent facial feature. Then she saw that a few of the hairs in her soft brown eyebrows were white, and these invaders were thicker, as if to an-nounce on arrival that they were the bullies now in charge.

Was it the simple arc of aging, or did she have one more thing she could blame on losing her husband?

But then Lindsey smiled, and her eyes brightened. Her cheeks lifted, pulling back not just her mouth but also the potential jowls. It was as if the light had changed and the image before her was a version of her old self. Would it be possible to sleep while grinning? Because this was the look a man would need to see if one ever woke up in her bed. Lindsey hadn't fantasized about being in a reclining position with someone in so long that it felt ridiculous. She turned away from the looking glass and headed downstairs.

Would the guest she had invited show up?

And if so, when?

The day wore on. She kept busy with inventory lists and price comparisons for motel rooms on the island. By midafternoon her lightness of being had faded to disappointment. She took off the gold hoop earrings and changed back into her Hawaiian mom uni-form of baggy T-shirt and shorts. She didn't even lock the office door when she left, heading off to walk the beach.

As her feet scooped the wet sand, fine as flour, she thought back to the beginning, more than five years earlier. Paul had recommitted to surfing, which was something he had done when he was younger. She initially resented the hobby: With three kids at home and Sena being so young, she wanted his help on the weekends. But he had a way of making his personal time necessary in a way hers never could be be-cause he needed, he said, *to think*.

As if she didn't need thinking time? She was teaching two upper-division ecology classes, working at last on finally finishing her dissertation in atmospheric reanalysis-forced ocean simulation, and raising three kids. But then Paul proved himself right because, in his telling, he'd been deep in contemplation as he paddled to shore after two hours fighting for a decent wave when he looked up and EnGenStor appeared like a vision in the sky. He said he saw the application as if it had been written line by line in the gray clouds.

Was that even true?

It must have been.

Yet as she walked into the softer sand she had to wonder if it wasn't something he'd been working on for weeks, months, even years. Maybe the final piece of the puzzle happened in the water, but she doubted his story, although he did come home that afternoon looking possessed.

Paul barely slept for the next forty-eight hours. He sat at his computer, rarely taking time to eat, his fingers typing on his keyboard in a language that meant something only to him. The following week he scheduled a meeting to resign his well-paying tech job.

Beforehand, she and Paul had done an inventory of their lives. Lindsey remembered her husband saying, "I'm forty-one years old. Maybe it's all been leading to this!"

"It feels that way. We're set up. My job. The house. The kids."

Paul added, "Don't forget a dog, a cat, and a goat. The goat is the only one who pulls his own weight."

They'd purchased the billy because the blackberry bushes at the edge of their property were fierce and the goat was a better solution to keeping them in line than weekend pruning shearers. Plus, the smelly beast made their toddler happy. She too was fierce.

Paul told Lindsey that when he walked through the office lobby after quitting his job, he noticed the glass in the overhead light fixture was cracked and there were scratches on the receptionist's desk. The big fig plant in the corner had yellowish leaves and was dying. The whole place looked different. He knew at his boss's "Good luck, Paul" there would be no two weeks of wrapping things up. No good-bye party or farewell dinner. His email was locked and his parking card deactivated. Paul Hill was deleted from the system. The assets of the business left the building at the end of every workday, and he was a liability now—he was the competition. He'd had an idea, a brilliant one, and that made him instantly a threat to his former employer. At least, that's how he'd explained it to her.

But as Lindsey watched the surf lap the O'ahu shoreline, she tried to analyze what he'd told her. Why hadn't his colleagues gathered in some way to wish him well when he left? Weren't those people his friends? Had they tried to do something and he rejected it? That was possible. She realized now that he had the ability to move on from situations without looking back.

Nothing was the same after Paul gave notice. Lindsey went to work, but every day in the classroom somehow mattered less. She'd come home to find her husband on the phone, mostly pacing in a headset around the yard. She told people later that he raised money to start EnGenStor with only two phone calls. It was probably two hundred calls, but saying two was a better narrative and that turned out to be a big part of a new business enterprise. It was only two calls that really mattered, because there were rival groups of investors vying to go into business with Paul Hill. He and Lindsey had no idea if he picked the right one, but considering what happened, she wondered if it would have made any difference.

The early months of the new company were a series of meetings that took up every waking minute. She heard Paul repeat his standard speech about the new enterprise, and he didn't need to be rested or even sober in order to deliver the pitch. He confided in her that he must be experiencing what an actor feels doing the same show night after night. He knew how to take his audience by surprise and calculate where the laughs would fall. When he was talking to tech people, he revealed just enough analytical jargon to make their heart rates rise. When he was speaking with investors, he played the part of clueless genius ripe for the picking.

But he was so happy. That part she knew she was remembering correctly. He was becoming a big shot and he liked it. To the outside world her husband seemed to get better-looking and more interesting by the day. Being the face of the new venture meant he needed expensive haircuts. Great suits. The best-fitting jeans, Italian shoes, and cashmere sweaters money could buy. She didn't remember whose idea it was, but there were photo shoots for press articles, and she was sometimes included.

Then he wanted her to go with him to New York on an important trip, and he suggested she quit teaching. It took her by surprise. He'd always been proud of her career. At one point he had been pushing her to consider going to medical school. Her understanding of biology made her a perfect candidate. When she gave notice at the college, she felt numb. She told the chair of the department that she would be back, but it didn't feel like anyone believed her. They had all heard about Paul's company. They knew about the changes. After that, she traveled with Paul on most of his trips. It was a blur of great hotels, museums, and plays mixed in with expensive sushi with lawyers and the investment team. She smiled when she was with him, and it was mostly sincere.

She missed her kids when they were out of town, but she was having a good time.

He was having a great time.

The future looked incredible.

Yet she could admit there were days when she missed her students and the routine of a job. She didn't long for staff meetings or grading papers, but she had been proud of her paycheck. It had been necessary. The new company had changed that. Now she could see that she and Paul had been happiest when they had nothing. That was a cliché but absolutely true. And there was a corollary: Her family had been the most miserable when they'd thought they had it all and then were confronted with the fact that it wasn't going to last.

After the paperwork was signed, she and Paul owned 17 percent of his new business. They had both thought it would be more, but the suits came in and split things up, and 17 percent of potentially millions and millions of dollars was still going to be a lot. What was important, Paul had explained, was that he had control of the operation. They were the majority stakeholders after the pie had been sliced, resliced, and divided again. They still had the most important piece.

She felt the sand change and become abruptly pebbly. She stepped on something sharp and looked down to see the edge of a shell. It had been positioned on the perfect angle to cut into the ball of her foot. She watched a line of blood appear. The vibrancy of the red hit her.

Paul was dishonest.

That was the hardest part for her to admit.

His new business venture had been brilliant. It had changed their lives. That part was unassailable. But he had broken the law.

Paul had always been a man of contradictions. He was competitive and aggressive, but could be exceedingly kind and generous to complete strangers. He was self-involved, but had a good heart. And in the pursuit of something bigger than the life he and Lindsey had built, he was capable of making colossally bad decisions.

Lindsey took off her sunglasses and wiped her eyes. The sun cut through the billowy sky, casting shadows on the sharp mountains that tumbled straight into the ocean. She had on a hat, but she could feel that her skin was burning. Hawaiian rays were intense. Then the breeze kicked up off the water, and the sun disappeared abruptly behind fast-moving clouds, providing the relief of momentary shade.

She should have turned back earlier. She'd be late now to pick up the kids.

From what Olivia could figure out, the school's social power players were on the football team and the cheerleading squad. Football seemed to be the sun, moon, and stars at Kahuku. The second tier of social status was a group she thought of as the Water People. Some of these kids were professional athletes, which Olivia had to admit was no joke. At this high school you could be a pro surfer and still show up for math class. But Carlos had explained that the really great surfers didn't go to school. They got their diplomas online because they were making a living bobbing around in the water. According to him, the best girl surfer in the world should have been in the junior class. Olivia had been uncomfortable in the water even before her father lost his life in the ocean. She found it ironic that her mother had chosen to take her and her siblings to live in a place where the crashing waves were a constant soundtrack.

But Olivia could see that people didn't bow down to just the pro surfers and the football players. All athletes were in the top social tier. The stars of basketball, baseball, track, wrestling, and even water polo were school somebodies. And music was a way bigger deal than at her school on the mainland. That was just one more thing she'd never master. It was too late for her to play an instrument well, and her singing voice was for crap. Walking down the wide corridor she saw the weekly meeting of what was called Christian Fellowship. There were cute guys (football players) who looked like they were into that. But after losing her dad in a surfing accident she knew there was no God. She didn't do modern dance and she had never been part of the theater crowd. Out back in the far corner of the parking lot she noticed a group of kids who seemed like they might be druggies. Or else they just liked to smoke cigarettes and drink coffee. She knew she wasn't any kind of rebel, so that wasn't an option.

Olivia walked toward the back exit staring at paper flyers on the walls for air riflery, girls' volleyball, and the upcoming football homecoming weekend. She saw notices for SAT exam dates, community fundraisers, and a shuttle van scheduled to take juniors and seniors to meet college representatives from the mainland at a hotel on Waikīkī. There were pep rallies, service assemblies, and something called Zumba Under the Stars. There was a Pasefika meeting and multiple library events, one of which featured a lecture on mental health.

She wondered when that started.

Carlos met her under the big banyan tree and they walked across the wide expanse of concrete away from the school buildings toward the carpool line. "Olivia, it's okay to tell me stuff. I won't say anything to Mom. When we saw the therapist after Dad died, she said to let people know how you feel."

Olivia felt an uncontrollable wave of emotion rise up inside her. "What's that supposed to mean? I don't have anything to tell you. Sure, okay, I miss Oregon. I miss knowing people! I really miss our old house and the old neighborhood more than I miss the big house. I even miss the crap apartment on Sunnyside, which is crazy because the shower in that place was like someone was standing on a stool spitting on you."

Carlos mumbled, "Yeah, I really don't miss the apartment shower."

Olivia's internal wave was crashing hard. "I want to be able to order online like we used to do. I'd like to get food delivered and listen to my friends talk about each other. I want to go to a shopping mall and think about cool bands and be—"

He interrupted, "And be an asshole?"

"We were never assholes."

"We sort of were."

She didn't respond. He continued, "When we had all the money. After we moved to the big house."

Olivia shrugged, but she was drawn into the past. "Remember when they first hired Alba?"

"And I thought Dad said she was an 'oh, pear,' which was totally mean but it made sense when we met her because she had a big butt and small shoulders."

Olivia laughed.

It was working. He was making her feel better.

Carlos continued. "In the beginning I felt bad for her because she would hang up our clothes and towels and make our beds. It was like we had our own maid. Then I got used to it."

"Yeah, and she cooked all that food with gravy. Before that no one made us gravy."

"Plus, she did my homework sometimes."

Olivia was genuinely outraged. "No way."

"I didn't ask her. She just went through my backpack and started going over the assignments."

"Wow. That's crazy."

"Everything was crazy back then. Sena only wanted to eat orange food. And wouldn't wear shoes."

Olivia nodded. "But Alba figured out Sena could read."

"Yeah. When Sena got hold of the weekly schedule and saw she had a swimming lesson!"

"She wasn't even four. She was really difficult. Dad was the only one who was allowed to comb her hair."

Carlos ran his hands through his red curls. "Dad always stood up for her. Maybe she was his favorite."

Olivia looked out and saw the Crown Victoria inching forward in the carpool line.

"Do you think she understands Dad did that illegal stuff—before he died?"

Carlos sighed. "I doubt it. I barely do."

They stopped talking as they headed for the car.

"How was school?" Lindsey asked.

"Painful" was all Olivia would offer up.

Carlos shrugged. "It's going pretty well for me."

Lindsey tried to think of something positive to say but only managed, "It's natural to feel like an outsider."

Olivia saw her mother's toes clench in her flip-flops. Good. She was making her uncomfortable. Why should she be the only one worried about everything? Then her mom surprised her by saying, "There are a lot of Indigenous Polynesian people in Kahuku. And a lot of *hapa* kids. That's the Hawaiian word for 'mixed.' Their families came from the Philippines, Japan, China, Korea, and Samoa."

Before Olivia was angry. Now she was insulted. "I know what *hapa* means, okay?"

Instead of being hurt, Lindsey looked to Olivia like she felt sorry for her, which was even worse.

Carlos piped up from the backseat. "I have a shit-ton of freckles and red hair and a Spanish name and I'm left-handed. We have to just go with being different. I think it could be good for us to be outsiders."

"But I want to be an *insider*," Olivia said.

Sena, in the backseat, joined the conversation. "Sometimes a person doesn't get to choose."

10

———

Sena was finally allowed to move to the desk closest to the window, where she could appear to be looking at Mrs. Kekoa while at the same time have a view of the sky. As she sat there, Sena's probing mind usually focused on one of two things: the ever-changing weather or her chickens. Maybe, she thought, she would be a scientist when she was grown up and she would study climate. Or the effect of climate shifts on birds. Oregon had all kinds of great clouds, but Hawai'i was even better because the forms came and went much faster, and they didn't press down on the world in the same way as in Portland. Here what she saw was more sky than anything else. The weather on the planet was changing. Sena decided she might make that her life.

But then there were the chickens. Tink was her favorite. The rust-colored bird had taken to running to greet her as soon as she got out of the Crown Victoria. Her secret was that she gave the birds treats. Sena had salvaged the old sheets that her mom had thrown in the trashcan, and had spread them on the always-damp earth under their house. Early one morning, when everyone else was asleep, Sena took four of the empty Rubbermaid plastic containers that were in the laundry room. She walked toward the south edge of the property, where bamboo grew on both sides of a footpath, and filled the tubs with the fallen yellowy bamboo leaves, which covered the ground like a mat. They were tough and thin, many split by the wind but as close to hay as she could find. Sena crawled under the house, dragging the Rubbermaid containers with her. She turned them on their sides on top of the old sheets and spread the bamboo leaves, finishing off her project by sprinkling uncooked rice on the new bedding.

The chickens took to the setup immediately.

Sena rightly believed that she was the only one operating a motel. She worried about the birds when she was at school. They were vulnerable to attack from mongooses. She'd never heard of a mongoose until moving to Hawai'i, and decided the name was just plain wrong. A mongoose was not a goose. It wasn't any kind of bird. It was a rodent.

At dinner that night, Sena explained, "The mongoose shouldn't be in Hawai'i."

Olivia put a forkful of mac and cheese into her mouth. "Says who?"

Sena gripped her fork. "Says me!"

Carlos was genuinely intrigued. "What's a mongoose?"

"A furry animal. If a rat, a squirrel, and a cat had a baby, that's what you'd get."

Carlos nodded. "Sounds cool."

"They're not. They're like weasels with furry tails, but they aren't cuddly. And they like to eat meat. They love chicken." Sena crunched her paper napkin into a tight ball. "They came to the Big Island in 1883 because a sugar plantation owner thought they would help control the rats. So he brought Asian mongooses over in cages on a big boat."

Carlos considered. "Is it mongooses or mongeese?"

"It's mongooses because they don't have *anything* to do with the birds, which is what I already said."

"I missed that part."

Lindsey turned around from the sink, where she was filling water glasses. "I haven't seen a mongoose since we got here."

"That's because they're sneaky." Sena had stopped eating and her face was getting red. "Many people on the island are very mad because the mongooses kill the birds and they also eat turtle eggs and the lizards that kill the insects, so that means more bugs everywhere. But that's not even the worst part. Rats are awake at night and mongooses are awake in the day! So it was a doomed plan from the start."

Olivia couldn't help but look in her mother's direction as she muttered, "A doomed plan. They're out there."

The following morning, Lindsey overslept and spent too long untangling Sena's wild hair into something she could braid into submission. Her younger daughter had been in one of her more irritating moods and insisted on giving her mother "a beauty treatment of her own" in return for sitting still to have her hair done. Sena found Lindsey's brown eyeliner pencil in the bathroom and drew arches on her mother's forehead above her actual eyebrows. The dark marks made Carlos laugh. Even Olivia found her mother's face amusing. The sound of her kids' giggling was irresistible, so Lindsey let Sena apply shimmering pink lipstick to her mouth, ignoring the outline of her lips.

By the time Lindsey had organized Sena's sack lunch, they were running late, so she stayed in her old nightgown and didn't remove the makeup for the drive to school. Since she never got out of the car during drop-off, what difference did it make?

A half-hour later she returned to the motel to find a silver Jeep parked on the gravel and Chris Young waiting in the wicker chair on the front porch of the office. At his side were two cups with a logo she recognized from a place in Kahuku. He raised an arm as she parked the car, calling out, "Good morning."

She didn't know if he heard her reply of "Holy shit . . ."

Lindsey looked down at her nightgown. She had driven in bare feet and wasn't even wearing her flip-flops. Or a bra. Her hair was piled high on her head and held in place with a red chip clip, which had been used only a half hour before to secure a large bag of Terra Real Vegetable Chips. She had on her boxy black glasses and a second set of eyebrows courtesy of Sena. She glanced into the rearview mirror and could see that some of the shimmery pink lipstick that extended far beyond her mouth was also stuck to her front teeth. Lindsey wiped her lips with the back of her hand and felt the lip gloss spread to her right cheek. She silently cursed her younger daughter as she inhaled, exhaled, and then got out of the Crown Victoria.

She returned Chris's greeting with a fumble of words that were supposed to be "good morning," but sounded to her own ears like "kid warning." She then walked up to the bungalow, smiling stiffly. "If you could give me a second. I took the kids to school and. . . ."

She didn't even finish the sentence. She swept right past him and was certain she heard a small laugh mix in with the slam of the screen door as she headed up the stairs.

Moving as if she were in some kind of competition, she scrubbed off the second set of eyebrows and the pink lip gloss, brushed her teeth, and combed out her hair. She didn't slather her legs with Tahitian vanilla body lotion or find her gold hoop earrings, but she put on a bra, slipped a floral sundress over her head, and jammed her feet into her sneakers.

Lindsey came outside only four minutes later, having transformed into something that made Chris Young get to his feet. He was the one who seemed unnerved now. He handed her the full cup of coffee. "It's probably not very warm."

Lindsey smiled. "Thank you. Warm enough."

"I'm sorry I showed up unannounced. And so early. I didn't have your number or I would have called."

"Not a problem. My daughter Sena was in charge this morning. For the record, I usually don't wear a clown face and my pajamas to school drop-off."

He shrugged. "I'm a fan of pajamas. Though on the fence about clowns."

Lindsey took a big gulp of the coffee and was grateful it was cold. She looked back into the office as if she'd left something important inside, which prompted him to say, "Don't let me get in the way. I'm sure you have all kinds of things to do getting the motel ready."

She let out what sounded like a sigh but was actually the release of an anxiously held breath. "It's pretty overwhelming. My strategy is to pick a single thing and make that my next assignment."

"What's today's plan?"

"I'm still figuring that out." She needed new plumbing, a real painter, a roofer, and a carpenter. She sighed. "You wouldn't happen to be a licensed electrician?"

His exuberance caught them both by surprise. "It's your lucky day."

"Don't be cruel."

"Okay, maybe I'm not licensed. But close. My uncle had his own electrical business. I worked for him with my cousins every summer when I was growing up. He had us on ladders or in crawl spaces fishing down wires, installing fixtures. By the time I was in college he handed over whole jobs to me. I'm serious—I know electricity."

"That's amazing."

"So what's going on? Is there a switch that doesn't work or—"

She stopped him. "You're on vacation. You don't want to look at dead electrical outlets."

"Show me one."

"Come on—if you weren't here, what would you be doing today?"

He looked uneasy. "I'd probably hike the Hau'ula Loop Trail. Then do some writing later in the afternoon."

Suddenly she had a vision for her morning. *What the hell*, she thought. *Why not share it?* "Okay. What if you look at a few of the outlets and then I play hooky and we both go for a hike? I haven't done anything like that since I got to the islands. I walk on the beach, which is great, but I'd love to try something new."

He took a moment to answer. "Sounds good."

Lindsey turned with an attempt at chipper competence and he followed her inside. She'd just invited herself to go with him on a hike. She didn't know a thing about him. She pushed away the thought that it was a bad idea.

Carlos had brought in one of Rangi Kalama's toolboxes from the shed and left it in the front room. Chris found a screwdriver and they headed upstairs. Lindsey was relieved that she forced her kids to make their beds every morning; it was messy in their rooms but nothing to be embarrassed about.

Chris started popping off the electrical plates, but he didn't even look closely at anything before telling her, "Normally I'd say a dead outlet could be a GFCI reset or even loose wiring, but it looks like nothing in here has been changed in years. So probably a circuit blew."

Two of the outlets in her bedroom upstairs didn't work. And neither did the light in the narrow hallway or a wall outlet in the bathroom.

"We need to check the fuse box."

Lindsey had no idea where it was, but Chris didn't even have to consult the Kalamas' tattered notebook. He was certain it was outside. As they started back down the stairs, Chris glanced up at the fishing net hanging from the ceiling. "I bet this netting went up decades ago. It's so great."

Lindsey looked at the collection of shells and glass floats trapped behind the diamond-shaped netting. "The Kalamas believed that change wasn't inevitable. I guess I admire that about them."

"Or maybe they simply decided that upgrading isn't always an improvement."

Lindsey didn't want to start an argument, yet she couldn't stop herself. "But isn't that kind of a risky position in the motel business? I mean, people don't want towels that feel like sandpaper and lights that don't work."

"Agreed. There's not a lot of charm in a dark bathroom."

Lindsey didn't believe he truly understood her point until moments later he opened the rusty metal cover and looked at the electrical panel outside.

"Wow . . ."

"Not 'wow' good, right?"

"You don't see glass fuses like this very often—super old-school. They screw in. That metal alloy ribbon carries the current. If it's overloaded, the ribbon melts, and that opens the circuit."

"Right." She had taught biological science, but her knowledge of physical science was spotty.

"These things protect against short circuits that might cause a fire. But it looks like the load is too much for most of these fuses."

Chris picked up several of the dusty glass cylinders, which were stacked in a row on the bottom of the panel box. "These are all blown. Plus, I don't see a main breaker."

"But there has to be one—right?"

"Maybe not. It's how you turn everything off at once. It's a safety thing. It doesn't look like there have been many upgrades."

"So the wiring is unsafe?"

"At the very least you need a new electrical service panel."

He shut the rusty metal door of the box. Lindsey tried not to look as deflated as she felt. "I bought the property sight unseen, and I only got the place because I put in my offer that I wouldn't tear anything down. I'd keep running the motel the way it is—"

He interrupted her. "I can do it."

"Do what?"

"Fix the stuff. We'll have to go to an electrical supply store. I'll need to be able to turn off the main. . . ." He stared up at the wires. "And that's always tricky. You'll have to invest in a good ladder."

She was confused. "You're not serious?"

"It's a challenge. And now that I've seen what's going on, I'd be worried if you didn't immediately replace some of this stuff. It's a serious hazard."

Chris took his phone and began looking online for electrical supplies. Lindsey could feel herself growing more anxious. "How much would you charge? I've got a budget for repairs but—"

He shook his head. "No charge. But it's going to take the better part of a day. Maybe longer. We probably have to go to Honolulu to get what I'll need."

"You can't just rewire my motel for free. I don't even know you."

"I'm offering to change out your service panel. Not rewire your motel. And I *want* to do it."

"I have to pay you." She was firm.

Chris turned, and his eyes met hers with what felt to Lindsey to be more of a challenge than an act of charity. "Okay, then. How about this—I put in the new service panel and you let me stay in one of the cottages. Just a few days. The one you've painted red. Best view."

Lindsey felt a combination of excitement and bewilderment. She didn't answer, but took a seat on the bench next to the office.

"Yes." That was all she could get out. Then she added, "I have three kids. Two daughters and a son. You met my youngest. It's not that quiet around here."

If three kids were a surprise, he didn't show it. Then she realized he'd been upstairs and seen their bedrooms.

He smiled. "That's cool. I like kids."

After going under the house, he delivered more bad news. "The wiring is all what's called knob-and-tube. You really don't see that anymore. No one should use a hair dryer or even the toaster until it's been replaced."

"So it's not just getting the service box?"

"Panel. That will make things safer. But this whole structure needs to be rewired."

She looked away, hoping it might appear she was thinking critically, when in fact she was clenching her jaw in an attempt to keep from screaming, "What the bloody *hell*?"

She glanced back and saw he was waiting expectantly. Apparently, there was more to share. He pointed beneath the office. "You've got a very active chicken situation going on under there that will need to be cleared out."

"That's just Sena. She's decided they're pets."

"There are sheets, plastic tubs, water bowls, a mess of bamboo leaves, and stacks of old phone books. Pretty much all of it is covered in bird shit. Chickens carry bacteria. Salmonella and campylobacter. Pretty soon the smell alone would mean you'd have to clear it out. But it all has to go for me to get under there to work."

"Wow . . . I'm sorry."

"It's not your fault."

"Of course it is. I didn't even know my daughter had been under the house."

His voice, calm and reassuring, brought her back from the edge. "Let's just do this one step at a time. I can start on the service panel. There's time to get the stuff out from under there."

Lindsey flashed on a new problem. "Do I need to get a permit?"

"That's up to you. I'm not licensed. And they'd insist on that. But I'll do all the work to code. The requirements are available online."

For the briefest of moments, she was skeptical. It wasn't as if she could ask for references. What if he did something wrong and the office burned down? She pushed the thought aside because apparently the office and the cottages were all about to burn down anyway. Olivia had already fried the upstairs bathroom outlet while blowing out her hair.

The hike and the swim were off. She couldn't help but feel disappointed. Then she remembered she'd agreed to let him live in one of her cottages. So she'd have someone to hike and swim with in the future. If nothing else, there would be another adult on the property. A possible friend.

11

At the Home Depot in Pearl City, Chris filled a cart with supplies as he explained he was going to increase the amperage when he replaced the service panel. Moving down an aisle with framed mirrors toward the cash registers, Lindsey caught sight of herself. She was a freckled white Englishwoman walking alongside a handsome Black man in hiking shorts. She looked out of place. He didn't. Nearly everyone she saw was some kind of ethnic mixture. There was no racial majority in Hawai'i. She knew more people identified as Asian than any other group. It was so different from Oregon. She wished she could have claimed that diversity was why she had picked Hawai'i. But that was a lie. She hadn't done any kind of sociological research. She had simply scrolled through island real estate listings late at night when she couldn't sleep. It was an impulsive swing, not some kind of well-executed plan.

By the time they arrived back at the motel, Lindsey was running late to get the kids. She was always on time or even early for school pickup, so she was certain her children would be worried. Or irritated. Olivia would probably be both. Carlos was going to stay after school to watch football practice and had a ride home with a classmate, so at least she would only be late for two kids.

When Lindsey pulled up to the elementary school parking lot, Sena was the last one waiting with the man in a yellow vest who supervised the drop-offs and pickups. Lindsey hadn't even come to a full stop before she shouted out the window to her daughter, "I'm so sorry, sweetheart. I lost track of time."

Sena didn't look in the least bit upset. She had her backpack and carried a book. She climbed in the Crown Victoria and before the door shut she was pointing at a page. "I want you to see something."

Lindsey glanced over. When her daughter showed an interest in living things it felt so validating. They both shared a love of the natural world.

"Look. It's a centipede. They have giant ones here. This is real size. They bite and it *really* hurts." Sena's finger was pointing to a photograph in the book.

Lindsey tried to keep her eyes on the road but at the same time sneak a peek at the insect, which appeared in the picture to be as long as her hand.

"So you're interested in centipedes?"

Sena turned the page to another photo of what looked to Lindsey to be an even more alarming centipede. Sena continued, "They are everywhere. But guess what? The chickens *eat* them."

Right then and there Lindsey would have committed to taking in as many chickens as possible, because the last thing she wanted at her motel was a mini-snake with legs. But Chris had warned her about the fowl carrying salmonella and campylobacter. Lindsey taught science. Those bacteria were real. She was thinking how she might segue from the insects to Sena's relationship with chickens when her youngest daughter said, "Mrs. Kekoa said that centipedes are ʻaumākua."

Lindsey waited, but Sena didn't explain, so she asked, "ʻAumākua? What's that?"

Sena shut the book. "Mrs. Kekoa says ʻaumākua are what Native Hawaiians call ancestors—that means people from their past—that live around them. Only not as people. As spirits."

Lindsey nodded. She knew there was more coming.

Sena continued, "Common ʻaumākua in Hawaiʻi are owls. We have those at the motel. They can help—if you leave them alone.

Mrs. Kekoa said that owls rescue lost souls of dead people and take them to where they belong. But things like lying can bring bad stuff from the 'aumākua. They aren't all good. Even if you think so at first."

Seven years on the planet with this child had taught Lindsey not to push back when Sena fixated on something. But she had to ask, "Is this what you're learning in class? They're teaching you about the Hawaiian spirit world?"

Sena stared out the window. "You were late, so I got to talk to my teacher. I'm gonna learn more about 'aumākua on my own now."

Lindsey nodded "Okay, sweetheart. That sounds interesting."

Sena's voice was low and ominous (at least to Lindsey) as she whispered, "We just have to hope that the centipedes don't decide to come into the cottages. That can happen if they are part of some- one's 'aumākua and get mad at us."

Lindsey decided to postpone the talk about moving the chick- ens out from under the house until her daughter wasn't so focused on evil spirits. She wondered how Paul would have dealt with the 'aumākua. He had been close to his youngest child and had always comforted her. Lindsey wished she had the same ability.

Olivia had a scowl on her face when Lindsey arrived, but she thankfully had nothing to say about centipedes, owls, or the unseen Hawaiian mystical world. Her voice was icy as she got in the car. "You're late."

"I know. I'm so sorry. There are electrical problems at the motel and—"

Lindsey stopped apologizing because it seemed obvious that Olivia wasn't paying attention. She was watching a group of boys vigorously stomping in unison on a sports field. Sena looked over at the kids. "What're they doing?"

Olivia mumbled, "It's called haka. The P.E. teacher said it came from Māori tradition. I guess it's some kind of war dance."

Lindsey put the car in drive and carefully pulled away from the curb. "So, a lot happened today."

Neither of her daughters responded, so she forged on. "I discovered that the whole motel needs to be rewired. But the good news is I already found someone to do it. He's going to live right on the property, which will be really helpful."

Olivia gave her a sideways glance. It turned out she was listening. "Some electrical guy is moving in? That's weird. Doesn't he have his own home?"

"He's not normally an electrician. He's just visiting the island on vacation. He's a writer."

Sena looked interested. "Does he write books or for a magazine or the internet?"

"Books."

"What kind of books?"

"I don't know the titles. You'll have to ask him. His name is Chris."

Olivia was concerned. "You have to back up. I don't get it. You hired a writer to wire the motel? Did you get some kind of great deal? Did you find him on Craigslist?"

"He was a guest of the Kalamas for years. He used to stay at the motel with his wife."

Olivia pressed on. "So the Kalamas sent him to come fix stuff? That's good. Did he get the plug working in the bathroom?"

Sena pulled her insect book close to her chest. "I might be a writer when I grow up. I want to talk to him."

"Thank you, Sena. That's the right attitude."

Lindsey reached over and turned on the radio. "This is Island 98.5, your home for island reggae."

Olivia talked right over the announcer. "Repair guys get to look at all your personal things and see what you're doing and you don't know them but they suddenly know you. I hope he's not creepy. Because repair guys can be creepy."

"Olivia, that's an awful thing to say."

Olivia only shrugged. "You need to watch more horror movies."

"You need to change your attitude. We need a lot of help and we're lucky to get it."

Lindsey turned up the radio even louder. It was no longer possible to have a conversation. She realized her heart was pounding. All day she'd felt a new anxiousness to add on to her confused grief. But this didn't need analysis. Maybe that was the problem with having been married for so long. That's what almost two decades of Paul Hill had done to her. She was riddled with loneliness. She missed adult companionship. She wanted it so badly that she'd allowed a total stranger to move into one of the cottages. Olivia's concern was legitimate.

Lindsey tried to push down her conflicting emotions, working to make herself strong, but when she put on the signal to turn off the highway into the motel, she heard Sena's voice. "Mama, why are you crying?"

Olivia went down to the beach and sat on the hard-packed sand just far enough from the waves to stay dry. There was no way all of her mom's gushing tears were her fault. Before they got out of the car, Lindsey had wiped her face and then blown her nose. But then Olivia watched as her mom pulled out the elastic that was holding up her hair and glanced up into the rearview mirror to see how she looked. What was that about?

The answer stepped out of the office onto the porch. The vacationing writer who was also some kind of electrician turned out to be cool. Olivia did a quick inventory, noting he was a Black man with small ears, and eyes that were sort of far apart. They were big eyes, so it made his face look open and friendly, not like a fish. He might have once been an athlete, because for an old guy (he had to be at least forty) he was pretty ripped.

No wonder her mom had on earrings.

But Rangi and Pearl Kalama hadn't sent him to help. He'd just showed up. Because, according to her mom, he used to visit the motel with his wife. She had died and he put her in the ocean in front of the motel. Sena had whispered to Olivia on hearing this news: "That means now she's just sand and algae."

Olivia found the idea of spreading someone's ashes pretty gross.

But still, she wished they could have done that with her dad. Of course, there would have been a big argument over where to put him. She would have voted for the path by the river in Portland because that's where her dad had taught her to ride her bike when she was six. She could see Carlos saying Dad should be in the ocean, since he liked to surf. But he'd *died* in the water, so that didn't feel right. Olivia remembered reading how a bunch of South American Indigenous cultures had practiced endocannibalism. She liked the word. What if she took her dad's bone chips and hid them in oatmeal, which she sometimes made for everyone for breakfast? Only later would she explain the grit was their father. Then, as she had been told more times than she could remember, he would truly live inside them. Olivia started to laugh. She wanted to tell her brother and sister, but it was doubtful they would think that "Dad oatmeal" was as darkly funny as she did.

Olivia was still staring at waves and listening to shore birds when Carlos got home. He came down to the beach and took a seat next to her in the sand, extending a bag of sweet Maui onion potato chips. Olivia scooped up a handful. "You know they don't make these in Maui."

Carlos shrugged. "Wherever they make them, they taste good." He crunched a mouthful of chips. "I met Mom's new electrician."

"Yeah?" She hoped it didn't sound like she was interested.

"He told Sena he was a ghostwriter. I like ghost stories."

"Don't be an idiot. That means he doesn't put his name on the stuff he writes."

Carlos dug the heels of his shoes into the sand. "If I did all the work of writing a book, I'd for sure want credit." He looked over his shoulder. Sena, followed by four chickens, was heading toward them. He turned back to his big sister. "Incoming."

Sena dropped onto the sand next to her brother. The chickens stayed at a distance, having stopped to peck at a piece of seaweed that was covered with sand flies. She had news.

"Mom's new worker is a pescatarian."

"Really?" Olivia asked.

"That's what he said. He told me he hasn't eaten chicken in ten years."

"I'd never be able to do that. I love Chicken McNuggets," said Carlos.

Olivia rolled her eyes. "You like anything from McDonald's."

"Because it's all really good." He glanced over at his little sister. "A ghostwriter means he doesn't put his name on his books."

"He told me. People will pay money to get their own name on stuff they didn't write. It's cheating. But he said if they're famous enough, it's okay to cheat."

Olivia liked being an expert. "I think that's what Trump did on his SATs. Paid someone."

Carlos got to his feet. The chip bag was empty. He held it upside down and little bits of salty potato shards were picked up by the wind. The chickens scurried after them. "McDonald's has fish sandwiches. Maybe we can talk Mom into going there for dinner."

Olivia gave him a sly smile. "I bet we can talk her into all kinds of stuff now that the ghostwriter's here."

Her brother and sister went back up to the office, but Olivia stayed at the water's edge to think about school. Her counselor had strongly suggested she join an extracurricular activity, and she had settled on the Computer Repair Club. The next meeting was tomorrow. She didn't care much about fixing computers but felt it would look good when she applied for college. Olivia assumed everyone in the group would be doing their own thing and leave her alone. She'd show up a few times and then stop going. Hopefully no one would notice.

By the time she got to her feet to walk back from the beach she could see that the ghostwriter had the lights on in the red cottage. It was strange to have someone else on the property.

Olivia came in to find her mom in the kitchen making a meal. She'd forgotten that some of her mother's food was pretty great. After her dad died, they ate mostly take-out and heated-up frozen stuff. She couldn't be mad about it. For a while no one had been very hungry, and cooking reminded them of their dad. Plus, for so long her mom seemed too sad to stand over a stove.

"That smells good, Mom."

"I'm making eggplant parm. And ziti. What do you think about starting the salad?"

Olivia knew this wasn't a question. It was interesting that orders were often delivered as inquiries. Especially by women. Olivia opened the refrigerator door and stared in wonder at the packed shelves. "Wow, where did all this food come from?"

"Chris bought it."

"The repairman? Are we allowed to eat it?"

"Of course. He bought it for us. He's got his own little refrigerator in his cottage."

"Holy shit." Olivia couldn't help but be impressed.

Carlos came down the stairs. "Yeah, I should have told you. That's how I got the good potato chips."

Olivia was caught between being happy that someone understood the value of mozzarella sticks and fresh salsa and being suspicious of such a person's intent. She pinched two grapes from a bunch and popped them into her mouth. "So I guess he's our first motel employee."

"He's not an employee. He's a *guest*. And I'd like you to be pleasant at dinner."

"I'm always 'pleasant.' And I hope all the guests buy us food *and* fix our broken stuff."

Carlos started for the doorway. "Are you guys going to fight? Because if you are, then I'm going back upstairs."

Both Olivia and Lindsey said at the same time, "We're not fighting."

Olivia realized it was hard to work up much of a case against the guy, especially after he walked into the kitchen and took over the job of making the salad dressing, which turned out to taste better than anything she would have come up with.

During dinner, Olivia tried to strike a welcoming tone. "So, Chris, I heard you're a writer. What kind of book are you working on?"

"I don't have my next project yet. I turned in my final manuscript right before I left for Hawai'i."

Carlos asked, "When you're a writer, you can just work from anywhere—right?"

"Pretty much. As long as I have good internet. Of course, it helps on some projects to be able to go to a library."

Sena had her insect book in her lap and was eating while staring at bug photos. She kept her eyes on the page. "Libraries are the most important places in any town."

"Agreed." He smiled, but she didn't take her eyes off a picture of a moth.

Lindsey chimed in. "Sena learned to read when she was only three and a half. Since then, we just can't stop her."

Olivia wanted to tell her mom not to brag about that, but she was trying hard to stay *pleasant.*

Carlos reached for another piece of garlic bread. "I don't know what I'll be when I grow up, but maybe a writer."

Olivia couldn't stop herself. "I doubt it."

Sena turned the page of her book. "To be a writer you have to be a reader."

That put an end to that line of conversation.

Carlos looked up from his pasta. "Chris, there are a ton of turtles in the water right in front of the motel. I've seen one every time I've been in. I saw a turtle that was the size of the office coffee table. Do you want to go out with me tomorrow or on the weekend to look?"

"Maybe. We'll see."

Olivia could tell he wasn't really interested. She begrudgingly had to give the guy a measure of respect. Not everyone wanted to see a turtle the size of a coffee table.

12

Lindsey lay under the thin blanket feeling a slice of warm tropical sunlight slowly inch up her thigh. The kids were all still asleep. The rooster had crowed off and on for the last hour. His morning alarms were layered into the waves and ever-present wind, which, when it hit the rafters at the right angle, made a shrill whistling sound. Lindsey's hand went to her face and her fingernail accidentally scratched her left cheek. She felt a deeper pain inside. The day before had gone well. The dinner with Chris and her children had been without incident, but this morning she hoped he'd step out of his cottage and announce he'd had a change of heart.

Because she had.

It was all a mistake.

She'd gotten what she wanted, which was to spend some time with a man. But she had woken to find her interest was gone. She didn't have the energy to search for clothes that made her look good. Or worry about her hair. She had too much going on to think about another adult. Was she supposed to get him breakfast in the morning? Figure out his lunch? She didn't want to explain her life. Or listen to any of his personal history. She felt more comfortable with her own sorrow.

She had exercised bad judgment.

She thought experience would have cured her of that.

Lindsey slid out from under the sheet, grateful that at least he hadn't appeared interested in her romantically. She glanced down from the second-story window. Just the sight of his clean silver Jeep parked near the dirty Crown Victoria felt wrong.

He was still in the red cottage when she left with the kids for school, but she took her time heading back, sitting in the car at a turnoff along Kam Highway for over an hour to watch the waves. When she finally returned to the motel there was a cup of coffee and a cinnamon twist in a waxy Ted's Bakery sack waiting on the wicker table by the front door. It wasn't hard to find him. Old sheets covered with bird shit were piled alongside the south wall of the office, along with a mound of packed garbage bags with feathers poking out the tied tops. Chris, wearing blue rubber gloves and a face mask, was on his knees under the structure, clearing out the last of the detritus from the chicken encampment. Her heart sank.

"Oh my God. I'm so sorry. You should have waited for me to help."

It was impossible to see his expression. "No problem. It's all done now. I'm going to throw this stuff in my Jeep and take it to the dump—which they call a 'convenience center.' I saw online there's one right in Lāʻie."

"No. Let me do it. I'll drive the bags over."

"You've got your own checklist. Plus, my car's a rental."

She wasn't sure how to respond. He sounded as if the decision had been made. It was like trying to pay a restaurant bill with someone who already had their credit card out. She managed, "Okay. Let me know what the dump costs."

"Will do."

She then added, "Thanks for the coffee. And the donut."

"You're welcome."

He went back to the cleanup. Maybe he was feeling some version of the regret she was experiencing? Without saying anything else, she headed down to the beach for her morning forced march. She knew there would be nothing leisurely in today's step counting. She would substitute one anxiety for another. Better to think about Paul than the stranger who was dealing with the mess her daughter and a flock of feral chickens had made. It was more comfortable to open an old wound than to worry about current drama.

Lindsey let her toes grip the sand. She couldn't remember who had first suggested private school for the kids, but she distinctly recalled a turning point the afternoon she got a flat tire while driving her Prius home from doing car pool. It had to be towed on a flatbed to the dealership. She phoned Paul to explain that the salesman was suggesting she get four new tires, not just one.

"They're saying the Michelin all-season radials. That sounds okay—right? Do you want to look up the brand?"

She heard Paul suck in air. Was he irritated she'd called for his advice?

But it turned out she wasn't reading him correctly. His inhale was a product of his excitement. "Hold off on that."

"Paul, they're shot. The guy showed me. The tread is gone."

"Let's just get rid of the car."

"Because the tires need to be replaced?" She was confused.

"No. Because we should get you a Tesla. I like the red one."

"A red Tesla?" She started to laugh.

"Shouldn't we have one great car? What do you think? We'll take turns driving it."

"I don't know. Aren't Teslas really expensive?"

"The company will pay. It's cheaper for us than buying new tires. I swear. It's a business expense."

"But the Prius really isn't that old and it runs great and—"

"You'll love the Tesla. I promise."

They both loved the new car.

Paul got a second one (midnight blue) six weeks later. As he explained, "It's not right to have a good car and a bad car. Who really wants to share the good one?"

It was a slippery slope. She remembered the first Christmas they didn't put up their own holiday decorations. Instead of a lone painted plywood reindeer on the lawn and the random candy canes that they'd shoved into the always-wet winter grass, there were sparkling globes hanging in all the trees. At night the property looked like a sweet holiday card.

But soon that house was sold. She traced the first signal of the relocation to Paul clipping his toenails into a paper bag. It was something his mother, when sober, had insisted upon. It was late at night and he'd just taken a shower. He looked at her and said, "Did you know self-storage units are the fastest growing part of the US commercial property business?"

"Really?"

"The stuff we are all storing ultimately costs more to save than to toss."

"We aren't pack rats."

"No. But we've outgrown this place. We're overflowing. We're not going to go rent a bunch of storage units."

"We should give stuff away. Our closets have so many things we never wear. Let's Marie Kondo the place."

"People don't want our junk. Charity bins are at capacity. You can't just ship the stuff overseas anymore." He kept clipping his nails. "We need to move."

Lindsey remembered it was hard to follow his logic. "Because the Goodwill doesn't want donations?"

"Babe, we've got so much extra money. So why not spend it?"

"I dunno. I mean, we like it here. The kids have so many friends in the neighborhood and—"

Lindsey could see from the look on his face that the fifty-fifty split on who was the boss was shifting.

The next day her husband announced, "I need to exercise more. I ordered a Peloton."

"Okay. How big is it? I mean, where are we going to put it?"

"We'll figure out something."

Only now did she fully realize that one way to get a new house was to buy enough stuff that they'd literally be forced out. Paul's new Peloton was wedged into their bedroom. The new ski equipment he bought that winter was piled in the garage alongside the new skateboards, scooters, and electric bikes. But she had to admit that it wasn't just him. Her wardrobe went through a major upgrade, with shoes and handbags that were stored in buttery-soft dust bags. The Amazon and UPS drivers stopped several times a day at the house. Moving was inevitable.

She and Paul had both been in favor of finding property that would be their home for many years. Forget the next step up. They would just go for it in a big way. Back then her mom made the long trip across an ocean every February. It would be great for her to have her own place on those visits. And if they had a real guesthouse, they could get a live-in nanny and that meant Lindsey could go with Paul on more of his business travels.

She thought they'd look for months or even years, but the Realtor was "highly motivated." The property she found was listed for a lot more than they wanted to spend. They wrote the offer anyway, which was accepted only two hours later without a counter. Lindsey didn't sleep that night, but Paul took eszopiclone and was snoring away at her side in minutes. His last words before he nodded off were, "The new house needs to have good things. Not this junky stuff."

Lindsey, still sitting up in bed, gazed across the room at a bureau in the shadows. She remembered finding the treasure at the Salvation Army before the kids were even born. She loved the strange brass handles. The carved wooden feet. She stared at the chest of drawers and felt herself questioning her own judgment. Was it beautiful or ugly?

The bureau didn't make the cut. Almost nothing did. An interior architecture firm, headed by a woman who always wore layers and layers of beige linen, took charge. She insisted that most of the tile at the new house should be replaced with custom squares made from family images. "Narrative style" was all the rage. Lindsey had never heard of it and then found herself picking out dozens of photos to be used for the project. She only remembered once asking Paul about financing.

"We're paying cash for the house with an advance from the company, which is then converted to a loan on paper."

"But it's still a loan."

"No, sweetheart."

"So the business owns the new house?"

"No. We own it. But it's in the company's name."

"Which means we own 17 percent of the house?"

"You're not listening."

"I'm trying. It's just so much money. Even if we're borrowing from ourselves."

"Lindsey, that's how it's done. At some point the business will journal the money over as a bonus. All we need to worry about is the tax liability. The richer you are, the more money you owe. It sounds crazy, but it's true. We want the debt. We'll *need* the debt."

"Okay . . ."

"Sweetheart, you borrow because you *can*, and you spend because money needs to change hands. It's not a static thing. Currency is transactional. It has to flow."

After they closed on the house, Lindsey couldn't remember having another conversation with Paul about money until the only conversations they had were about that.

Lindsey stopped to reapply sunscreen. She'd been on the beach for thirty minutes, starting right on the edge of the water, but gradually moving further into the waves, which now lapped her knees and thighs, occasionally threatening to knock her over. She was rude to leave Chris to haul away her garbage. And yet as she retraced her steps back to the motel, she returned to her life in Portland and her pace slowed. She was in no hurry to get back.

As she and Paul had entered a new world of affluence, they let go of their old habits and routines. Once you stop performing basic tasks, Lindsey realized, you lost the ability to do them. It was possible spellcheck would make people illiterate. She used to draw maps to get places. Now she wondered if anyone did that. The calculator on her phone did the simplest math. People might be hardwired to want more and do less. Maybe the first cave dwellers who had the brilliant idea to make a better tool felt the need to find a bigger cave. Was there something in modern culture, in the economic system, that pushed people in this direction? That conditioning might start so early that a person didn't realize it was even happening. It wasn't just Paul who changed. She went along with the choices. Maybe in some cases she initiated them. But blame felt better than shame.

She didn't actually miss the expensive house when they were forced to move, because her heart had never been in it. And they hadn't lived there that long. There were different zones for heating and cooling, and everything was hooked up to a Wi-Fi system that was voice activated. Windows and doors would open and close, lock or unlock, with blinds that parted without lifting a finger. But the system got confused and heard voices on the TV and initiated actions, like preheating the oven or pausing a dishwasher cycle without ever being told to do so.

That was not a comfort.

Neither was hearing the garage doors open at 3 A.M. because one of the kids was up late, and the electronic ears heard a snippet of a video game soundtrack. The long driveway at the new house turned out to be, Lindsey decided now, what money was all about: getting away from other people.

At the old house, doing yard work had been a weekend family affair. But she and Paul never clipped back a single rosebush or pulled one weed on the new property. The kids certainly never again picked up a rake. They were too scheduled to do anything like that. Paul was told joining the country club would be good for business. The initiation fee was the price of a mobile home, and non-refundable. There was also a minimum monthly spend as a club member. This was to guarantee the dining facilities were used enough to justify a high-level cook. The chef wore a tall black hat that Sena thought meant he was related to Abraham Lincoln. During Sunday brunch he made the rounds to every table to ask how people were enjoying the food. The first time this happened, Lindsey thought it was special; later, the man's presence while she was chewing only annoyed her. Lessons were a big part of club life. Olivia and Carlos were being taught golf and tennis. Sena sat under an umbrella by the pool for hours with coloring books and a satchel filled with plastic Peppa Pig figures. She refused to join the Preschool Fun Klub and entertained herself.

In the old neighborhood, kids were everywhere, skateboarding on the sidewalks and trying to sell lemonade or recklessly cross the street on a scooter. Now, though, the kids were in private school and that was a club of its own. Besides the steep tuition, there were so many events. The social pinnacle of the school year was the annual fundraiser. Everyone knew Paul was making a splash with his new tech company. Lindsey remembered getting the call to sign up for a ten-year giving program that locked in their donation level. They were setting an example to the community, which would later be framed as a cautionary tale, but until that happened, they were trail-blazers, leading the fundraising drive, with their names in gold lettering on the school's year-end thank-you booklet. She had always kept her maiden name. She was Lindsey Sisley, yet the school had listed Paul and Lindsey Hill on the donor board. It was official; she had become a different person.

The silver Jeep was gone.

Lindsey climbed the uneven wooden steps to look in the front window of the red cottage. There was a T-shirt folded neatly over one of the bamboo chairs and a computer bag resting on the round table. She felt his presence as if he were in the room.

In the office, she found a note on the large wooden desk:

> I'm off to town to drop the trash and pick up more supplies. Text if you need me to get anything.

Lindsey took out her cellphone and entered the number he'd written down, feeling uneasy that he'd come in the office when she wasn't there. She told herself he'd probably just been looking for her, not snooping around. Maybe she'd been too friendly the day before. She had always considered herself a shy person until Paul pointed out that she wasn't timid or reserved, so why did she think she was? Lindsey took a seat at the stately old desk and opened her computer. Today she was going to work on finding a plumber. She felt fortunate that her mother had been a good role model for dealing with home repairs. She had always said, "A skilled plumber isn't cheap. And a cheap plumber isn't skilled." Lindsey was glad she didn't recall her mum using the expression about electricians, though doubtless she would have.

Olivia had dressed for school in a way she hoped would make her blend in with computer nerds. In Portland they wore lots of layers, and not just because Oregon had so much raw weather. People seemed to hide in their clothes there. But here, when it was eighty-plus degrees every day, with the sun bouncing off everything, layers were harder to pull off. Olivia had decided on a T-shirt with a cotton overshirt and a short black skirt with printed leggings. She finished the ensemble with black leather ankle boots. She figured with the school's air-conditioning she'd be okay, but it turned out she was wrong. Olivia spent the whole day uncomfortable, feeling overdressed and sweaty and even more out of place than normal.

The computer repair club listed room 112, which was one of the science labs, as their meet-up spot. Mr. Wong, the physics teacher, who had short hair and glasses and often wore a shirt that said YOU MATTER, UNLESS YOU MULTIPLY BY THE SPEED OF LIGHT SQUARED, THEN YOU ENERGY, was the club's advisor. Olivia walked through the doorway with her eyes downcast, which is why she didn't notice the person heading out of the room until they awkwardly bumped shoulders. She spun around to say sorry and realized it was Koa Kahale. She hadn't seen Koa since her mother hit him with the Crown Victoria. This was exciting; he was into computer repair! But then she realized he was exiting the room. *Fleeing* was a better word. He was getting away from Mr. Wong as fast as possible and yet he still was able to mumble, "Sorry, Olivia."

It took her a moment to fully absorb that he knew her name.

And then he was gone.

Nine other computer repair club members were already there. Eight boys and one girl, who she would learn was named Nova. She was holding hands with a guy named Cookie. Olivia had seen these two leaning against a locker licking each other's ears the day before. *Get a room, people.* But then she remembered her family had come to the island to run a motel. Was that what most of the guests were going to be doing in the cottages? Olivia's negative spiral was interrupted by the arrival of another repair club member, who came through the door announcing, "Sorry I'm late, guys." She looked up to see Haku, the guy who had been so aggressive about his spot outside. He met her gaze.

"Today we're adding a new member to the club," Haku told the group. "This is Olivia Hill. Her family bought the Kalamas' motel, where my brother used to work."

Olivia felt her lower lip twitch involuntarily. "Your brother?"

"Koa."

Olivia's face must have revealed her disbelief.

"Stepbrother. I know. You're surprised because I'm so much hotter—right?"

A few of the other kids laughed. Olivia didn't.

Haku put his laptop on a desk. "Chill out, Olivia. It was a joke."

Olivia exhaled and felt a surge of something close to optimism. One way to get to know Koa could be through Haku. She smiled at the group and said, "Let's talk about reinstalling operating systems."

Sena couldn't believe what her mother was saying. Everything for her chickens had been not just removed but thrown away. "Driven to the dump" was what her mother told her.

Sena silently unfastened her seatbelt and then opened the back door on the right side of the Crown Victoria. She already had one leg dangled out when her mom screamed, "*Sena!*"

Lindsey slammed on the brakes, causing the car to screech to a halt as Sena pulled her foot back inside. Lindsey then grabbed her daughter and held her close. "Are you all right?"

Sena waited to be released, which happened as her mom exploded. "That was incredibly dangerous! You could have seriously hurt yourself!"

Sena didn't answer. She gritted her teeth. She could see her mom was upset, but she wasn't sorry.

"You've lost your privileges!"

"What privileges? You didn't ask about taking my stuff away." She shut her eyes and barely heard the explanation of chicken bacteria causing unsanitary conditions for people. Sena was so furious she thought about running away from home. Only she didn't have any friends to take her in, and there wasn't even a neighbor who might have a garage where she could hide. She was stuck living with her mother, who now was a traitor. But Sena knew it was Chris Young who was responsible. He said her chickens might be sick and that Sena had to stop taking care of them. He shouldn't have been under the office and he shouldn't be allowed to stay in the red cottage. If only she hadn't wanted rice cakes that night, none of this would have happened.

But she would get even.

She would get her revenge.

13

On Saturday morning, when Chris left to buy electrical supplies, Sena went to his cottage. She thought she'd need to climb through a window to get in, but the front door wasn't even locked. Once inside, she moved around, looking at everything very carefully.

It was irritating to see that he did a good job making the bed and that there weren't dirty dishes in the sink or random things lying around. In the small closet, she found his suitcase, which was empty because his clothes were on hangers. The stuff in the drawers in the bamboo bureau was arranged in a neat and organized way, which only made her angrier. Even his leather shoulder bag was hung up.

His laptop looked new.

He had an iPad and a bunch of chargers.

He had mini-binoculars on the counter.

He had breath mints in a small bowl.

He had a leather pouch in the bathroom with a razor, shaving cream, extra blades, and lotion. He had Band-Aids, pain reliever, and vitamins. He had dental floss. His toothbrush had soft bristles.

His toothpaste said it was for sensitive teeth and gums, and was powered by baking soda.

This was not right because he was not a sensitive person. He didn't care about chickens.

Sena squeezed out a long nurdle of toothpaste and washed it down the drain. Would he notice the tube was now half empty? She had one more act of vengeance. Sena slipped off her sneakers. A layer of sand had accumulated under the rubber insoles. She tilted her shoes on an angle and then pulled back the top sheet and sprinkled the gritty particles in his bed. She then replaced the covers, put on her shoes, and exited out the back door of the cottage. She felt a measure of satisfaction in seeking justice on behalf of the island's birds.

Standing under a palm tree, Sena surveyed the crime scene. Her mother was inside the office, probably plucking her eyebrows. Sena didn't remember her doing that before Chris Young arrived. Her brother was eating in the kitchen. Olivia was doing something on-line. The chickens were scattered everywhere. Sena's flock had relocated immediately to different spots on the property. The smaller ones found places to roost in trees; the fatter ones who couldn't fly sought out bushes. The birds returned to their wilder state.

Sena went to sit in a swing that Rangi Kalama had made from fishing net. She swayed back and forth for almost twenty minutes, rocking herself to the sound of the waves. She was jolted out of her comfort by her mother's voice.

"There you are. I was looking for you."

But her mom wasn't angry and she didn't say anything about the toothpaste or the sand in the bed, which was both a relief and a disappointment. Everyone was supposed to participate in a group project to trim back the plants growing on either side of the long driveway that went out to the highway. The night before, her mother had tried to make it sound fun, but they all knew it was never going to be anything but hard work. She claimed it was a family project, but then Chris appeared and said he'd join them.

Olivia was the first to quit after pretending she pulled a muscle in her back. Sena gave her a look but didn't say anything. Then Carlos announced he was done because he was going to see friends on his new bike, which was actually an old bike but new to him. He'd gotten it from a kid named Pano. Sena wondered if someone nearby was now missing a bike. The man in the hardware store in Hale'iwa had said, "Here in the islands we have lots of *love* and lots of *thieves*."

He said this when he was ringing up a cord for her mom's computer, and her mom had laughed. When they got home, her mom noticed the package had been opened and the cord inside looked old. Someone had switched it. When she plugged it in, it didn't work. Sena saw that she wasn't laughing then.

With Olivia and Carlos gone, it was just Sena and Lindsey and Chris working to clear back the overgrown plants. Sena was given the job of picking up the cuttings. Lindsey had big clippers and she hit a rusty metal wire that was hidden in a tangle of unruly vines. The clipper blades bent and she walked back to the office to get another pair and also to bring out water. This left Sena alone with Chris.

The sun was high in the sky and it was very hot. Sena could see he had done more than Olivia, Carlos, and her mom combined. He was a hard worker, but she didn't want to give him credit for anything. She stayed at a distance, filling black plastic bags with clippings as best she could. They were getting closer to the main road when Chris stopped. He wiped his forehead and looked at Sena. "I think we should call it quits."

"But we're not done."

"It might be better if the section up ahead stays overgrown. When your mom's ready to reopen it can all be trimmed back."

Sena's voice was cold. "When you start a job, it needs to be finished."

"Okay. Let's wait and see what your mom says."

"She'll just agree with you."

"We don't know that."

"She let you stay in the cottage and she let you borrow our big saucepan." Sena squinted up at him with defiance. "She wears earrings now."

"You don't want her to wear earrings?"

"I don't want centipedes. They can be evil spirits."

"You've seen centipedes?"

Sena felt herself getting more upset. "Under the office."

"Really?"

"I don't make up stuff. Also, there are centipedes where the dead palm fronds are stacked."

"Do you want me to get some kind of insect poison?"

Sena exploded. "Are you crazy? The chickens eat the insects! You'll kill all the chickens!"

He nodded. "Sena, I'm really sorry that we had to move the birds." She didn't look at him. He kept going. "It was a health thing. I know we've explained that but—"

Sena's right hand, which was gripping a garbage bag, let go and she turned and ran down the drive. When she rounded the curve, she met her mom. Sena hissed at her, "Everything in the world is connected. You need to explain that to him."

The look on her mother's face said she had no idea what Sena was talking about.

Later, Sena sat at the end of her big sister's bed while Olivia moved around the room trying to put things in order but somehow making more of a mess. She tried to explain what had happened, but her big sister only said, "Well, yeah, I think it's totally weird that he's living in the cottage, but on the positive side my blow-dryer works. And the lights don't flicker when the refrigerator goes on. That's because of him."

"There are other people who can fix things on this island."

"Yeah. But maybe it's good for Mom. She's not as sad. I think it helps her to have a friend."

Sena bristled. "He shouldn't be here." She picked up her insect book, but before she left the room she looked back at her big sister. "Mom doesn't need him as a friend. She's got us. I don't trust him. Not after what he did with Tink and the other chickens."

Sena was just a seven-year-old kid, but Olivia couldn't stop thinking about what she had said. There was no disputing that having functioning electricity was a big plus, but Chris had changed the dynamics of the place. Olivia couldn't help wondering if he was up to something. She had searched for "Chris Young" online, but it was too common a name. There was a country music singer, a celebrity chef, and a baseball player all named Chris Young, and they were hogging up all the webpages. Olivia searched "Chris Young author" and "Chris Young ghostwriter" and "Chris Young science writer." There were people with that name who wrote books, but she couldn't connect any of them to him. If she'd been a real snoop, she'd have gone to his cottage and poked through his things. But Sena admitted she'd done that and come up with nothing but the fact that he made them all look like slobs. Apparently even his socks were in a neat stack. Plus, if her mom ever knew she went into his cottage she'd go off her trolley, to use one of her own expressions.

There was just one thing Olivia couldn't shake. And it was minor. Maybe not even a thing. Olivia had woken up in the middle of the night, missing her thin, cotton blanket. She looked over in the shadows to see that her little sister wasn't in her bed. Sena had taken Olivia's cover and was sleeping on the floor with her knees touching her chin and her head on a stack of books. It looked so damn uncomfortable. Olivia wanted her blanket back, but she decided, in a rare act of sisterly generosity, to leave her sister alone.

The moon was full and the room was bathed in long shadows. Something made Olivia walk to the window, where she was shocked to see a person standing on the lava chips. It was Chris Young. He was pacing, obviously agitated, as he spoke on his cellphone.

Who was he talking to at 4:06 A.M.?

Then she remembered that it was 7:06 A.M. on the West Coast and 10:06 A.M. in New York. Olivia wished she could hear what he was saying. She stayed watching him pace for a full five minutes. Then he finally pulled the phone away from his ear and headed back into his cottage.

As Olivia retrieved a blanket from the hall closet, she thought about the possibility of sneaking a look at his cellphone and going over his call history. She could do a reverse search of the numbers. Only she knew that wouldn't happen because she'd have to cut off his arm to get his phone. It was always with him. But there were other ways to keep an eye on him.

Carlos loved his sisters and his mom, but without his dad in the picture, conflict in the family had a way of escalating. He was sick of being the one who tried to calm everyone down, so the ghostwriting electrician was a gift. Plus, the man could do things. He was encouraging when he spoke. And he asked Carlos questions, which was a form of respect he wasn't getting from anyone else on the property.

When Carlos got home from his bike ride, he saw his mom and Sena in some kind of discussion down on the beach. Chris was outside the office threading new wiring from the upstairs down through the wall to the ground floor. Carlos took a seat to watch, explaining, "Sena's still mad about the chickens. She can really hold a grudge. One year she scooped up her Christmas presents and threw them in the fireplace. She was only three, but no one could stop her. She had asked for a live penguin, which of course she didn't get."

"I guess she's always loved birds."

"All animals, really. She's had to say good-bye to a lot of pets. Our dog died when she was little. Then our cat when we moved. We couldn't take our goat to the big house because they had strict homeowners' association stuff."

"That must have been hard."

"Sena cried so much about the goat, my dad went around the rules. The property was pretty big, so I think he realized the neighbors wouldn't know. Dad bought her a pony, which was actually a miniature Icelandic horse."

"I've never seen a miniature Icelandic horse."

"He was named Snorri. And pretty chill. But he had sinusitis and it gave him a real snotty nose."

Carlos could see Chris was amused and that made him happy, so he kept talking. "When all my dad's problems happened, Mom sold Snorri so we could move to the apartment. But losing Snorri hit Sena hard."

"I understand better now about the chickens."

"Yeah."

"Can you hand me that voltage tester? It's got an orange handle."

Carlos looked into the toolbox and located the probe. He lowered his voice. "What really happened with our cat is the moving truck ran him over. We weren't home and he got out. But my mom said the cat ran away because she didn't want Sena to know."

"That was probably easier for her."

"Yeah. But not easier for my mom and dad. Sena made them put up lost-cat flyers all over the neighborhood. She wanted to drive back to the old house all the time to look for him. They should have just told her the truth. Only I didn't mind going back to our old street. We knew all the neighbors. At the new house we had a really long driveway and you couldn't hear anyone having a barbeque on the weekends or someone's screen door slamming shut."

Carlos didn't know why this made Chris laugh. "But you liked the new house?"

"We all thought it was really cool in the beginning. It was so big. You had to use an intercom to find people. Dad wasn't home very much since he was always working. And Mom was really busy, too. We didn't do very many things as a family except take fancy vacations. But then Dad made a mistake at work and the company got into trouble—" Carlos abruptly stopped. It was hard for him to continue, but he exhaled and kept going. "A few months later my dad drowned in a surfing accident. There had just been a big storm and he shouldn't have been out in the water. He was a good surfer but not a great surfer. At least that's what Mr. Cole said. He was our old neighbor."

"Your mother told me. I'm so sorry."

"It took a long time for us to get stuff sorted out. Two whole years. We stayed at friends' houses and for a while at a motel. Mom sold most of our stuff and we ended up in the apartment."

"Well, you're here now. You all picked a great place to start over."

Carlos managed something close to a smile. "I think so. But I'm the optimist of my family."

14

The kids were at school. Chris was working on the electrical situation. Lindsey, notepad in hand, sat on the porch. The second plumber to give an estimate had come and gone and the roofer was again a no-show. She was making progress, but another week had passed and she increasingly felt the pressure of her undertaking.

Looking out at the motel property, she was comforted by the beauty of the place. There were more shades of green than she'd ever thought possible. She squinted and turned the trees into triangles. The bushes into scallops. The cottages into squares. Everything fit in place with a visual harmony that defied explanation except for one thing: the two telephone poles with their low-hanging electrical wires. The power lines were awful.

Was she focused on the metal filaments because Chris was installing a new service panel? The wires looked so out of place. It was like the annoying internet dish, which despite being mostly covered up by now-dying greenery didn't belong. With so many things necessary to reopen the motel, it wasn't logical to fixate on electrical lines. Only she couldn't stop herself. She suddenly wanted the poles and wires gone.

She opened her laptop and did a search only to find that the utility company agreed with her. Since 1966, developers building on more than four lots had been required on Oʻahu to bury the electrical lines. Now 40 percent of the island had underground utilities. This meant the current wasn't as vulnerable to extreme weather, which made going below ground an all-around safer option, especially in light of the hazards of the more intense storms brought on by climate change.

After waiting on hold for an eternity, which her phone showed in reality was twenty-three minutes, she reached an employee at the power company who said he would schedule an appointment at her property and take a look at "what she had going on in terms of utility lines."

She was encouraged until the man added, "But the first thing you need to do is check the cultural overlay map for your area."

Lindsey wasn't sure what he meant. "What's a cultural overlay map?"

"It shows the geography of your property with the known human history."

"It's been a motel for over eighty years."

"Archaeological sites aren't obvious. Shoreline property has a real chance of holding something significant."

"I'm still not sure I understand."

"Before we consider burying power lines, we need to know whether it's appropriate to dig. There are ancient burial grounds on the island."

"Really?"

"Years of plant growth, weather, and people have removed obvious signs."

"But two generations of the same family ran the place. The buildings are all original."

"That's aboveground. We're talking below. There's a woman in charge of the cultural overlay maps for your part of the island. You'll need to get in touch with her. Depending on what she says, we will discuss the steps to take your electrical lines underground. I can give you her direct contact information."

Lindsey hung up and stared at the name and telephone number she'd scribbled on her notepad. She didn't dial. A kind of paralysis took hold. What if she was sitting on a burial ground? What did that even mean? She had to make certain Sena never got wind of the possibility. She could feel herself starting to spiral, which was interrupted by Chris asking, "Is everything okay?"

She looked up to see him standing a few feet away. She hadn't heard him approach.

"I'm not sure. . . ."

"Did you get bad news?"

"No." She was flustered. "Well, maybe. I had this idea that I should put the telephone poles and all the wiring underground."

She'd been avoiding him when the kids were at school. It was one thing to talk when her mini-bodyguards were around, but it felt different when it was just the two of them on the property. He made her tense. She guessed he could feel that. His eyes slid off into the distance. He was making a point of not looking at her.

"Putting the lines underground would be a good thing, I think. If you have the money."

His agreeing lifted her spirits. She had told herself she wasn't going to become dependent on his approval for decision-making, but she couldn't help feeling reassured.

"Is it complicated?" he asked, adding, "I mean, everything is, I guess."

"The utility website says they are encouraging people to bury the wires. But when I spoke to a person there, he said I have to start by seeing if the land is culturally important."

He nodded.

She continued, "They have a person with maps. Digging might unearth something."

He brightened. "Maybe you're sitting on buried treasure."

"I just hope not a bunch of decaying bodies."

Silence.

Lindsey knew she'd sounded flippant, and she regretted it. He'd put his wife's ashes in the ocean in front of the motel. She couldn't read his expression. Her mother had a lifelong habit of laughing when situations grew uncomfortable. Lindsey had made it a priority not to repeat this irritating mannerism. But she had to force herself not to erupt in some kind of awkward titter.

"I guess I'll give the lady a call."

Lindsey didn't expect her to show up the same afternoon. And her timing was such that she was already at the office when Lindsey arrived home from school with the kids, so there was no keeping anything from them. As she steered the Crown Victoria around the wide curve, they all saw a blue Toyota parked right next to the silver Jeep. Mia Manu was sitting on the porch with Chris having what looked like a lively conversation.

"Who's that woman?" Sena asked.

"I don't know," Lindsey answered.

"She's pretty," Olivia observed, making Carlos glance over with interest.

Mia Manu looked to be somewhere in her late thirties, with curly dark hair that cascaded down her back. She appeared athletic, fit, and confident as she got up from the porch steps and headed toward them. Wearing loose-fitting green linen pants with a white linen shirt, she was waiting with a hand extended when Lindsey opened her car door.

"We spoke on the phone. I'm Mia Manu with SHPD."

Sena was concerned. "Is that a police department?"

Mia laughed. She bent down to explain. "No, sweetheart. I'm from the State Historic Preservation Division."

"What's that?"

"It's part of state government. We work to make sure Hawai'i's past is protected."

Lindsey shot Chris a look. He was on his feet, watching at a distance. It didn't feel right to be irritated that he'd been talking to this woman. But what had he said? And why did that matter to her?

Mia continued explaining to Sena, "We have three divisions— architecture, archaeology, and history and culture. I'm part of history and culture."

Lindsey noticed that even Carlos was paying close attention. Only Olivia seemed uninterested. She grabbed her backpack from the floor of the Crown Victoria and started toward the house. Mia rose from her crouch in front of Sena. She was taller than Lindsey.

"So are you here because the motel is so old?" Sena asked.

"No. I've come to see if it would be possible to dig on the property."

Lindsey joined the conversation, addressing the group. "I'm thinking about putting the electrical lines underground." She pointed and everyone looked up at the poles. "Wouldn't it be better without them?"

No one responded.

They all went inside, and Mia took an iPad from her shoulder bag. Lindsey gave her the information for the motel's internet, wondering why she couldn't just investigate in her own office if all she was going to do was look at something online. As if Mia could read her mind, she explained, "It's best to be onsite when I run the program." She pulled up a complex map with a pulsing blue dot in the center. No one spoke until Mia said, "Interesting . . ."

Sena leaned close to the iPad. "Did you make a discovery?"

"We're in a gray area."

Lindsey asked, "Where you can't tell something?"

"No. A gray area in the GIS means possible detection."

"What's GIS?" asked Sena.

"Geographic system mapping—it's a computer program that shows data in relation to set positions on the surface of the Earth."

Carlos edged forward. "What kind of data?"

"Plants, buildings, streets. The state's GIS also has known historical and physical property changes. For Hawai'i, nature is part of culture."

Sena piped up, "Because in Hawai'i the landscape is the most sacred." She then added, "Mrs. Kekoa told us that at school."

Mia smiled. "Mrs. Kekoa is right."

Lindsey wasn't looking entirely at the iPad. She couldn't help but notice there was no ring on Mia's wedding finger as she typed additional commands into the program.

While the iPad reloaded, Mia asked Carlos, "You're in school in town?"

Carlos nodded. "I'm in middle school and my big sister is at Kahuku High."

Mia flashed her thousand-watt smile. "My ex-husband is a counselor there! Ed Lam."

Lindsey only heard the word "ex-husband." Being divorced was so different from being a widow. No wonder the woman was so sunny and cheerful.

"We met with him on our first day," Carlos said. "He was really nice."

Mia nodded. "Yeah. He's great."

Then why, Lindsey thought, *did you end up divorced?*

Mia turned to Olivia, who was standing in the kitchen doorway. "Could I trouble you for a glass of water?"

Olivia didn't move, and Lindsey answered for her. "Of course. But can I get you a cup of tea? Or coffee?"

Mia shook her head. "Water's great."

Lindsey looked over to see Chris move a chair into place for Mia. He was making her feel welcome, which was what Lindsey should have done. Carlos then cleared off some of the things on the large wooden desk, giving Mia more space as she removed a notebook from her shoulder bag. Lindsey started for the kitchen and her son called out, "Mom, I'll have some water, too." Then Carlos turned to Mia. "We have cookies and a pretty good chip selection if you want a snack."

Mia Manu left thirty minutes later, having made an appointment to return with two coworkers the following week. The bad news, as far as Lindsey was concerned, was that there was enough data to support what Mia referred to as "minor excavation."

Carlos had pressed her. "So you think there might be something here?"

"We just don't know," said Mia. She then added, "But this is a very special place, and we wouldn't be the first people to think so."

It felt to Lindsey like a compliment and a warning. Before Mia got into her car she brightly proclaimed, "The best thing about this job is that I never know what my day will be. It was really cool meeting you all."

They stood together on the gravel and watched as Mia's car disappeared around the curve. Sena was the first to speak. "I might do that kind of job when I grow up."

"Her ex-husband is Olivia's counselor. What are the odds?" Carlos said.

Olivia's expression was sour. "When you live on an island, pretty high."

Carlos asked his mother, "Can I stay home from school next Thursday? I'd like to be here when they dig. They might find artifacts."

"No. School's too important to miss."

"But Mom—"

Olivia shot him a look. "Relax, Indiana Jones. I doubt they find more than rock."

"Lava," Sena corrected her. "And Mia was a really nice lady."

"She was," Chris agreed.

Lindsey only nodded. The telephone poles and the sagging power lines no longer looked like such a big problem.

15

The next morning, instead of continuing out of the carpool lane to head home, Lindsey turned into the school parking lot. She was filled with indecision, torn between going back to the motel and heading across the island to the warehouse stores to buy supplies. She shut off the engine and watched as teenagers streamed into the buildings, moving at different speeds and with different levels of enthusiasm.

She knew that every family's story was unique. The most important thing Lindsey believed she could give her children was her love, which was why she had left Portland. If she'd stayed in Oregon, she feared she'd become a version of her mum. Lindsey's mother was a good parent with good intentions, but after her husband died, she stopped growing emotionally, and whether she realized it or not, her world was all about limitations. Her favorite form of relaxation was to take out the family photo albums. She'd make herself a pot of tea, sink into the woolly chair by the window, and stare at pictures that captured moments no longer possible. Her mum had no interest in experiencing anything new. She forever had one foot planted in the past.

That was the emotional lesson Lindsey had learned growing up in the old stone house in Wales. What she had learned in Portland after the rush of new money was that wealth wasn't an achievement. What had made Paul Hill the happiest was coming up with his brilliant idea. It wasn't what happened after that. It was creating something. Doing something.

That was why she had bought a motel.

She needed to force herself to be active in the world.

"Good morning."

It took a moment for her to realize someone was talking to her. Lindsey turned to see Ed Lam several feet away. He nodded in her direction. "Everything okay with the kids?"

"I think so."

Ed took a few steps toward her car. "It's a big adjustment. A new school. And coming in when the semester has already started."

She nodded. "So far so good, I think. I guess they're in the settling-in phase."

"Once they make friends you should see less anxiety."

"Right. That makes sense."

Silence. Then he filled it. "So, you're thinking of putting your power lines underground."

Lindsey's face showed her surprise. "News travels fast."

He smiled. "It might be an island thing."

"Or a small-town thing."

He laughed. "It's a small-town-island thing."

"The utility department wants soil samples. Your ex-wife is in charge of that."

"She told me she was out at the Mau Loa. She's fantastic at her job."

"Yes. I can see that."

"She said you have a great guy from the mainland doing electrical work."

Lindsey tried to hide her surprise. "Chris. He's really helping me out."

"Unfortunately, there's a building boom going on around here right now. You're lucky to have found him."

"He found me, actually." She wasn't sure why that was important to clarify.

"Mia said he's going to take a look at her new garage. There aren't any outlets in there. She didn't realize when she moved in. He'll let her know if it's a big deal getting power."

"That's great." She found herself continuing. "Chris is a writer. Not really an electrician. But he knows his stuff. I mean—I think he does. Let's hope so. He's basically rewiring my whole motel!"

She laughed. It was her mum's nervous laugh. The one that signaled unease and discomfort. But he didn't know her mother, so hopefully he didn't find it irritating. Lindsey noticed the fingers on his right hand moving as if he were playing an invisible piano that ran alongside his leg. She wondered if he was anxious, or if he was just one of those people who had a lot of pent-up energy. She put her hands on the steering wheel. "I'll let you get to work."

She thought he looked relieved.

"Please feel free to check in with me anytime."

Lindsey started the car and drove out of the parking lot. She no longer felt conflicted. She had to get home and see that Chris was there. She couldn't stop herself from tailgating the slow-moving truck in front of her. Twice she almost rear-ended the vehicle. But she couldn't back off. This was not the way to drive on Kam Highway.

Chris had been on the property for two weeks and the cottages were almost all rewired. He wasn't fast at the work and he wasn't slow. He was methodical and careful, stopping often to check what he'd done. An early riser, he was awake before the rest of the family, and usually went out running. He came back, sat down at the computer to check email, and by the time Lindsey returned from dropping the kids at school he was at work. There were many days when he had to go to Honolulu for supplies. One minute Lindsey wished she'd never met Chris Young, and the next she felt anxious at the thought that he would be leaving soon. But that conflict seemed to have resolved after Ed Lam's exchange in the parking lot.

Lindsey didn't think of herself as a competitive person. Someone who was competitive wanted above all to win. When Paul died, she'd decided life was about being able to tolerate losing. That's what separated the weak from the strong. So if she wasn't competitive, was she jealous? The thought was deeply uncomfortable. She stepped hard on the gas and almost hit the truck ahead of her. People were talking about her. She would give them something to talk about.

Olivia stared at herself in the reflection of the art room mirror and took inventory. Her hair was light brown, just a shade from being something that would attract attention. It was dull, more beige than honey. Her eyes were blue, but not piercing blue. They were the kind of blue that looked gray, which she read meant that it was possible she came from the Algerian Shawiya people of the Aurès Mountains of Northwest Africa. But probably not. She was average height for a girl, which placed her on the tall side in Hawai'i, and she was neither thin nor chunky. Her ears and nose were totally near the middle of the bell curve of regular-looking. But she had a larger-than-average forehead. She knew that in early modern times a big forehead was considered elegant. Women actually changed their hairlines by plucking out strands to achieve a look that she was born with. But no way did she wish she lived in 1580.

Olivia turned away from the glass. She wondered why she couldn't be like Carlos and be open to new friends. There were kids at school who had been nice enough; she knew she was the problem, not them. All kinds of people had parents die when they were kids. Some never had two to begin with. She'd read that nearly one-third of American presidents had lost a parent at a young age, but she didn't see herself as a political figure. On the other side of that equation, criminals were three times as likely to have only one parent. She wondered what the Venn diagram looked like for presidents who were criminals who had lost a parent. Having a ton of money and then not having money was a pretty rough thing to have happen, but it wasn't like she'd lost her right leg, which Riley Furtick did in eighth grade when he fell off his dirt bike.

It was possible, she decided, that she had been pretending to be okay for so long that she wasn't sure how she felt about anything anymore. Her mask of indifference never came off.

Olivia walked into room 112. She was early. But Haku was already there. In the two times the club had met, she hadn't been able to get any information from him about his brother. Haku looked up at her and muttered, "Hey."

He was slumped in his chair, one hand holding up his head as if it weighed a hundred pounds. He seemed sad. She couldn't stop herself from asking, "Is everything okay?"

He managed only a shrug. From what she'd witnessed, that was unusual. The kid had a relentless personality. He wore people out. At least he wore her out. But unplugged Haku was worse than the electric version. She pressed him. "Did you get some bad news?" He didn't answer. She added, "That's happened to me before."

He lifted his gaze. He didn't say anything but he didn't need to. She knew the look. She suddenly forgot all of her own shit and said, "Do you want to get out of here?"

He was confused. "What's that supposed to mean?"

"Ditch club."

"What would we do?"

She thought of the last time she'd been carefree, truly happy. Then it came to her. "Do you want to go bowling?"

He looked at her as if she'd just asked him to take off his pants. She pressed on. "Where do people bowl around here?"

"At The Hub."

"What's that?"

"It's the student center. On the BYU campus. It's not far from your motel. You don't have to be a college student to go in there."

She smiled.

He managed a half smile in return.

She reached out and grabbed his arm. "Let's go."

He had a pickup truck. The windows were down and the wind whipped her hair. He wasn't sitting close, but there was an intimacy in being together in the moving vehicle. They had ditched computer repair club. That was wrong. He was the president and he should have been there. But she could see that whatever was bothering him was being left behind. It was the same for her. She didn't have to pretend that she hadn't suffered emotionally. She felt for the briefest of moments completely free.

They parked the truck and walked onto the small campus. There were students going places, but they didn't look that much older than she and Haku were and, from Olivia's perspective, no wiser. They did appear more conservative than most of the islanders. The students didn't wear short-shorts or crop tops. The boys had shirts with sleeves and some wore belts with pants, which was something she never saw at her high school. She knew Haku was coming back to his old self when he started saying hello to anyone who passed. They were all courteous in return.

"Before this was a school for Mormons, it was a *pu'uhonua*," Haku told her.

"And that is?"

"A sanctuary city."

"I'm not sure what that means."

"Hawaiians who messed up—didn't follow the laws of *kapu*— came up here to avoid punishment."

"What kind of things got them in trouble?"

"You weren't allowed to cross the king's shadow."

"Okay . . ."

"Or eat turtle meat."

"I won't."

They'd reached the student center. Haku opened one of the double doors. She headed inside, saying, "I need to warn you. I grew up in Oregon. It rains a lot."

"Yeah . . . ?"

"Rainy weather makes a good bowler."

Carlos had wanted to be a garbage collector when he was little. He loved the big trucks, the way their mechanical claw could lift a container up into the air and powerfully swing it overhead with ease.

His mother used the term "trash man" because she was from Wales, and when he was four years old that's what he was for Halloween. The paper name tag his father affixed to his khaki shirt said CARLOS. A neighbor, not knowing that this was the actual name of the red-haired kid with the pale skin, laughed hard as he shouted, "Carlos! That's so funny!" The man thought the tag was brazen political incorrectness, causing the sensitive little boy to burst into tears.

He would never wear the outfit again.

Carlos moved on to worship firefighters and police officers. His parents gave him a fire truck birthday party when he was five years old, complete with an inflatable bouncy fire truck, which took up the whole backyard at the old house on Emerald Street. He had a collection of toy ambulances, and silently played games where his porcelain animals were EMTs arriving at disasters to heroically sort out trouble. He pretended in subsequent years to be interested in chess camp and coding camp and space camp, but his heart was never in it.

What he really wanted to do was help people in distress.

Then in a blink of an eye, everyone around him was in that state. Losing his father only heightened an impulse that was already there. He felt certain he could have saved his dad if he'd been there. He was a strong swimmer and he fantasized about heading straight into the white-capped waves, a shirt in hand, which he'd wrap around his father's chest as he towed him to shore through the rolling black water. If it was destiny that someone had to die that night, he would have filled his own lungs with ice water. Because if just one person could survive the storm, it should have been his dad.

More than once, he'd been told by people who had good intentions that he was now "the man of the family." He wasn't sure what that even meant for someone his age. It sounded pretty sexist, and he knew his mom and sisters wouldn't be cool with it. Maybe that's why he liked having Chris Young living in the red cottage. Listening to him explain what he was doing made Carlos feel good. He wanted to help his mom fix up the motel. They needed to be self-sufficient, emotionally and financially. That was part of what the last two years without his father had taught him.

But if he was really going to be useful at the motel, he needed to learn how to fix things, which was the impulse that led him to the toolshed. There was some level of organization inside the wooden structure, but it was known only to the Kalamas. Olivia had never once even looked inside. Sena's chickens never came near the place, so she wasn't interested. And after his mom moved all the sharp tools up into the rafters, she had too many other things to do, so she kept her distance.

Chris hooked up a large battery-powered light that hung from the center beam, and Carlos began to treat the place as his personal clubhouse. He was fascinated by the buckets of screws, nails, latches, and hand tools.

He went over the checklist that his mother made, which included looking at the hinges on the doors and trying to figure out ways to return the old screens to the windows. But after the woman from the state said they would need to do excavation on the property, Carlos couldn't stop himself from wanting to dig. He found a pickaxe, shovels, and hand trowels, which he thought would be useful. He didn't want to tell his mom, or Chris, that he planned to nose around in the dirt in an isolated area where he couldn't be seen. The mass of greenery between the motel and the highway was a jungle. It was thick with plants and insects, in most places essentially a swamp of brackish, dark mud. Even if Carlos could hack his way to a spot that was out of eyesight, he would pay for the decision with welts and bites. Carlos was a pincushion for mosquitos and flies, and because there were so many in the thicket, spiders were everywhere. Everyone in the family knew Carlos was afraid of spiders. They didn't even have to be black widows, which, apparently, were on the island. Just the sight of a cane spider or a striped-legged garden spider made his heart race.

He came up with a solution. The floor in the shed had long ago rotted out. Most of the wide planks were gone in the back and the dirt below was like crust to the touch.

Carlos cleared an area and, with a hand shovel, started to dig.

16

When Lindsey got back from drop-off, Chris was out. So she went for a long walk. Every day on the beach was different. The dynamic nature of water caused areas that were firm with fine sand one moment to be mushy and pebble-covered only hours later. Lindsey knew that the tide was one very long wave that moved around the world. It didn't stop or start; the tide and wind were constant and relentless. Walking here was different from walking on the sidewalk in Portland, where changes were less obvious and linked to the four seasons. Here the rain fell, the sun came out, the wind could be a whisper and then a howl—all in a single hour. But the temperature was always warm, consistent, tropical, driven by trade winds, which were unpredictable enough to suddenly swirl in a new direction without warning.

When she finally returned to the motel, Chris was up on the roof of the cottage farthest from the office.

She remained on her porch in the shredded shade of the palm trees, checking prices on her laptop, making lists. It gave her time to go over what she would say, how she might approach him. But he disrupted her plan by announcing in a very nonchalant way as he came down from his work, "I'm stopping early today. I'm heading over to Haleʻiwa after I clean up. Mia—the woman from the state cultural office—just got a new place. She needs some electrical advice."

Lindsey wanted to ask if that's what he did now—gave electrical consultations to single women over forty. Was Mia over forty? Probably not. She answered brightly instead, "That's so nice of you."

He smiled in a way she felt might be ironic and then headed to his cottage.

Lindsey watched him go. For two weeks she'd been polite. Warm enough. Grateful for all that he was doing. But she had been careful to keep her distance, and he had done the same. She was anxious around him. She wondered about the expression "butterflies in the stomach." Was that what he was doing to her? She was out of practice with whatever she was feeling. Her legs pressed into the wicker chair. The hot midafternoon air was still. Soon the wind would pick up and the palm fronds would rub against each other and the smell of the salty ocean would be more present. Mia Manu had shifted the ground under Lindsey's feet. She felt as vulnerable as the shoreline. And something inside was moving.

Early on at the community college, Lindsey had taught a class on the anthropology of reproduction. The accepted science was that humans were the only species that exhibited "covert sexual signaling." This was in sharp contrast to the animal world, where there were very set behaviors to signal the readiness to mate. Most animal indicators involved ritualized movement, a form of dance. The female typically called the shots, standing by to make a selection after a male showed off what he had. But in animal populations where the females outnumbered the males, the situation flipped. It was on the females to strut feathers, click tongues, and attract attention to signal they were willing and ready.

Lindsey closed her laptop and went inside. After giving it a lot of thought, she came out wearing one of Olivia's T-shirts. It was tighter than the shirts she usually wore, with a lower neckline.

She wasn't sure how to let him know, after two weeks of playing emotional dodgeball, that she was interested in him. This was all she had.

But the silver Jeep was already gone. The waves were bigger than usual and she hadn't heard him drive away.

It was close to dinnertime and Chris wasn't back. Lindsey wondered if he was still checking out Mia's garage, or if they had gone together for a swim at a secret beach or a drink at a bar only locals knew about. Maybe he'd decided to drive over to the other side of the island. He was a city person. This was the country. The locals even called it that. He might have "island fever," penned in by all the surrounding water. That form of psychological distress was real.

Olivia had been dropped off by a boy in a blue pickup truck. She looked happy, which brought Lindsey unexpected joy. Carlos was doing something in the toolshed. Sena rocked back and forth in the hammock with a chicken in her lap. It didn't look natural for a bird until she realized her daughter was feeding the hen uncooked instant oatmeal to keep it wedged in the crook of her small arm.

Lindsey decided to make pasta for dinner the way Paul had always done, not with red sauce but lemon and cheese, cracked pepper, and basil. It was easy and the kids liked it. They didn't think of the meal anymore as their father's spaghetti. She put a lid on the pot and pushed it to the back burner. Maybe she'd go the extra distance and bake cookies. She had a composition journal with a black-and-white-speckled cover where, ever since she was a teenager, she had jotted down recipes, starting with favorites from her mum and her nan. Curled yellow scraps of old newspaper and magazine clippings, articles she'd torn out and for the most part never tried, were stuffed between the crinkled pages. Nearly everything she wanted to cook was available online now, but she still found comfort having recipes in one place, even if she rarely consulted them. The cardboard-covered journal had traveled to every kitchen she'd ever lived in since leaving Wales. Cookware, plates, glasses, and appliances had all come and gone. Only the black-and-white journal survived.

The cover was sticky to the touch, with a dark red spatter stain. Lindsey grabbed a dish towel from the counter and tried to clean the splotch, which proved hopeless. She tossed the cloth and begin flipping the journal pages in search of instructions for Nan's treacle cookies. But when she landed in the right place, there was a piece of folded paper taped over the recipe. Lindsey pulled off the adhesive, and the page ripped. She felt a stab of pain. She stared at the torn page and then slowly unfolded the paper. She recognized Paul's handwriting immediately, even though the letters were smaller, more crunched, and without his usual flair.

She read:

1. I maintained too much control.
2. I didn't let the businesspeople do the business part.
3. If I was a chef, I bought all the right ingredients for a great meal and then tried to put it together after I'd kept everything out on the counter too long. I let the fresh food spoil.
4. BECAUSE THE COMPANY TOOK TOO LONG TO LAUNCH.
5. By the time I realized the problem, someone else had a better version. I was blindsided by the team in Finland.

I hope you can forgive me for leaving you on your own with the kids.
   I hope you will forgive me for seeing no other way out.

She closed the journal and sank to the floor.
She used to make treacle cookies all the time.
They called them molasses cookies in America.
He had assumed she would keep doing that once he was gone.
He was such a fool.

Lindsey had wondered ever since the first horrible phone call from the highway patrol officer if Paul's drowning wasn't more than an accident. She wasn't the only one who questioned his intent. They were flat broke, yet he'd taken out an expensive two-million-dollar life insurance policy only eight weeks before he died. As she came to learn, beneficiaries can collect on life insurance if a person's life ends by suicide, but only if it is at least two years from the date the policy was issued.

She had filled out so many forms and then agreed upon request to allow the hard drive on Paul's computer to be copied. The insurance company, American Security, also asked to review his iPad history. The representative claimed all cases got scrutiny, but it was clear that this was something more. The company needed affidavits, and Lindsey was required to give a deposition. In order to collect, she'd had to retain a lawyer and threaten to sue. She didn't have the money to pay for hourly legal advice; her arrangement meant she had to give the attorney part of her payout. The insurance company took over two years before issuing her a check. She would have written a scathing Yelp review, but that seemed too mild a revenge compared to what she'd been put through.

She had never lied. She had looked for a note, for some kind of message from Paul, but she hadn't found anything. Until now. She felt both better and worse. But she wasn't going to tell anyone. What was done was done. He hadn't been in a surfing accident. He'd unhooked the leash from his surfboard and purposely swum out into those enormous waves. He'd wanted his lungs to fill with ice water. He'd wanted his life to end. And he hadn't had a problem leaving her and the kids behind.

Lindsey took the note and went upstairs to her room. She shut the door and dropped down onto the sagging mattress. She sat for a long time, her body trembling slightly, her heart fluttering with what she knew to be tachycardia. She felt as if her chest might explode. She tried to slow her breathing, to calm herself.

Lindsey finally opened the folded piece of paper and read the words again. She felt sorry for him and at the same time enraged. Her right hand squeezed his note into a ball. She pressed harder and harder until the paper was compressed like a rock. It was so much easier to see the way things had gone wrong now that she had some perspective. Paul's company had been scooped by another form of the *same* brilliant idea. He could have sold their shares and walked away with enough cash to hold his head up high and keep his family afloat. Other people would have come in to clean up the mess and salvage something from the wreckage. But he didn't. He got rid of his critics. He took on more debt. Then he broke the law. Maybe that was what finished him. He created false expenditure reports and began transferring corporate money into his personal account. The company was already in negative numbers.

At the time, she hadn't been privy to any of the specifics of what was really going on, but knew things were bad and getting worse. It wasn't just the company that was floundering; so was her husband. He wasn't sleeping. He lost weight. She got him to see a therapist she'd found online. She didn't want to ask anyone for a referral. It was important, Paul kept telling her, that they make it look like the company was doing great. But nothing could stop the bank from foreclosing on the house, which the company owned.

After Paul stopped taking a weekly salary, Lindsey contacted the college and asked for her old teaching position back. But that job had been filled and the school was going through cutbacks. They had a hiring freeze, so she couldn't even return as a teaching assistant. The downward slide was fast. An auction house listed all the big-ticket items from the house to raise cash for their delinquent tax bill. But the sale didn't bring in what they'd expected, and after their commission was deducted, Paul and Lindsey were back to negative numbers. In what felt like the whiplash of a car accident, they withdrew from the country club and put the kids back in public school. The private lessons ended. The expensive dinners. The nanny. The cleaning woman. The gardeners. The car leases. The subscriptions to everything from a dozen pay TV services to the wine-of-the-month club. The manicures, pedicures, blowouts, skin creams, personal trainers, eyelash tints, and facials—the list went on and on. It all came to an end.

She told Sena that they were boarding her pony, but Snorri the miniature Icelandic horse was sold on Craigslist. The government no longer allowed importation of the animals, so Sena's faux pony was the one thing they'd bought that showed a profit in the two years of putting at least five figures a month in charges on their credit cards.

Lindsey found a sublet on the Eastside of Portland. It was just a short-term fix. The owner demanded cash (after checking their credit report), and the money for Snorri provided that. By the next rental, four months later, Lindsey had learned her lesson. She used her mother's name on the application and never brought up Paul or the company. Americans seemed to naturally believe British people; it felt to Lindsey as if they were hardwired to defer to the accent.

The third rental had two bedrooms and a pantry off the tiny kitchen that had all of the shelves and the door removed. Olivia and Sena were in one bedroom. Lindsey and Paul took the other. Carlos got the pantry, which he said smelled like cough syrup. But he was happy because the place had only one TV and he could watch from his bed. At the dream house there were screens in every room. Even the bathrooms. It was no wonder they'd hardly spoken to each other when they lived there.

The day before the final move, Paul flew down to San Francisco in a last-ditch effort to save EnGenStor. Lindsey didn't ask the specifics. She was over the details of their failure. She just wanted him to walk away and find a new job. He was qualified to do all kinds of things. Paul returned late that night and didn't try to sugarcoat it: The ship was sunk. The credit cards couldn't be tapped for more cash. There was a lien being filed against them by a list of debtors who wanted money for the offices and equipment rental.

Lindsey drove to the Home Depot and asked two guys standing on the curb if they'd move boxes in exchange for Paul's clip-in Peloton cycling shoes and a bag of her overpriced high heels. They agreed but without a lot of enthusiasm, and only after arguing among themselves at length over who got the pricey stilettos.

She might have appealed to friends for help, but she hadn't been in touch with people from the old neighborhood in months and she couldn't face the new friends. It was easier to keep the Circle of Disaster small. Lindsey had even been lying to her mother.

They'd only been in the last sublet for eighteen days when a severe storm hit the Pacific Northwest, bringing high winds and torrential rain. It had barely subsided when Paul decided to go surf.

Lindsey regretted that they'd fought that morning. She'd had tears in her eyes and nothing but anger in her voice when he walked out the door.

How could she possibly have known she'd never see him again?

But at some point earlier he had taped a note in her recipe book. Was it the morning he went surfing or the day before? It took twenty-seven months for her to consider making Nan's treacle cookies.

Had he really believed his family would be better off without him? Had he thought so little of himself at that point?

Love wasn't innocent.

17

It was Sena who noticed something was wrong. They were eating at the table in the kitchen, and the fifth chair where Chris often sat was empty.

"Mama, your face is red."

"I got too much sun."

"Because you forgot to wear your sunscreen?" Sena asked.

Lindsey nodded. Sena didn't let it go. "Is that why you aren't having dinner?"

There was barely any food on Lindsey's plate. "I had a really big lunch, sweetheart."

Sena's chin rested on her palm. "What did you eat?"

Lindsey's mind went blank. She didn't answer.

Olivia put down her fork. "Mom, are you okay?" Carlos stopped chewing.

"I'm sorry. I'm just thinking about—"

"About lunch?" Sena asked.

Lindsey looked around the table at her three children. They were each special in their own way. They were what she and Paul had made together. They were what he left behind.

"About what, Mama?" Sena was more insistent.

"About your dad."

Sena got up from her chair and slid into her mother's lap. She reached up to encircle her neck. Olivia silently got to her feet. She put an arm around her little sister and the other arm around Carlos, who had joined Lindsey on the other side. Sena pressed her lips against Lindsey's ear and whispered, "We love you."

No one ate the treacle cookies.

The kids cleaned up the kitchen and sent Lindsey upstairs to rest. She climbed into bed, her legs heavy, as if they were swollen from some kind of assault. Her shoulder refused to relax into any position that made the mattress feel comfortable. With her fists pressed into her face, her thumbnails against her lips, she counted each inhalation and exhalation, trying to take in as much air as possible, hoping to slow down her racing mind.

Nothing worked.

Lindsey wedged a pillow between her knees to even up her right hip as her toes curled and uncurled, twitching as if not part of the rest of her body. With her eyes closed she could see nothing but the page of the cookbook and the taped message. She wondered how Paul could have ever thought she would understand. She would never fully accept the fact that he had been in so much pain and she hadn't been able to help. She had heard him but hadn't listened. She hadn't understood the depth of his despair.

An accident might involve bad judgment, foggy thinking, or just plain bad luck. It was absent intent.

But he *meant* to leave them all behind.

Instead, he died and took part of her with him.

The next morning when Lindsey got back from dropping the kids at school, she asked Chris if she could help with the wiring. Perched next to him on a stool, ready to hand over materials and tools, she spoke in a new way. Her voice had an urgency that had been absent. "Would you tell me about your wife?"

He stopped what he was doing, surprised at the question, but remained silent. She waited. He pointed toward a new switch, and when she gave it to him, their fingers touched. She pulled her hand away and brushed the hair off her face. Then, his back to her, he said, "She worked for my publisher. She was in marketing."

"So that's how you met? Because of work?"

"There was a lunch and she was there. I sat next to her."

He turned, and she could see his face in profile. She didn't want to be pushy, but she longed for more. "Did you know right away? Was it one of those love-at-first-sight things?"

"No, but I was intrigued. That's what I remember."

"And she was beautiful?"

"She was. When she spoke, I could feel my anxiety ease up."

"You have anxiety?"

"Who doesn't?"

"You hide yours."

"I'm on vacation in Hawai'i."

"Working every day rewiring an old motel."

He shrugged. "I had all kinds of plans for my life back when I first met Cassie. I didn't want to fall in love. But her laughter got me. And her optimism. I needed it."

"How soon after you met did you marry?"

The smile that spread across his face was more open. He didn't mind telling her. "We did everything out of order. First we bought a house together."

"Before you were married?"

He nodded. "Then we took a big trip to Europe. Neither of us had ever been. We went everywhere. Saw so much."

"Like a honeymoon?"

"Totally. But budget travel. Food from markets eaten sitting on low walls and park benches. We were gone for two months."

"That sounds amazing."

"It was. When we got back, we found a rescue dog. Marcus. Then we were married and started trying to have kids. . . ." He'd been talking while at the same time threading wires from an outlet up to a switch. He stopped. Lindsey straightened. When he spoke again his voice no longer had any bounce.

"Cassie's doctor found a lump in her neck. She had a sore throat. He was just running his fingers under her jaw to feel her glands. He wanted a scan, because he said he always erred on the side of caution. I went with her to the appointment three days later. We didn't think there was anything wrong; it was just an excuse to take a few hours off from work and grab a nice lunch together."

"You found out right away?"

"The radiology assistant had just seen Cassie's scan. I was heading down the hall to join my wife and the woman asked if we had kids. I answered no, and she murmured under her breath without thinking, 'Thank God.' That's how I knew my wife was in trouble."

"Oh my gosh . . ."

"There was life before that moment. Then after."

"I'm so sorry."

She wanted him to stop, but she'd started this. He had more to say. "She was trying to get pregnant, but it had been almost a year. We wanted children. We had an appointment with a fertility specialist on the books, which we canceled and always pretended we would reschedule. They say every cancer is different and there is always reason for hope, but hers was advanced when they found it."

Lindsey felt like she should say something, but all she could do was nod. He went on. "Cassie told everyone she was going to beat it. They did the operation right away to remove the tumor. Chemotherapy. Radiation. More chemo. Then, after her recurrence, a stem cell transplant. It was over three years from start to finish. She fought every day, complained much less than I would have. She worried more about me than herself. That's not an exaggeration. That's the kind of person she was."

He turned his back to her again. He held the needle-nose pliers. She watched his hand grip the handles hard.

Grief was isolating.

Lindsey got to her feet. "I'm going to make a pot of tea. I'll be back." There was nothing she could say that would make a difference. That much she knew to be true.

Olivia had been looking for him. She hung around her locker, but he didn't come by between classes. There were 208 people in their class. At least that's what she thought the counselor had said on her first day. They had different schedules, but the school wasn't that big and she should have been able to find him. At lunchtime Olivia didn't eat in the cafeteria, but she stood in the doorway surveying the room. He wasn't there. After her last class, her eyelids heavy as she gathered her things, she heard a voice. "Hey . . . Olivia . . ."

She turned to see Koa. He had a backpack over his shoulder and his skateboard jutted out the top. One of the wheels was spinning. "Haku said to tell you he wasn't coming to school today."

"Oh . . . I wondered."

"Sorry. I was supposed to let you know this morning. He wanted me to make sure you had his telephone number."

Olivia wordlessly gave him her phone and he entered the digits. "Is he home sick?" she finally asked.

"No. He had to go to a court thing. In Honolulu."

She nodded as if that was as normal as a dentist appointment. "Right. Thanks." She took back her phone realizing she could finally have an actual conversation with Koa. She could ask questions about when he'd worked at the motel. Or what he thought about school. But she didn't. She stood awkwardly in silence until he turned and walked away.

Olivia had a friend in Portland who had gone to court because she drove without a license. Another kid she knew had to go before a judge after underage drinking at a house party where she almost froze to death after passing out in an unheated garage. She wondered what Haku had done. He didn't seem like the kind of guy who was dealing drugs or stealing from a 7-Eleven. She wanted to find out what was going on, but not be, as her mom sometimes said, "too chopsy." She didn't like pushy people, even though she wondered if she could have been described that way once.

Olivia went outside to wait for her mom. Kids were getting on buses and bikes, crossing the street to go down to the beach or walk home. She watched the chaos of the end of the school day, wondering if she should text Haku or just give him a call. Choices were such a burden. She felt certain the world would be easier without so much technology. She decided to ask Haku a question her friends in Oregon had put to her so often it had lost all meaning. She sent a text: *Are you ok?*

Three dots appeared. Olivia remembered her dad calling these "typing awareness indicators." He could be such a nerd.

She heard the text beep and looked down to read, *I can drive you home. I'm just down the street.*

Olivia called her mom and said she didn't need a ride.

She got into the front seat of the pickup and fished around for the seatbelt. "How come you weren't in school?"

"Custody hearing." He sounded drained, as if he was talking about someone else.

"Of what?"

"Me. My mom moved to the mainland. She's in Utah. I live with my dad and Koa's mom." He put on his turn indicator and pulled out of the parking lot. "Have you been to Utah?"

Olivia had gone to Park City to ski a few times, but she shook her head. That had been another lifetime. She'd been a different person. She wanted to hear more, but he turned the tables on her.

"So what happened to your parents?"

There were so many answers to that question. The easiest was to say her dad died in the ocean during a storm. Most people didn't need more details. But she wanted to hear about his mom in Utah and why his parents got divorced and what it was like to have a stepbrother. It had to be a fair exchange.

"My dad drowned two years ago."

She could see this wasn't news to him. Koa had worked at the motel. The Kalamas knew the facts. Maybe most of the kids at school had heard a version of her story.

"My dad started a tech company. In the beginning it was going well, but then a few years later he had a reversal of fortune. That's what the newspaper called it when he died."

"What's that code for?"

"His big idea wasn't so big. I swear one day we were ordering all kinds of stuff online and the next day no one was supposed to use a credit card."

"And everything changed." He sounded as if he spoke from personal experience.

She continued, "We had a nanny who said she was going back to Sweden, but then I ran into her at a movie theater and she was with the new kids she looked after. She was really embarrassed. I knew I should be worried because she bought me popcorn, and she was all about saving money. Right after that we lost our house. And moved a few times, always to smaller places that cost less. My parents started selling things. They were fighting all the time. Then my dad went surfing in a big storm and he drowned."

She stopped talking. She wondered if he felt sorry for her. She wished she hadn't told him so much. It had just come tumbling out. She pulled her legs up onto the seat and grabbed hold of her ankles. She wanted to be small. Her chin rested against her kneecaps. More silence. Too long. Uncomfortable. She wanted out of the truck, but Haku spoke. "My mom took off with my dad's best friend." His voice was as even as if he were saying, *My mom does yoga.* He then continued, "But what are you going to do? You just have to say—"

She finished his sentence. "Two tears in a bucket."

Haku started to laugh. There was a sweetness to it. "I never heard that."

"It's from my mom. Instead of swearing. I've got a little sister who's only seven."

"Got it."

18

He had to put the ladder down into the pit in order to get out. That's how deep it was.

Carlos had slowly, carefully, dug a hole, now two feet wide and four feet deep. He kept assuming he would soon hit solid rock and the project would come to a natural end, but so far that wasn't the case. He had made an opening at the rear of the shed by moving two boards, allowing him to shove his full dirt pail out the back. This gave him an area hidden from view. Carlos set up an old window screen to act like a sieve. It was painstaking, but he forced the soil through the mesh with one of the Kalamas' old squeegees. Before his family had moved to Hawai'i, he had heard about a curse from Pele, the goddess of Hawaiian volcanoes. If someone took a rock or shell from the islands and brought it home, she would seek revenge. But this was home now, so he hoped nothing he was doing would make Pele mad.

Carlos had done some research. There were three types of dirt: sandy, clay, and loamy. He thought the categories sounded like names for puppies. He was surprised that the spot where he'd decided to dig wasn't hard-packed. It had an unexpected softness and the moisture content changed daily, which he decided might have to do with the tides. His first revelation was that there were a shocking number of bugs living underground. Squishy gray grubs, ants, and tiny white mites were everywhere. So were roaches, earwigs, and wire worms, which were the orangish larvae of future beetles. But, fortunately, no spiders. In the beginning the insects almost stopped him from digging until he realized they could be easily pushed aside. When he wasn't at school or off doing something with his new friends, Carlos was in the shed digging his hole, which he covered every night with a tarp. He had unearthed rocks, bottle caps, and plastic scraps that didn't seem very old or interesting. And yet he kept going. It was his project and it was his secret. At night he dreamed that he no longer had fingers; his arms ended in trowels.

On the afternoon of the day before the woman from the state office, Mia, was supposed to return, he was crouched on the ground, sifting through fresh dirt that he'd just dumped behind the shed, when he found something. He assumed it was a piece of a shell. Sena had put up a chart on the wall in the bathroom that identified puka, cone, miter, and drupe shells. He couldn't help but stare at the different shapes and learn the names. Now, as he dug, he found auger shells, once home to snails. There were parts of sand crabs, cowrie shells, and sunrise shells, in many sizes, but this piece was different. It was a shard, almost the length of his little finger, with a very specific shape.

Carlos went back inside the shed and pulled the tarp over his hole. He then took what he'd found and went down to the beach where he kicked off his flip-flops, which the kids at school called slippers. He waded into the waves, his hand immersed in the water. The caked dirt washed away as he realized what he was holding wasn't a shell but a piece of bone. It was shaped like the letter *J*, but with two interior barbs. He lifted it close and discovered there were marks carved into the bone and a small hole at the top. He'd seen this shape before, on a surfboard. And in a different form as a tattoo on the PE teacher's arm. It looked like a thick fishhook, but it had to mean more.

Carlos wanted to shout to the world, or at least to his family, about his find. But at the same time, he decided this thing might be too important. It could be very old. Maybe even a historical artifact. He put the treasure into his pocket and headed out of the water up the sandy shore back to the motel.

Once inside, he drew a picture of what he'd found and went out to where Chris was working on the purple cottage. The guy knew a lot. Maybe he could help.

"Do you know what this is a picture of? It's a local thing I think." Chris put down his pliers and took the piece of paper in hand. "A *makau*."

"Yeah. It's a fishhook—right?"

"I think at this point it's a cultural symbol."

"Of old times in Hawaii?"

Chris pulled his iPad from the work bag at his feet. He typed, then read, "'Today it stands for safe passage over water. The *makau* is a symbol of human connection with the sea, its creatures, and the fragile balance of life on the islands.'"

"That's pretty cool."

Chris lowered the iPad. "It's supposed to bring strength. They have a big collection at the Bishop Museum in Honolulu. Maybe we could head into town and see."

Carlos nodded. "I bet Sena would want to go with us."

"Town" was what the kids at school called the city. He liked that Chris was talking like someone who lived here.

"We just need to figure out a time before I go," Chris added.

Carlos was silent. Of course, Chris would be leaving someday, but that wasn't something Carlos wanted to think about. "And we still haven't gone swimming. We have to go snorkeling together."

Chris put his iPad back into his work bag and picked up his reaming pliers. "I'd better get back to it."

Carlos had his right hand inside his pocket, and his fingers wrapped around the *makau*. He wondered if it was his imagination, or if he was standing taller.

Lindsey took a hanger from the tiny bedroom closet. On it was the only outfit left from the time when there had been money to spend on impractical clothing. She had not worn the white linen dress with the matching jacket in three years and had thought twice about bringing it to the islands since the idea of ironing the thing was ridiculous. Plus, she wasn't going to any weddings, cocktail parties, or charity events here. Lindsey slipped the dress over her head and the fabric fell like a soft curtain around her body. She looked at herself in the mirror. She looked good.

But it was too obvious. She took off the dress and returned it to the closet. Mia was supposed to be arriving any minute. Carlos wasn't at school, after complaining of a bad sore throat. She hoped to hell it wasn't strep. He was going to spend the morning in bed, but he had asked to go sit outside and she'd agreed. She knew he wanted to watch the state workers take soil samples. Or whatever they would be doing.

Carlos was waiting on the porch when she went downstairs. He didn't look sick, but he did cough when he saw her. Before she could ask how he was feeling, Mia's blue Toyota, followed by a white truck with the seal of the state of Hawai'i on the door, came around the wide curve and parked. Chris was close by, doing something at the telephone pole. He was the first to greet her when she got out of her car. Carlos was on his feet heading to join them.

Lindsey watched as Mia and Chris said hello. They were courteous, not overly familiar. She felt herself relax ever so slightly as she headed down the porch steps. Carlos was already peppering Mia with questions.

"What happens if you find something? What do you do?" Carlos asked.

"It depends on what it is."

"What's something cool you dug up before?"

Mia laughed. "There's a lot under our feet. The first Polynesians were here three thousand years ago. We're looking for evidence of their lives."

"And that's in the dirt?"

"Yes, but most of the time we only unearth natural decaying material—seeds, animal bones, shells."

"But you have found other stuff? Important things?"

"We've come across evidence of plants and animals that are no longer in the islands."

"They're extinct?"

"More than forty different species of birds are now gone. Some long before the Polynesians were here, but the real wave of animal extinction happened in the last two hundred years. Along with all kinds of insects that have vanished."

"Because of people?" Carlos asked.

Mia nodded.

Lindsey spoke up. "In the UK they started a Remembrance Day for Lost Species. Now it takes place all around the world."

Carlos was intrigued. "I never heard that."

"It's at the end of November."

Carlos looked from his mom to Mia. "Maybe we should do something for that this year. I bet Sena would be into it."

Mia smiled at him. "That's a great idea."

A man and a woman in green work clothes, after consulting Mia's electronic map, selected a spot right next to the curve in the driveway to begin. They had a collection of tools, the most interesting of which was something Mia called a bucket auger. She explained to Carlos, who stood mesmerized at her side, that it would make boreholes and they would analyze the soil samples they extracted back at their workplace.

"What would keep us from putting the power lines underground? What kind of discovery?" Lindsey asked.

Mia's tone was official. "Evidence of human remains. If this was a burial ground."

Lindsey didn't respond, but Carlos did, pointing to Chris. "He put his wife's ashes out there in the water."

Mia glanced over at Chris. "Which is actually illegal. You need to be three miles offshore to do that." Chris looked guilty but didn't say anything. Mia continued, "Human ashes don't dissolve in seawater. The fragments—bone chips and grit—scatter onto the sea floor."

"Is that bad for the fish?" Carlos asked.

Mia softened. "No. It's okay for ocean life." Chris looked relieved.

Lindsey couldn't shake the idea that she was standing on a cemetery. She stared at the auger. "How far down can that thing drill?"

"Seven meters—that's twenty-one feet—is the maximum. But so close to the ocean we almost always hit lava before that."

Lindsey saw her son's eyes widen with excitement.

The survey was quick, and in under an hour the two vehicles were gone. It was like getting an MRI or some other sophisticated medical test. The results would be conveyed at a later date. The good news was that the workers didn't find anything obvious when they took the samples. Mia explained that they had once hit a human skull, and on another occasion had come across an ancient wooden paddle.

Carlos, saying his sore throat felt a lot better, went out to his shed to do something with the tools. Chris got in his Jeep not long after and left. Lindsey was uncertain where he was going but didn't want to pry.

Trying to distract herself, Lindsey reviewed her calendar. She had six weeks until her proposed "soft opening," when she intended to have guests in two of the cottages. She had already done the fun part, ordering new pillows, twenty-one sets of white organic cotton sheets, and twenty bathmats in the different colors of the cottages. She had spent way too much time looking at the options before placing her first order for hotel amenities kits, picking the product that was advertised as having a "clean grapefruit scent." They were priced at $4.95 for each kit and included shampoo, two mini soaps, and skin lotion. She purchased 240. Storage, she was beginning to realize, was going to be a major issue. Pearl and Rangi Kalama had used the two extra bedrooms upstairs for supplies. She wondered how the kids would feel giving up part of their rooms for rolls of toilet paper and cleaning products.

The least fun part of reopening the motel so far had been coming up with policies for bookings, cancellations, refunds, and the dreaded marketing of her cottages. She was surprised to see that even small motels used what were called OTAs—online travel aggregator sites. Expedia, Travelocity, and Trip.com were the vicious brokers who took

15 percent of every booking. Lindsey hoped a day would come when she would make reservations for the cottages like the Kalamas had, without worrying about finding new guests.

It was Chris who had offered advice that echoed every day as she moved forward: "Underpromise and overdeliver." He believed she should put an emphasis on the rustic, old-style island experience, selling what he called an authentic Hawaiian vacation. But he had also voiced a warning. Chris said a friend ran a small business and had been sued for a slip-and-fall accident. She needed to have insurance in place for unforeseen calamities.

It was overwhelming. But while everything she read seemed firm on the fact that professional photographs were important for marketing, Lindsey went another way. She asked her three kids to take pictures. The results were both predictable and unexpected. The single best shot, they all agreed, was from Sena. She had been on her belly on the gravel aiming out at the yellow cottage with the blue ocean visible in the background, when a rust-colored chicken stepped in front of the lens. There were three layers of narrative in her image. Somehow the picture said it all.

Olivia got a ride home from school on Friday with Haku. She asked him if he wanted to come inside, but he shook his head. She felt good about both things. She wanted to be polite, but she really didn't feel like hanging out with him in front of her mom or brother and sister. After she opened the car door she turned to him. "You're my first friend here."

He answered, "Maybe someday I'll be more than that."

She couldn't look at him. His words derailed her. She shut the car door and hurried toward the office.

Olivia went upstairs to find Sena waiting for her. "Mom made bouillabaisse for dinner."

"That's cool."

"She didn't make it for us. It's for Chris."

"It tastes good. That's what matters."

"No. What matters is that we only have it for special. It's for celebrating."

"So maybe we're celebrating that he didn't get fried when he connected the electricity from the telephone pole to the new panel. I guess that's pretty dangerous."

"No. The bouillabaisse means she likes him."

Olivia made a face. "It's not like she's going to date him or any-thing. She's way too old to be thinking about hooking up with guys."

"She doesn't think she's too old."

"Well, she is."

Olivia hoped that was the end of the conversation. Sena grabbed her insect book and slid off the bed. Her final words to Olivia were, "You only make bouillabaisse if you really care."

That night at dinner Lindsey worked to find a topic that would keep everyone in a bright place. No mention of Sena's chickens or the school day, no discussion of the motel website or reserva-tion software. But when the kids were talking, she found herself watching Chris with such intensity that she lost the thread of the conversation. His face had few lines. His hair had just the first hint of gray at the temples. His athletic body was draped into the chair directly across from hers with an ease that said he either was tired from the day or had grown comfortable with her three children. They always sat with the kids as buffers, but Sena made a point of moving her seat as close to her mother as she could get once the bouillabaisse was set down.

Chris stared at the yellow concoction. "It looks amazing."

Carlos looked excited. "It has saffron. And orange peels. That's part of what makes it different."

Lindsey reached for Olivia's bowl. "I can serve you guys."

Chris got to his feet. "Let me help."

As he took the ladle Sena began eating her mound of plain rice, muttering to the table, "It's just fish stew with a fancy name."

After dinner, Chris insisted on leading the cleanup of the kitchen, and Lindsey sat on a stool pretending to go through her list of motel business on her laptop. In reality she was watching his back at the sink. But when she shifted to look at the dark glass of the window, she realized that he was gazing at her reflection, too.

The kids were all asleep when Lindsey climbed the stairs to her room. She slipped out of her shorts and T-shirt and put on the white linen dress. She looked at herself in the mirror, wondering what she would do differently if she could start over. The big decisions didn't seem as important as the small ones. If she and Drew hadn't gone to that brunch all those years ago in Portland, she might have married him. She didn't doubt that she would have lived with happiness, if not grand passion. But she wanted adventure, or at least she thought she did.

And then there were her children. Not marrying Paul would mean no Olivia, Carlos, and Sena. That was unthinkable.

Lindsey knew the white linen would wrinkle, but she lay down on her bed anyway. Chris was almost finished with the electrical work. The one subject she never brought up with him was his plan for the future. But she knew that at some point he would climb into the rental Jeep and drive away. Maybe that was about to happen.

There was no great virtue in pretending she didn't care.

19

He agreed to go hiking on the trail at Hauʻula.

She told him that she had the morning free because the computer system at her bank was down and she wasn't able to meet with the officer about her new merchant account. It was a lie. But instead of feeling bad about that, she felt only excitement.

Lindsey was filled with both unease and expectation as they started up the steep path. Coral creepers, with pink and red flowers, wrapped around the trunks of towering trumpet trees. Ferns and thick pili grass choked either side of the trail. It was a lush, emerald-green tropical forest and the wet air was heavy with the smell of mulch, at once sweet and rotten. It was late morning, but the sky was growing dark. Giant clouds propelled by a westerly reverse flow appeared from out of nowhere. They blocked the sun and then just as quickly shifted, opening holes for brief but hot shafts of light.

The first part of the trail, which was a loop that began as a very steep climb, was difficult for Lindsey. She kept her head down, working hard to stay at Chris's pace. It took just under half an hour to reach the highest point, where the vegetation gave way to an open area that stretched along the coast, as jagged ridges ran parallel to the ocean in a breathtaking vista. But Chris didn't stop long enough for her to even catch her breath. It felt as if he was trying to get away from her when he started down the winding backside of the less-used side of the trail. It was midweek and no one else appeared to be in the rainforest. Their aloneness, in a place so dense with life, pushed in on Lindsey. Her heart raced, and sweat ran in rivulets down her spine. They passed through a grove of towering octopus trees and were on a steep section of the narrow pathway when he seemed to quicken the pace. It was possible that moving fast was easier on this level of incline. His feet barely hit the ground before rising again.

Lindsey struggled to keep up, not wanting to admit he was moving too quickly. Her eyes darted back and forth from the ground to his fleeing calves. Every step required concentration, and as she crossed a small stream, not much more than a trickle surrounded by a swarm of insects, her right foot landed at the wrong angle and her ankle turned. She lost her balance as if she'd stepped on black ice. She landed hard, splattering dark muck across her face, neck, and T-shirt. Lindsey called out in panic and then cursed as she pulled her hands up from the tar-like earth.

Chris stopped at the sound of the fall and spun around, shouting from below on the trail, "Are you okay?"

Lindsey tried to stand, but her feet were unsteady and she fell again, this time getting mud on the front of her shorts and all over her thighs. Chris took off in a sprint to help her. "You're okay. Just take your time."

He stepped toward her, hand outstretched, and he, too, lost his footing in the slippery stream.

Once they were both down in the wet ooze, her humiliation evaporated.

Then they started to laugh so hard they were barely able to breathe. Small flies and gnats buzzed in the air as the gray clouds, barely visible through the canopy of two tiers of leafy green trees, shifted again and rain fell from an exploding sky.

Chris, still wheezing with laughter, got to his feet first. She was so worried about her balance that she stayed on her knees. He reached for her, this time with a stable grip, and pulled her up as the rain came down harder, bouncing off everything green, pelting their bodies. He had her by the arm and the elbow but instead of stepping away and finding her own stable stance, she lifted her head and looked into his eyes. She wasn't laughing anymore. She pressed herself into his torso, her legs against his. And then she shut her eyes and kissed him full on the mouth.

It wasn't a soft, sweet kiss. It was anxious and desperate.

And it was 100 percent her doing.

He didn't pull away. The rain fell harder and he kissed her back. His mouth covered hers and they lost their balance and fell again, landing in the mud and the ferns. They were all over each other, tugging on clothing. He had one hand up her shirt when a loud crashing sound stopped them. The noise was aggressive, feral, and frightening.

Lindsey turned her head to see three wild boars trampling down the hillside in their direction. One, a sow, was enormous, over two hundred pounds, with a pair of bottom tusks jutting out from its jaw. The other pigs were small, with snouts displacing greenery as if their noses had swirling propellers attached to the ends. They chomped down on roots, fungi, insects, and the corms of the bulbous water plants, sending leaves and dirt flying. Because Lindsey and Chris were on the ground, the pigs didn't see them, and with the rain coming down so hard, they weren't able to pick up a human scent. But they were on a collision course.

Chris and Lindsey pulled apart. He scrambled to his feet and, through the dense foliage of the rainforest, locked eyes with the giant sow. The creature jerked to a stop. Lindsey swallowed a scream. The smaller wild pigs squealed and then ran in the opposite direction. But the bigger beast stayed rooted to the ground.

Chris raised his arms high over his head as he confronted the animal, shouting, "*No!*"

The defiant sow met his gaze straight on, shook her filthy body, sending mud spiraling in all directions, and then she crossed the hiking trail and went straight over the steep edge, crashing through the thicket of green below.

Lindsey only heard it, as she was running down the trail as fast as her legs would carry her. The adrenaline surging through her body transformed her into some kind of superathlete. She jumped over fallen logs and sailed in a single leap across a stream. She didn't stop for over a quarter of a mile, until she reached the point near the beginning of the loop where the trail flattened out. By then she was breathless and near collapse. When she turned around, she saw Chris coming down the trail, mud-splattered but steady.

Lindsey waited, her heart pounding. Her hair hung in a wet, mud-caked mane. As Chris got closer, she met his gaze.

"That was insane. I thought they were going to attack us! They came out of nowhere!"

He took what she could see was a big breath, followed by a slow exhalation. "It's all fine. The small ones were probably her piglets. We startled her. That's what made her aggressive."

The intimacy they had just experienced disappeared. A shield had gone up. She fumbled for the right words, but all she could manage was, "I overreacted. I know that. Sorry."

"No. It's fine."

"Really. Sorry. I was scared."

"No worries."

She hated that expression. She wasn't worried; she was explaining herself. But Chris saying "no worries" was going to now make her worried. She didn't move as he stepped around her on the trail, heading downhill toward the asphalt road in the distance. The rain was still falling, making it difficult to speak without shouting. But there was nothing for her to say. She was silent, watching the raindrops hit her bare legs and wash the mud down her calves into her soaked socks.

They finished the state park loop and walked in silence to his Jeep. A wave of intense exhaustion hit Lindsey. Up ahead on the shoulder of Kam Highway she could see the vast gray ocean. She wanted to go straight into the water, wash herself off, and start over.

"Should we jump in the ocean? Get rid of all this mud?"

"I'd rather rinse off at the motel."

There was no room for discussion. She tried to smile, but he wasn't looking at her. He unlocked the Jeep, then took a seat to remove his filthy hiking boots. He grabbed two towels from the backseat and handed her one. She thanked him, but wasn't sure if he even heard her voice.

Once they had the car doors closed, it stopped raining as if a switch had been flipped and the clouds turned off. Like him. He rolled down the window on the driver's side, and when he stepped on the gas a gust of outside air blew in, causing her to shiver involuntarily. It was the first time she'd been cold since arriving on the island.

Lindsey could feel a wall between their seats, and with every curve in the road it became more solid. She wanted him to say something to reassure her, but he was silent, focused on driving. She was so relieved when he turned off the highway to the motel that she allowed herself to speak. "I'm going down for a swim. Join me?"

He shook his head. "Not this time."

He parked and she opened the Jeep door, tossing her muddy boots onto the lava chips. She got out and headed barefoot across the tough, spiky grass. He didn't want to swim with her. She was suddenly conscious of the fact that she had never seen him go in the ocean even once. She wished she had suggested they make tea in the office or, better yet, open a bottle of wine and laugh about falling in mud and surviving three rampaging wild hogs.

Once on the shore, Lindsey forced herself into the water, taking no pleasure as she swam out just far enough to look like someone who was enjoying it. That is, if he was even watching.

She came up from the wide beach just in time to see him emerge in dry clothing from his cottage. He went straight to his Jeep, started the engine, and lurched into reverse.

There was no text from him on her phone, and in the minutes and then hours that followed, no missed call.

In the afternoon she picked up the kids from school, and he wasn't there when they got back to the motel. She tried not to think of him, but with every passing second that became more difficult. She went to his cottage and felt relief to see his suitcase still in the closet and his muddy, wet clothing still hung outside on the back railing. He had to return at some point. It was just a matter of when.

She cooked dinner for the kids and found herself moving from anxious to angry. She sent a text message asking if he'd be joining them for pasta, and he didn't respond. Carlos set the table, and when he put down a plate for Chris, she managed to say, "He's not coming for dinner."

Carlos lifted up the plate with a shrug. "Is he sick of our food?"

Olivia looked up from her phone. "Maybe he's sick of us."

Lindsey and the kids cleaned up after dinner, and she asked Carlos to leave a dinner plate at the front door of the red cottage. Two hours later, when Chris still hadn't returned, she went out and took away the uneaten food. She peeled back the tinfoil to see that everything was covered with ants. They had been working at a feverish pace to haul away the bow-tie pasta.

Just after midnight she finally heard car tires crunch on the lava chips. She stood in darkness looking down from the upstairs office window as his Jeep rounded the curve into the parking area. He was driving too fast and came to an abrupt stop, almost hitting a palm tree. His head was downcast, and he walked with a sluggish, unsteady step. She realized he'd been drinking. She was suddenly furious. She had waited for Paul to come home the night he was swallowed by the ocean, and she would never get over the anxiety of those hours. There was only one thing worse than the dread of not knowing about a loved one's safety, and that was to have your most awful fear proven right.

She could hear the palm fronds slapping against the tin roofs. Katydids and crickets rubbed their wings together to make a repeating overlay of chirps. An owl hooted in the distance. The waves repeated their unyielding song. She stopped herself from going straight to his cottage and screaming that he'd hurt her in a deep, awful way. Instead, she climbed into bed with a mix of exhaustion and anxious despair keeping her awake. Finally, she allowed herself to turn on her phone on the night table. The glowing numbers in front of her showed 3:07 A.M.

Damn him.

Damn him straight to hell and back.

She threw off the sheet, went into the bathroom, and pushed open the window. Outside the moon was nearly full and she could see a slice of reflection on the silver ocean. A light was still on in Chris's cottage. Good. So he, too, couldn't sleep. Or maybe he was so drunk he hadn't even bothered to turn off the light. He'd pay for that with bug bites. A sudden gust of warm wind caught the window and slammed it shut. She recoiled and bumped straight into Olivia, who was standing directly behind her. They both shrieked as Lindsey cried out, "You scared me!"

"You scared *me*!"

"Olivia, what are you doing up?"

"Going to the bathroom. What were *you* doing staring out the window?"

Lindsey didn't answer. Olivia slid down her underwear as she took a seat on the toilet. "Were you spying on your island crush?"

"What's that supposed to mean?" Lindsey was glad the room was dark because she knew her face was red with embarrassment.

"Really, Mom, like you don't think we see you geeking out over him?"

Lindsey's reaction was too big and too fast. "What you see is *appreciation*! Christopher's been a huge help around here—we're all bloody lucky to have him come to our aid!"

Olivia reached back and flushed the toilet. "You sounded very Welsh just then."

"I will take that as a compliment."

"Don't."

When Olivia stood up her tone had changed from teenager to angry roommate. "Since he arrived, you've been using my makeup, wearing my earrings, and even borrowing my clothes, which is so *not right*. You're taller than me and bigger. It's not like my stuff even looks good on you. You're stretching it out in all the wrong places!"

"Your lack of generosity is ex-traor-dinary!" Lindsey did in fact sound very much like she had just arrived from Wales.

"Chill out, Mom. Carlos said the guy's leaving soon."

The statement was a gut punch. "What?"

"Carlos is the king of bad intel. But he might be right for a change. The man *is* on vacation in Hawai'i. Or he was until he turned into your handyman. At some point he's got to go back to wherever he came from."

Olivia headed out the door, but not before adding, "As Gran would say, 'Don't fanny around.' You better make your move."

Lindsey was humiliated. But there was a positive side to being called out by her daughter. The fatigue she instantly felt was so overwhelming that when she put her head on the pillow, she was sound asleep in minutes.

20

Lindsey opened her eyes and realized the sun was too bright. She'd overslept. The morning would now be a fire drill, rushing to get everyone out to the car in time for school. She jumped to her feet, shouting for the kids to wake up. Then the day before came flooding back to her.

In the bathroom, she scrubbed her teeth as if her tooth enamel was the baked cheese in the bottom of a burnt lasagna pan. When she spat out her frothy saliva, it was pink with fresh blood. Lindsey turned on the faucet and used her fingers to push the goop down the drain. She had to get Chris back on the hiking trail. She had to fall into his arms again, only this time there could be no interruptions. What were the chances that feral pigs would appear twice on that steep path? In her mind's eye she saw her children crouching in the green ferns on the hillside and heard Sena whisper, "Cue the wild boars!"

Maybe this was all the kids' fault.

Sena was probably driving Chris crazy with her obsession with chickens. Carlos pestered him daily about the electrical work, always wanting an explanation for what he was doing, always asking about going snorkeling. Olivia's teenage moodiness could be a buzzkill. Lindsey stared at herself in the mirror. She was blaming her children for keeping away a man. None of this was the kids' fault. If anything, Chris had probably hung around longer than he intended *because of* her kids. He could no doubt see how much they needed another adult around.

Lindsey pulled back her hair and slipped an elastic band over the snarl. She headed out of the bathroom burning with shame.

The kids had breakfast on the run, and when they went out to the Crown Victoria, the Jeep was gone. That wasn't unusual, but the sight of his empty parking space pushed her panic button. Lindsey tried to steady herself as the kids piled into the car, hoping she sounded calm. "Chris left early this morning."

Olivia and Carlos stayed quiet, but Sena answered, "He was up with the chickens."

"Did you see him?"

Sena nodded.

"Did you speak to him?"

Sena shook her head.

Lindsey had one final question. "Did *he* speak to you?"

"He said 'See you this afternoon.'"

Lindsey exhaled and her shoulders visibly lowered as she smiled at her younger daughter. She just hoped the kids couldn't feel her anxiety meter fall.

It seemed like the whole class was excited about Pajama Day. Sena stared at the pictures put up on a big bulletin board from last year's event. Most of the teachers came to school dressed in onesies, which seemed like Halloween costumes. The principal had on a bright yellow pineapple suit, and the hood came with a spiky green crown. Sena knew there was no way he slept in that.

"Pajama Day is on the eighteenth. So start planning what you will wear!"

Her teacher was giddy with enthusiasm. Sena could see the other kids move their heads close together to discuss. They were buzzing like bees in a hive. She didn't understand the interest in wearing pajamas all day, especially since everyone already showed up in shorts and T-shirts, which looked pretty much like something you could sleep in.

Her teacher continued. "Are there any questions?"

Sena raised her hand. She had been careful not to ask much in the classroom. And she had let Belly beat her in a spelling contest the day before. She was keeping a lot inside. Only this pajama situation was connected to something called Spirit Week, and that was intriguing.

"Sena?"

"Pajama Day is part of Spirit Week?"

"Yes."

"Is that when we will be talking about Hawaiian spirits?"

A few of the kids looked like they were holding in laughter. The teacher answered, "When we think of Spirit Week, we are referring to *school* spirit. That's why we're doing a fundraiser for the food bank."

Sena's voice gave away her disappointment. "So there won't be anything about the Hawaiian spirit world?"

The teacher managed a smile. "I think it's a really nice idea to think about including that."

Sena couldn't tell if she meant it or was just trying to put an end to the conversation. It didn't seem from the other kids' faces like they thought it was a nice idea.

Sena took in a deep breath. "I've been thinking about it because the Kalamas' *ʻaumākua* was an owl."

A kid named Lark who sat in the back and was usually quiet spoke up without raising her hand. "My family's *ʻaumākua* is an *ʻio*."

Sena didn't wait to be called on. "What's an *ʻio*?"

"A hawk. My *tutu* watches for one who lives high in the trees behind our house."

Sena turned to look at Lark. Up until that moment she hadn't thought much about the girl having a bird name. But now it made sense.

It was the time of the week when the class went to the library, and minutes later Sena and Lark were seated next to each other at a long table. They were allowed to bring snacks, and Sena gave Lark one of her peanut butter–covered rice cakes, and Lark gave Sena part of her sweet potato pie. It turned out that Lark also was interested in bugs, so they looked for books about insects and birds. Lark explained to Sena that she was named after a bird that was known for singing.

"But I'm not very musical," she explained. "When we did the holiday concert last year, Mrs. Alanka put me in the back row and told me to just move my lips but not make any sound."

Sena was outraged. "That's horrible."

"Yeah. And it's not my fault. Singing is one of those things that you get from your genes."

"Which one is Mrs. Alanka? Does she teach first grade?"

"She's not at the school anymore. They said she got a job in tele-marketing."

"Good," said Sena.

The tardy bell rang, and Olivia barely made it into her seat. She took out a notebook and pretended to get ready for class, but she was thinking about two things. The first was why something called "fruit slush" was on the day's lunch menu, and the second was whether she had the guts to go to the just announced Princess and Frog Dance.

Back in Portland, a dance where a girl asked a boy had been called Sadie Hawkins, but her old school considered those events sexist, since it didn't matter anymore who asked who to go dancing. Calling a girl a princess and a guy a frog seemed more judgmental than Sadie Hawkins, who was apparently a woman who wore big boots and stepped on men's toes. At least that's what someone had told her back in Oregon.

She tried to imagine Haku dancing.

It made her uncomfortable.

The only thing more uncomfortable was imagining herself dancing in a room full of strangers. She shut her eyes and worked to banish the thought.

At the front of the classroom the teacher was talking about peer mentoring. He explained that "the ultimate form of peer mentoring was with siblings." Olivia felt a pang of guilt. She could probably do a better job in that department. She went back to thinking about Haku, only not dancing.

The day before they had been in computer repair club together. He knew more than everyone else about how to troubleshoot because he'd been taking computers apart since he was eight years old. She bet her dad would have found that pretty cool. Haku explained to everyone that the best place to begin was to try to understand CPU socket types, but the real action in a computer was understanding the motherboard, which was in charge of communicating all the critical electronic components of the system. No one ever called it the fatherboard.

That made sense to Olivia.

Because that's what mothers did.

They held it together.

When Lindsey returned from school drop-off, Chris was seated on the office porch, just as he had been the second time that he'd shown up at the motel. Sunlight filtered through the canopy of trees, falling in a perfect circle at his feet. Sena's fowl pecked at the ground nearby. Lindsey opened the car door with resolve. She couldn't help that her voice was higher in register, tense and tight, as she called out, "Good morning."

His answer was calm, measured, even reassuring. "Good morning."

All she could come up with was a dull cliché. "So, another beautiful day in paradise." As she climbed the first step, he handed her a small brown bag with a grease stain on the bottom. "Chocolate glazed from Ted's."

"You drove down to the bakery?"

"I was hung over. Sugar helps." He smiled for the first time, and she felt the knot in her stomach untwist one turn as she took a seat at his side.

"What's on tap for the rest of your day?" She hoped she sounded, as Olivia would say, chill.

"Not sure. I have to start thinking about work I guess."

"You've done enough here to last a lifetime."

He laughed. "No, I mean my regular gig."

"Oh." She tried to hide her concern. "You need to get back to writing?"

"I'd planned on being on O'ahu for a week. Friday it will be a month."

Lindsey looked toward the ocean and suddenly imagined letting the air out of his tires and then locking him in his cottage. She gripped her chocolate donut. She had to meet this freight train of heartache head-on.

"So, you're going to leave soon?" She pulled the donut from the waxy paper and took a bite, unable to taste the sweetness as she waited for his answer. It felt as if she was chewing a sock.

"I have to get back to my office."

"You go into an office in Philadelphia? You don't write from home?"

He shook his head. "I rent an office downtown. I need the routine."

"So do you know what your next book will be about?"

"No, but I'm getting pressure to figure that out."

"They're just jealous—right? They know you're on the beach in Hawai'i?" Lindsey forced herself to swallow what felt like a golf ball of fried chocolate paste, then said, "Tell them I'm not going to let you leave."

He didn't answer, but after a long moment his arm reached around her back and his hand took hold of her shoulder. It was an act of kindness, she thought, yet just his touch made her release the rest of the donut. It tumbled off the edge of the porch and hit the ground. In seconds a half dozen chickens were pecking eagerly at it. Lindsey didn't even acknowledge her clumsiness. She forced herself to look up at him and when she did, she realized too late that she was crying.

His arm tightened around her back as he whispered, "Hey. Don't. You're going to be okay."

"No . . . I'm not."

"Lindsey—"

"I'm not going to be okay. It can't happen twice. It's not fair." He put both arms around her as she burrowed into his chest.

"What's happening twice?"

She choked out, "I lose . . . the bloke I love."

She winced, because she would always be Welsh and her words sounded like something from a corny songwriter. Only apparently not to him, because he lifted her chin and then pressed his lips right into hers. Not in a sweet, sad, sympathy-for-the-widow way. But in an urgent, wild-with-desire, hiking-trail-in-the-rain-times-ten way. Only now there were no wild pigs and no rain and thank God no children to wander up to the office.

There were only chickens fighting over a donut.

21

_____

Sena kept her gaze out the window. "The birds are all flying away from the water."

Carlos answered, "Because it's so windy." He caught his mom's eye in the rearview mirror. "Where are we going?"

"The surf shop."

Carlos pumped his fist. He'd been asking for new swim fins since they'd first arrived. "Yes!"

Lindsey didn't explain that her real reason for going to Hale'iwa was to buy Chris a present. While they hadn't spoken about their future together, she was hopeful. They had had a full week of a double life, keeping the newness of their relationship hidden from the kids. So many things were falling into place. They had all danced around the room when the first notification pinged on her cellphone indicating the motel had booked its first guest. Someone named Anne Herlihy. Coming from Westport, Connecticut. A party of two. She would be arriving in fifteen days. This meant income and the possibility of a real future. It was all worth celebrating.

Olivia was getting a ride home from her friend Haku, and Lindsey turned left, not right, on Kam Highway. The wind was blowing hard when they parked their car in front of the North Shore Surf Shop. Lindsey was struck by the fact that people were bustling about in more of a hurry than usual. Two men with plywood were out in front of the store with a drill and hammers.

Sena seemed happy enough to wait with one of her schoolbooks on a bench outside. Carlos talked to the workers, then explained to his mom, "It's supposed to get super windy tonight. They're boarding up the front of the store to protect the glass." Lindsey wondered if they should take any precautions at the motel. She'd talk it over with Chris when she got home. She remembered that the Kalamas had left plywood in the shed and wondered if that was what it was for.

Carlos already knew which swim fins he wanted. He found his size and put them on the counter, staring down into the glass case, which was filled with necklaces. The ones for men were on black cords, made from thin leather, and some had pendants—a shark's tooth, a silver "hang ten" fist. His eye caught a replica of an ancient *makau*. Carlos knew he had to have it, and since it wasn't expensive his mother agreed. Lindsey was feeling generous, and when they walked out of the store, she carried a bag of new stuff, excited to get back to the motel. But Sena was gone.

What started out as an annoying search turned quickly into a frantic hunt. Lindsey went in one direction and Carlos in the other. They ducked into the shops and the market, and then circled back to the car. No sign of Sena.

Carlos finally spotted his little sister on the other side of the busy roadway standing under the canopy of a large acacia tree. He darted across the blacktop to get her, and Lindsey's relief turned to anger as Carlos returned with Sena at his side. "You can't just disappear like that!"

Sena kept her eyes on the ground and didn't answer. Carlos leaned close to her ear. "We were worried about you. Tell Mom you're sorry."

But Sena wouldn't say she was sorry. She slid into the front seat of the Crown Victoria, her hands balled in tight fists.

Lindsey's voice was loud. She wasn't yelling, but she was close to it. "Why would you leave like that? What were you thinking?"

Sena remained mute, turning her head away from her mother. Lindsey reached over and took her daughter's chin, forcing the little girl to look at her. "Sena, answer me!"

Sena shut her eyes, but that didn't stop tears from rolling down her cheeks.

Lindsey's anger dissolved. She dropped her hand. "You scared us. Don't do that again. *Please.* That's all I'm asking." She leaned over and kissed the top of her daughter's head. "I didn't mean to shout at you. I'm sorry."

Sena kept her eyes closed and Lindsey started the car. "Never cross the road like that. The traffic is too dangerous."

Carlos, forever trying to broker peace, asked, "Can we listen to music?" Lindsey turned on the radio. An announcer was in the middle of a weather report. There was a storm in the Pacific. It wasn't on track to hit the islands, but it would pass close enough to bring strong winds and heavy rainfall. Carlos piped up, "I bet there will be crazy big waves in the next few days."

Lindsey stared into the rearview mirror to meet his gaze. "Why's that?"

Carlos shrugged. "Because of the storm."

Olivia could see something was going on with her mom and Chris. He was becoming a part of things in small and large ways. He arrived every morning now with coffee and donuts before they'd even left for school. And twice he showed up to get Sena and Carlos, leaving her mom back at the motel to work on the upcoming opening. She understood why he rented the power sprayer to wash the tin roofs, but why was he being a carpool dad? After dinner every night, Chris now sat with her mom making spreadsheets and talking about everything from insurance policies to potential safety and security problems. Chris had installed lighting on the walkways (safety) and her mom had purchased small safes for each cottage (security). When Olivia listened to their conversations, she could hear them laughing. But what was so funny about "daily operating expenses" or "customer service procedure"?

Maybe Chris was staying because he felt sorry for them. He told stories at the dinner table about growing up and once even shared that his father had died suddenly and how hard that had been. Carlos listened intently to every word that came out of his mouth and always asked questions. He was honestly interested. Sena seemed to never be paying attention, but of course she was. Olivia admired that the little kid could be so focused on a book but still be aware of everything going on around her.

What was obvious was that her mother was so much happier.

Olivia wanted her to smile more and worry less. What good was thinking the future only held cloudy skies? Wasn't the reality that pieces of blue were always there, waiting to break through?

But patterns were forming.

Olivia felt anxious as she put her things into her backpack. Haku drove her home from school every day. She was becoming dependent on him, which felt mostly good, but also unnerving. Maybe, like her mother, she was getting into something and would have trouble getting out.

She found him waiting by his pickup truck. He always beat her, no matter how quickly she tried to get outside first. He had the doors open to cool down the inside, but her legs still stuck to the hot seat when she climbed in.

"So you know how I told you we have this guy living at our motel doing electrical stuff? He finished, but he's still there."

"You mean as a motel guest?"

"No. He's helping us get ready to open. I feel like my mom might be growing too dependent on him."

"You like him, right?"

"Yeah. I mean, not really at first, but he's okay now."

"Maybe it takes you a while to warm up to people." Olivia wasn't sure how to take his comment, so she ignored it. He waited and then added, "Have you snooped around? Tried to find out more about him?"

Olivia shrugged. "I googled him when he first arrived, but his name's too common. I couldn't find anything."

"You could look at his email. He uses your server, right?"

Olivia smiled. The idea connected her to her father. She was his daughter. She understood operating systems. "I'm not going into his cottage, but I guess I wouldn't need to if I remotely installed a keylogger program."

"You're impressive in so many ways." She thought he was teasing her, but his smile seemed to say he was serious. "I can be there when you do it if that makes it easier."

Olivia was surprised at the relief she felt. It seemed less like a violation to spy on someone if it was a joint effort, which she knew made no sense. It was like hacking with Evan Auerbach. She would never have done that on her own. "Okay. Cool."

He added, "I'm supposed to give Koa a ride home today. Is it okay if he comes, too?"

"Yeah, sure."

Just then Koa appeared. He opened the door and Olivia scooted over, wedging herself between the two teenage boys. They really couldn't be more different. Koa was tall and thin with long hair that hung over half of his face. He was like a wolf or a leopard, some animal that was sleek and moved with grace; that wasn't how she would usually describe a guy, but it felt like the only description for him. Anyone who could get hit on a skateboard by a car as big as the Crown Victoria and walk away was otherworldly. Haku, on the other hand, moved like he was carrying a bag of rocks, which was sort of true because he was always weighed down by his backpack, filled with his computer, his iPad, and books he checked out from the library. His every step was full of purpose, intention, and struggle. She could relate.

The brothers didn't say a single word for the entire drive to the motel, which was, according to Olivia's phone, fourteen minutes and twenty-nine seconds. When Haku swung his pickup across the road to turn into the driveway, Koa finally spoke. "You guys cut back the plants."

"Yeah."

They continued to the big curve, passing the once-turquoise 1940 Chevrolet panel truck without tires, which Olivia realized she had stopped seeing until Koa said, "I always wanted to fix up that truck." He laughed.

Olivia laughed, too.

Haku didn't.

The parking lot was empty. The Crown Victoria and the Jeep were both gone, which was *amazing* news. As they got out of Haku's pickup, Koa stared hard at the cottages.

"They look so different."

"We painted. My mom and Chris did most of the work."

She glanced over and could tell Koa liked the new colors. Up until this point she had been fairly indifferent to the new paint scheme. "Yeah. It's a total upgrade. Each color is for one of the islands," she said.

Haku didn't appear to have an opinion about the cottage colors or anything else on the property, which he had seen every time he dropped her off. He headed straight toward the office. But Koa took his time, looking around like he'd once owned the place. Olivia explained, "Everything's been rewired. We got internet. A lot of new stuff going on."

Koa seemed to approve.

Once they were all inside, Olivia went into the kitchen and brought out glasses of water, along with a bag of salt-and-pepper popcorn.

"Sorry we don't have lemonade or anything good."

"Popcorn is cool." Koa took the bag and ripped it open with his teeth.

Haku shot him a look. "Are you sure you don't want to just wait out in the truck?"

Koa raised his middle finger.

Olivia wondered if they were fighting over her. That didn't seem possible. She tried to focus and sat down alongside Haku on the old couch. She pulled out her laptop from her backpack. She wanted to look smart, but not like a show-off. She started typing.

Haku and Koa were both watching her. She explained for Koa's benefit: "The guy who's staying here is a writer and he says he works for different publishers, so he doesn't have a regular job. His wife died and he spread her ashes in the water on our beach because I guess they were really happy here. Since then, he comes to Hawai'i every year on their anniversary. Anyway, he's done all this stuff for us and I feel like we should know more about him."

Koa's mouth was filled with popcorn. "Did you look him up in the notebooks?"

Olivia didn't know what he was talking about. "What notebooks?"

Koa pointed to the drawers in the unmovable mahogany desk. "The Kalamas keep them in there. Dude and his wife would have signed in. With their address and driver's license. Mr. Kalama always wrote down that stuff. Super old-school."

So there were registries she could search? That was such a boring way of being a snoop. But it was embarrassing that she hadn't even thought about doing that. "I'll for sure check out the notebooks."

Koa continued to shovel popcorn into his mouth as he went to the desk. He opened the bottom drawer and took out one of the notebooks. Haku looked up at his brother.

"What are you doing? You can't just go looking through other people's things."

"Isn't that what you guys are going to do? Look at somebody's email?"

Olivia had to admit he had a point, but she kept her attention on her laptop as she opened a program that could monitor Chris Young's computer activity. She inputted the server information, feeling grateful that her mother had turned the internet network over to her.

Inside the jumble of letters and symbols that indicated keystrokes was an email address. Haku pointed at the screen. "So is that his email: CBright@AmericanSecurity.com?"

Olivia stared at the screen. She felt her cheeks burn. Her body experienced something she could only describe as an invisible gut punch. She abruptly shut her laptop.

She got to her feet and started for the office door. "You guys have to go. Sorry. I can't do this right now."

Haku stared at her, then asked, "What's wrong?" He and Koa

exchanged looks. Koa shrugged and started for the door, but Haku lagged behind. "Did I do something wrong?"

Olivia pushed the screen door and held it open. As Haku and his brother walked past her, Olivia mumbled, "Thanks for the ride. Sorry that you can't stay. I forgot I had some important stuff to do this afternoon."

Koa headed onto the porch and down the steps, but Haku stopped in front of her. His eyes searched her face. "Are you okay?"

Olivia shook her head.

"Do you feel bad for looking at his email? You did the right thing to stop."

Olivia was silent. Haku put his hand on her shoulder. "Liv, you can tell me."

She couldn't believe he called her by that nickname. Her dad called her Liv. She didn't remember ever telling him that. She felt her legs weaken. She needed to sit down, but the look on his face was so filled with compassion. She leaned over and lightly kissed him on the lips, then turned and went inside.

Olivia sank down into the old couch. Her eyes were unblinking.

American Security.

The company that had issued her dad's life insurance policy.

American Security.

The people who'd fought the death claim for two years until an Oregon court officially declared her father no longer living.

American Security.

The company that had finally written a check for two million dollars to her family.

Chris Young wasn't Chris Young.

He was C. Bright.

CBright@AmericanSecurity.com didn't have a dead wife whose ashes were covered in algae on the ocean floor. He had come to the motel to spy on them, to find out if his company could get the life insurance money back.

Did he feel so guilty about being a rat that he'd rewired their
motel?

Maybe.

No.

He'd probably installed electronic sensors and had been listening
to her family the whole time he'd been on the property.

He was a liar.

He was a total fraud.

He was the enemy.

Her father hadn't left a note. He hadn't said good-bye. So what if he'd
hugged her and Carlos and Sena too hard that last morning when
he dropped them off at school? No one knew that. They hadn't
seen the purple pancakes with the special blueberries he'd made or
heard the fight in the kitchen with her mom. That was private. Okay,
so maybe her dad had been depressed. Big deal. When she went to
the private school back in Oregon, half of her class saw a therapist,
and a whole bunch of them took medicine for psychological stuff.
Questioning your existence was just part of modern life.

Olivia looked down at her right hand and saw her fingers moving.
Small twitches. She placed her left hand on top of the shaking digits,
but it didn't help. The circuitry to her brain had been disrupted.

Was American Security trying to prove her father had died *on
purpose* while surfing? Olivia knew the score. Suicide invalidated the
life insurance policy.

Go ahead and prove that, Mr. Bright!

Olivia couldn't wait to tell her mom. She thought the ass-hat was
the kindest person in the world. What a joke! Sena had explained
that Hawai'i didn't have venomous snakes, but she'd added that there
were centipedes and they lived in the dirt, undetected by most people.
The insects had a terrible bite. That's what this guy was: a poisonous
creature right there on the property. Hiding in plain sight.

Olivia picked up her laptop and googled: "C. Bright, American
Security."

The first hit was from LinkedIn. She clicked the link to see him smiling right at her in the center of his profile page.

Chris Bright
SENIOR FRAUD INVESTIGATOR
AMERICAN SECURITY INC.
500+ CONNECTIONS

Have worked in the insurance sector for over fifteen years. Extensive experience investigating strategic response to high-value policy fraud.

So his name really was Chris. Olivia stared at the screen until the white spaces grew in size and the letters merged together into a watery jumble. The sound of tires on the gravel brought her back into the room.

Her mother was going to freak. Worse than freak.

Olivia realized that she had to be careful. She didn't need to include her little brother and sister in this. She closed her computer, and with the empty popcorn bag in hand, she tried to appear normal as she went outside and took a seat on the porch. Timing was everything, and she would make him suffer.

She would cat-and-mouse this liar.

Whoever said knowledge was power was right.

22

Where were you guys?" Olivia called out to the car.

Carlos emerged from the backseat with his hands full of new purchases. "Look! New boards and masks and—"

Olivia's eyes shifted to her mother. "That stuff's expensive."

Lindsey was cheerful. "We needed it. We'll share with the guests. How was school?"

"Okay."

"I like hearing that your new friend drove you home again."

Sena's favorite chicken, the red one named Tink, came out of the bushes and made a beeline for her. Sena scooped up the bird and pressed her against her chest. As she passed Olivia her voice was filled with edgy anxiety. "Mom said we're having chicken for dinner. I don't want anyone giving my hens the scraps. It's cannibalism."

Carlos handed Olivia a new snorkel. "We got one for you. No more clouds under the sea!"

Olivia was torn between her desire to check out the new swag and her excitement to reveal her knowledge about Chris Young/Chris Bright. But before she could say anything, his Jeep rounded the bend. This guy's timing was insane. She watched her mother's face almost physically glow. "Chris is back!"

Olivia's tone was hostile. "Yeah, I wonder what he was out doing."

Lindsey ignored the tone of her daughter's voice. Olivia looked over to see Carlos digging through the huge shopping bag. He called out, "Chris! We got you a new mask and fins!"

Olivia couldn't take it. She turned and headed to the office in what she hoped looked like an angry huff. No one, as far as she could tell, even noticed. But then the screen door opened and slapped shut and Sena reappeared, red-faced and antsy.

"Olivia, where are the birds going?"

She turned to her sister. "I just saw you with Tink."

"Not my chickens. The birds. The ones that are on the beach and in the trees. They're all in the air."

Olivia wasn't in the mood for one of Sena's Discovery Channel discussions. But her little sister did look upset.

"Sena, maybe it's because it's so windy."

"When we were driving home, I could see them all flying to the mountains."

"So there's a bird convention or something going on." She hoped that being funny was the way to get her little sister to leave her alone. "You could look online for an answer."

Sena went to her mother's laptop, which was on the mahogany desk. But she still had more to say. "Olivia, did you know there are a lot of things right in front of us that we don't see?"

Olivia nodded. The kid got that right. Sena continued, "An example is there are holes in eggshells and they're so tiny you can't see them but that's what lets the living thing inside an egg breathe."

"I didn't know."

"A chicken egg has about seven thousand five hundred holes. I don't know about a lizard egg. Also, a bullhead shark lays eggs."

Olivia touched her little sister's shoulder. "Thanks for telling me."

"Mom was too busy yelling at me in the car to hear anything. I've got a lot of important stuff but I'm not going to tell Mom right now."

Olivia managed a crooked smile. "Yeah. Me too."

They sat together as if they were a happy family, their plates on a tablecloth the Kalamas had left behind, patterned with red hibiscus flowers against a powder blue background. With her phone hidden from view in her lap, Olivia searched online for what a hibiscus flower symbolized. She hoped it was deceit. Instead, she read, "All hibiscus flowers are short-lived. This is considered a very feminine flower and is usually given or worn by women. It can symbolize female power."

Okay. Good. Because Olivia was ready to blow things up in a very powerful way.

Lindsey served spaghetti with red sauce to Chris and Sena, and then set out chicken with pineapple coleslaw and steamed rice for Olivia and Carlos. She had purchased a special sauce of shoyu, vinegar, and chili pepper. Carlos's new dive mask was perched on his head, holding back his red hair. Her brother's white-white forehead was exposed as he eagerly devoured his meal.

"Save room for dessert. I got haupia pie," said Lindsey.

Olivia tried to eat but was having trouble swallowing. The table talk was about how windy it was and how much it might rain from a storm out somewhere in the Pacific. She heard her mother ask Chris about boarding up windows, but barely listened to his reply. Apparently, she thought he was the expert on everything. When there was finally a break in the conversation, Olivia couldn't hold back.

"So, Chris, how do you feel about *secrets*?"

He seemed unfazed. "I guess we all have them."

Carlos stared at his sister, and her mom tried to change the subject. "This week is flying by so fast—"

Olivia kept her focus on Chris. "Tell us one of your secrets. Something big."

Lindsey shot her a look. "Olivia, that's rude."

"Yeah? Well, I think *dishonest* people are rude."

Chris cleared his throat and then looked at her. "Okay. I do have a big secret."

Carlos looked intrigued. "Really?"

Olivia was pleased to see that her mother's brow was creased in a way that seemed not just uncomfortable but tinged with apprehension. Lindsey asked, "What's that, Chris?"

Olivia added, "Yeah. Tell us."

Sena continued eating her spaghetti, but injected sourly, "If he shares, it won't be a secret anymore."

Olivia leaned forward. "Exactly." She knew she sounded smug. "Is there something we don't know? Something that would change the way we feel about you?" She was gaining momentum. "Mr. Chris *Young*, what have you been hiding from us?"

Chris looked around the table. "Okay. You win."

Olivia held her breath. Her mother didn't blink. Only Sena kept eating.

He sighed. "I hate the ocean."

Carlos confused. "What's that mean?"

"I was stung by a man o' war on the Jersey shore when I was a kid."

"A jellyfish?" Lindsey asked.

"They look like jellyfish, but they are actually something else. Anyway, I was a little kid and it's rare to get stung, only I did. It sounds crazy, but I've never gotten over it."

Olivia exhaled out her nose in irritation, but the focus in the room had shifted.

"Wow. *Really?* Is that why you don't go in the water?" Her mom was smiling in such a supportive, delighted way. Olivia couldn't believe that *not* swimming in the ocean made the liar even more interesting.

"Yeah. That's why."

Carlos reached his hand out and rested his fingers on Chris's forearm. "I can go in with you. I can keep my eyes out for jellyfish."

Sena added, "If he doesn't want to go in the water—no one should make him."

Her mother seemed to wholeheartedly agree. "Of course not. You're right, sweetheart."

Sena's eyes narrowed. "I wasn't a sweetheart when you thought I was lost at the surf shop."

Her mother ignored the comment and kept smiling as the conversation shifted to a discussion of fears, real and irrational. The only hiccup came when Sena finished her spaghetti and asked, "Why did you put your wife in the ocean if you don't swim? You can't visit her."

Chris was silent, but her mother jumped in to answer for him.

"His wife loved Hawaiʻi, so he was doing what she wanted. That was a noble thing."

Sena looked from her mother to Chris. "I don't know what was so noble about it. And also, that's not a word people really use today because we don't have kings and queens."

This made Chris laugh. It was a deep, full-throated eruption that caused Carlos and her mother to join in. Sena remained stony-faced.

They were still laughing when Olivia picked up her plate, saying under her breath, "I've got homework."

She didn't even pretend to study. Olivia went down to the water and sat on the wet sand until it was dark outside. No one came to check on her, which was the whole point of walking away. But it was too windy for any kind of meditative reflection, though the gusts coming off the ocean didn't stop mosquitos from finding her ankles. She would pay big-time for not having any bug spray.

Almost an hour passed and the wind was getting fiercer by the minute. Olivia wondered about the storm that was out in the Pacific. She pulled her phone from her pocket and typed, "Current weather on Oʻahu." But the motel internet wasn't working. She wasn't about to walk out to the highway for service.

Olivia didn't say anything about a possible storm when she came inside, or the internet, or the fact that she'd been sitting by herself on an empty beach in the dark, which could have been dangerous. Instead, she took a long shower, hoping that when she was finished no one in her family would find so much as a single drop of hot water left in the rusty old tank. Her little sister was already under the covers when Olivia came into the room.

"Sena, I'm going to bed."

"You don't go to sleep this early."

"I do tonight. I have a headache."

"I did what you said and I checked about the birds. The internet's out now, so it was good I looked before."

Olivia wasn't interested but Sena continued. "Birds have storm-warning systems. They are better than computers."

She couldn't help herself from pushing back. "Well, I don't know about that."

"Some people were studying warblers in Tennessee and a big storm was two hundred miles away and the birds changed how they were flying and got away from it."

"Good for the warblers, is all I have to say."

"That storm made eighty-four tornadoes and killed thirty-five people."

"Sena, I'm not sure you should read stuff like that."

"You're the one who told me to look online. The tiny birds knew more than the weather people. I just wanted you to know." Sena closed her book and hit the switch on the lamp. In the dim shadows everything was drained of color.

Olivia knew what she was doing was wrong. "I have a secret about Mr. Chris Young," she told her sister. "And it's *not* that he's afraid of ocean creatures."

Sena didn't answer right away. But she finally said, "I have a secret, too."

"About Chris Young?"

"No. About something more important."

"Yeah, well, my secret is a *pret-ty damn big deal*," Olivia retorted, then sighed. The sound was long, deep, and exasperated, because there was no reason to be mean to a seven-year-old. None of this was her fault. She softened. "Okay, Sena, do you want to tell me your secret?"

"No, because you'll say I'm a liar."

Olivia detected something in Sena's voice. She sounded tense, maybe even afraid.

"You have to tell me. I'm your big sister. If it's a problem, I'll help sort it out."

"It's a problem."

"So tell me."

"Like I said, you won't believe me."

"Go ahead, I'll believe you."

"Promise?"

"Yeah. I promise."

Sena whispered: "I saw Daddy today in Hale'iwa. He looks different. He has a beard. And glasses. He doesn't have any hair now. But it was Daddy."

In the beginning of the disaster, in the days and then months after he drowned, Olivia saw her father everywhere. There was a tall man in his forties with the same jacket getting into a silver car at the Shell station on Terwilliger. Then the man with hair the exact shade of brown bent over a little kid in front of the ice cream cooler at the grocery store. A runner in the distance in the park in the cold rain with his same long, floppy arms. A parent in the audience of one of the volleyball games at school whose head reared back as he laughed. All glimpses of imposters; never, of course, the real thing. The sightings went on for what seemed like forever, and then the fake dads started to fade away.

She didn't see him anymore in crowds or hiding in shadows.

It was such a relief.

But there was a deeper heartbreak as she realized his memory was disappearing. He was vanishing, and she would have to force herself every day to think about him.

Olivia whispered, "It was someone else. A guy who reminded you of Dad. That happens. I've made that mistake before."

Sena's voice was eerily calm but insistent. "No. It was Daddy. I saw him when Mom was in the surf shop. He was standing by a car on the other side of the street in the parking lot. He was watching me. That's why I crossed the busy road."

"Sena, Dad drowned in Oregon during the storm."

"No. He didn't. He's alive. I didn't tell Mama. I almost did, but she was really mad at me. So I decided it was going to be my secret. But now it's something we both know and I feel better."

Olivia tried to concentrate. Sena kept talking. "He said my name. He said, 'I love you, Sena.' Then he got into a car and he drove away."

Olivia stopped breathing. What the hell was going on? Their father couldn't possibly be alive.

But what if he was?

It would be such great news.

A miracle.

A dream come true.

In the dark room, the air turned as thick as sludge as Olivia felt herself split in two. She was physically in her bed—she could feel the back of her legs pressing into the lumpy mattress—but her insides started to crumble. Was it her soul that broke open? Particles of something fell down like rain into the room. They hit her face, which was suddenly wet. Olivia's hand reached up and her fingertips could feel the drops.

The most terrible day of their lives had started with pancakes. He'd made them special and then he'd gone surfing because the waves were really big from the storm. Maybe he'd been up all night, because he was wearing the same thing he had on the day before. He shouldn't have been in the water. Sena remembered they were going to go for tacos for dinner but didn't because they had to wait for Dad. He wasn't answering his cellphone, only they weren't supposed to worry because the battery might have died or maybe he lost his car keys. That had happened to him before. He could just have surfed too long and when he got out it was dark and he couldn't find the keys. Or maybe he had stopped to help people who were in trouble. Like maybe someone had a flat tire or maybe something worse, like having a heart attack. He didn't call because he was doing CPR. Or carrying the sick person over his shoulder to the hospital. He had carried them that way when they were really little. It made the blood rush to your head.

Sena thought he might be catching a dog because one time they were driving to the coast and they saw a black dog with white paws running along the highway. Dad had pulled over and was able to capture the dog by getting close enough to grab the collar. The dog was named Sally and was very afraid. Dad had a way of being calm when other people got excited. But he could get excited when everyone was calm. The owner's number was on the tag, and Sena remembered that they were all heroes when Sally was reunited with a woman in a pretty yellow dress.

It got too late for tacos that horrible night and no one was organized enough to order pizza. Olivia made scrambled eggs, and while she scraped the pan, which had a worn-out Teflon coating that she had heard Dad once say was probably giving them all cancer, Mom phoned the police. It was an hour later when a state patrol officer called back to say Dad's car had been found at the coast but he wasn't in it. It was late at night and the officers walked down to the beach, but they couldn't look for him in the water. They would do that in the morning.

Then people started coming over, the old neighbors from Emerald Street, and she remembered Mrs. Addison saying, "The kids should go to bed."

But no one went to bed.

People said not to worry and that everything would be okay, but everything was not going to be okay.

Sena curled up on the couch. She took her big sister's hand and said, "We'll see him again. I know we will."

Everyone wanted to believe her.

23

Paul Hill watched the sky darken as the last surfer got out of the inky ocean, leaving him alone. He hadn't slept more than an hour in two days. The waves were huge and he had so much water in his right ear that his balance was shot. He clung to his board, dizzy and raw, bobbing in the sea, lost in all ways that matter.

He'd had enough.

The ice-cold ocean made him numb, and that was as welcome as the pills he took, all legal and designed for people in high-stress situations. But the meds didn't seem to work right even when the dosage was increased. He'd thrown them all away that morning when he decided to call in the wrecking ball and operate the machinery himself.

He took a piss in his wetsuit and felt the warm liquid soak his crotch. He reached down and removed the ankle cuff from the board's leash. Nothing connected him to the surfboard now. He'd never felt so free. Or so tired. Or messed up. He reached back and peeled off both of his booties. He wanted his feet to freeze first, and for the rest to happen fast. He'd gotten his brilliant idea one day in the water, and he could make it all end in the same place.

He was suddenly aware of a sharp stinging sensation in his toes. He rolled off his expensive surfboard, separating himself from the only thing around him that could float. A crashing wave pushed down hard as he tumbled like a log, spinning out of control.

He lost all sense of where he was.

His eyes were tightly shut.

His fingers were clenched into fists.

Only then, in the cold reality of ever-eroding thought, he saw in his mind's eye a photograph taken three years ago. His kids were in the old house on Emerald Street. They were piled together in a single blue chair, looking right at the camera. This was before EnGenStor; it was a shot from the once brilliant past.

If only he could turn back the clock to that day.

Then more saltwater was forced up his nose. He fought with the image as he choked.

Olivia and Carlos disappeared from the blue chair.

Gone.

Everything was dark and heading to total black as fiery stabs pierced his arms and legs.

He gave in to the agony.

But Sena, in the damn blue chair, would *not* disappear. She sat staring right at him. Her steely eyes would not let go. Then her lips appeared to move and he heard her voice. It was so real. She whispered, "Daddy."

Paul opened his mouth to shout back to her, and water rushed in. He was choking on the salty swirl.

Sena, in that damn blue chair, forced him into a fight. He moved his mostly paralyzed arms and legs as a riptide pulled his body out to sea.

He did *not* want to die.

He thrust up his head. In seconds he broke the water's surface and managed to get a single breath. It forced his lungs open and he coughed violently. The saltwater was winning. He didn't try to swim against the ocean tide. The pain in his chest let up just enough for him to understand that if he could move, it would need to be at an angle to the land. The battle was on. The broken man versus the power of an unending current.

But he had a secret power.

He had Sena.

Paul stumbled out of the water, sharp rocks beneath his feet slicing into his heels. He could feel nothing below his knees. His hands were Ping-Pong paddles. He collapsed onto the sand, believing his death would be from exhaustion as well as hypothermia. But soon the wind forced his body into a crawl over the clumps of slimy seaweed to more jagged rocks and then finally the sandy roadside where he'd parked his car. After multiple attempts he was able to pry the hide-a-key from the wheel well over the back left tire. He looked up as the clouds parted, revealing a glimpse of stars.

No one knew about his backup safety kit, inspired by his crappy parents, who never, in his eyes, had a plan for anything. He kept an emergency set of clothes tucked beneath the spare tire and the carjack: old jeans, a sweatshirt, and worn running shoes. There was a crisp one-hundred-dollar bill in the jeans pocket.

He struggled to pull off his wetsuit. Standing naked in the dark, the wind howling around him, he felt an internal explosion. He was the only one really alive in this world. He fought his way into the clothing, glad he hadn't thought to add underwear to the emergency kit. His kitchen-mitt hands were regaining circulation, and he wrangled the spare tire and the jack back into place. He replaced the key into the magnetic box and shoved it up into the wheel well. His wallet, the clothing he wore that day, and his coat were all left inside the car. He took only the energy drink and the PowerBar from the glovebox; everything else was just as he'd left it when he first entered the ocean.

He headed down to the beach holding his wetsuit. In the dim light he watched as the wind erased his every footprint.

The tide was low and the hard-packed sand was easy to navigate as he chugged the energy drink and ripped into the PowerBar. Beach houses dotted the bluff just beyond dunes covered with tufts of swaying sea grass. The occasional porch light that glowed was triggered by a photocell. No one saw him trudge the five miles down to the small community of Neskowin. His family had stayed there almost a year before, a vacation rental Lindsey had booked online. Paul saw numbers the way an accomplished painter saw a composition. He didn't forget. He guessed the owners hadn't changed the lockbox code.

It was gratifying to be right after getting so much wrong.

Once inside the house, he kept the lights off, but moved the thermostat up to 85 degrees, conscious not to touch the dial with anything but the paper towel he tore from the roll in the kitchen. He knew his way around this place and remembered there had been wine in the garage. He opened a medium-priced cabernet sauvignon and drank the whole bottle. While sitting on the heating vent in the living room, he ate a box of Cheerios, followed by two tins of sardines. It was the first time his stomach had been full in three weeks. He vomited up half of what he'd consumed. He left the mess on the floor and went to one of the kids' rooms, crawled into bed, and fell asleep seconds after his head hit the pillow. He hadn't had that kind of deep slumber in months.

Paul awoke to late-afternoon light. It was impossible to know if the achy muscles and chills were from his escape from the ocean or prescription drug withdrawal.

He couldn't stop shaking.

Paul turned on the TV and watched the local Portland news. He was the lead story: "Tech entrepreneur presumed lost at sea." The Coast Guard, along with Portland Police Department cadaver dogs, were searching the beach.

What the hell had he done?

He cleaned up the stinking vomit, ate two cans of cold baked beans, drank another bottle of wine, and went back to sleep. But this time when he opened his eyes it was dark outside. And his head was clearing. He needed to contact Lindsey. He had to explain he was alive. He searched the house, but no one had a landline anymore. He curled into a tight ball and was overwhelmed with guilt and shame—and, increasingly, fear. He tried to sort out the last few months. He would be found guilty of embezzlement, or at the very least tax evasion. He would go to prison. His family would be tainted forever by his failings, which were crimes.

He couldn't stop crying.

He wished he had died in the ocean.

He stayed in the cabin for three days. When he finally decided to leave, he accepted that Paul Hill was gone. For him what had died were Lindsey, Olivia, Carlos, and Sena. To save them, he had to let them go. He understood he'd spend the rest of his life doing that. He'd taken out the life insurance policy. That was the only thing he'd done right amid a thousand decisions that were wrong.

He was in shock, which was another way of saying that he was still going out of his mind. It was midweek, and he calculated that the owners or any potential renters wouldn't arrive until Friday afternoon, if at all. So he twitched, warming himself in a scalding bathtub, as he tried to come up with a plan. He took a pink-handled razor from under the sink in the master bathroom. He had half a dozen cuts on his head by the time he was finished, but he was bald. His facial hair was growing in, and by the end of day three he had enough stubble to make his jawline disappear.

Paul found a pair of reading glasses in a kitchen drawer in the kitchen to complete his transformation. He was a bald man, with Vincent Van Gogh–like stubble and black-rimmed glasses. A plastic tub on the top shelf in the garage marked OWNERS' PROPERTY—DO NOT OPEN contained a warm down jacket that fit perfectly. There was a black leather shoulder bag hanging on a hook in the laundry room, and high-quality work boots in a utility closet by the water heater. He would have put money on the fact that someone with this much stuff would never think twice about a few missing items. He had been that man. He took it all.

On Friday morning he washed the sheets and remade the bed he'd slept in. He cleaned the bathroom, including removing the trap in the drain and disposing of the strands of his hair that had caught in the grate. He dug a hole in the yard, put in the dark curls, and covered them with sand. He was no longer trembling like a leaf, but his massive headache was playing with his vision. He took his trash to the neighbor's house, having determined that no one was at home there, either. It was midmorning when he wiped down all the surfaces one final time with Clorox, then closed the door and returned the key to the lockbox. He still had the one-hundred-dollar bill tucked in his pants pocket, and his wetsuit, along with a pair of yellow kitchen gloves.

It was low tide when he made his way down to the beach. As he rounded the curve in the shoreline, an eerie sight confronted him. Over two thousand years ago, Sitka spruce trees had thrived on this spot. They'd stood over 150 feet high, the third-tallest type of tree in the world. Either a powerful earthquake or the resultant tsunami had buried the area and preserved the bottoms of more than one hundred of the Sitka spruces. For years no one knew the stumps were there, but then a sequence of strong storms hit the area hard in the winter of 1997 and the dramatic shift in the sand revealed the remains of the past forest. Occasionally, when the surf drastically receded at low tide, dozens and dozens of stumps, covered with seaweed and barnacles, would be revealed on the pristine beach, as magnificent as any art installation and as confusing as a hallucination.

The Ghost Forest of Neskowin was now right in front of him.

Maybe his life story would mirror these petrified survivors. He had disappeared into the gray, violent ocean, but might continue to stand, unseen for years, to one day play a role in the landscape. The Ghost Forest of Neskowin gave Paul a shred of hope. The immediate needs of food and shelter were his first obvious concern, but once he got back on his feet, he would be the unseen family ghost. From a distance he would keep a covert eye on the people he loved.

24

Two miles down the beach, Paul watched three teenage surfers, two girls and a boy, get out of a battered maroon Subaru Impreza. The driver put the keys on the back tire. Paul waited until they were heading out into the waves, then pulled on the yellow dishwashing gloves. If the teens stayed in the water for any decent amount of time, he had two hours before they even started the search for their stolen car.

An hour and fifteen minutes later he drove into Salem, Oregon. He parked on a side street not far from downtown, careful to check for any surveillance cameras. He walked away, leaving the keys in the ignition. Maybe someone else would take the Subaru for a joyride. If not, he hoped police would locate the car without much of a search. As he headed down the sidewalk, he saw a dumpster behind a fence at a construction site. He threw his wetsuit over the chain link into the container. It landed with a thud. The rubber gloves followed. The last traces of Paul Hill were gone.

He found it ironic that while he'd never been a religious man, the first place he turned to for help was a church. At the Union Mission on Commercial Street in Salem, Paul took his place in line, eyes downcast, with a sense of superiority that eroded quickly. His story wasn't more important or interesting than that of any of the other people in line. They had all washed out of the system and needed help. A lost job. An addiction. A failed marriage. Crippling anxiety or depression. They were victims. And culprits. They had done harm and been harmed. They stood together, the crazies and the not-so-crazy, the addicts and the abused, outside the circle of society's protection, all waiting in a light rain for a meal.

He'd forgotten what it even felt like to have an appetite. His stomach was in pain from hunger. When he finally got his plate of stew, served with two hard rolls that tasted better than any artisanal bread he ever remembered eating, he had vertigo as he walked toward the folding tables to find a seat. They had been asked to pray before the line started to move, and he had surreptitiously looked up, hoping to find the other non-believers. But gratitude had a way of flattening ego, and the next time he stood in line for a handout, he knew he would be more sincere when he lowered his gaze to give thanks.

Paul slept the first night in Salem in a park, using for shelter what he had pulled from a recycling container. He thought about his kids playing with cardboard boxes. He could see the linen closet at the big house at the top of the hill in Portland. There were stacks of blankets and a dozen extra pillows. So much of everything. So little appreciation for any of it. But as he curled up with a strip of bubble wrap as his pillow, what he wanted more than anything was to check on his family.

The closest approximation to quenching the unquenchable desire was to go the following morning straight to the public library. He was there when it opened, along with a cluster of other people who looked as if they'd spent the night in an alley or hidden under a freeway underpass. He hit a snag when the librarian explained that he would need identification in order to access the computers. They were understaffed, so he waited until a woman left a terminal in the restricted area, then slid into her seat, confident that she hadn't properly signed out. He was right.

Paul went to the library's home page. The security they used was outdated and he quickly got past their firewall and into Salem's central library system. He scrolled through the list of library members and found a man his age named Jeff Ross. He copied down his address and the last four digits of his Social Security number, which were part of his unique, secure profile. Paul knew the first three digits of every Social Security number were determined by the zip code where the original application was filed. The second two digits represented the group number. The last four numbers were known as the serial number and didn't give away any clues. But two of the three parts of the sequence revealed in which state the number was issued and how long ago.

He might not have been smart enough to run a new company, but he believed he was clever enough to create a new identity. And he felt certain that Lindsey was strong enough to build a new life with their kids. He smoothed the front of his pants with the palms of his sweating hands. He wondered how many people died and got a chance to come back to life.

Armed with information, Paul returned to the front desk when a new person had taken over. He explained that his wallet had been stolen. He'd lost his library card and asked for a replacement. It was a risk. Salem wasn't a small town, but it was small enough. The librarian was helpful and had the system generate a new card, which would need to be mailed. Paul was given a yellow cardboard replacement to use until that arrived. Fake Jeff Ross had his first piece of new ID. He could legitimately use the library computers. Back in front of a pulsing screen, he created a Jeff Ross Facebook account. He then went to check on his family. As he stared at a photo of his wife, Paul gave thanks to computer pioneers Leonard Kleinrock and Douglas Engelbart, who in the year 1969 developed the system that first connected networks for resource sharing. They didn't get enough credit.

Lindsey's privacy settings restricted him from seeing anything but her main page, and it was a blessing. His oldest daughter, however, had nothing protecting her from a cyberstalker. Olivia's Facebook wall was filled with messages from teenagers, some of whom he recognized, but mostly from kids he'd never heard of, posting to say they were sorry about her dad. So many broken-heart emojis. So many yellow emoji faces with raised eyebrows, a slight frown, and a single blue tear. He scrolled through, reading as many posts as he could stomach. His right hand was shaking.

The snowball of identity theft moved rapidly when you knew what you were doing. Paul was able to gain access to the Visa card associated with the name Jeff Ross after searching a data breach, and he used the information to book an online Amtrak ticket from Salem to Sacramento. The train ride would be seventeen hours, during which he wouldn't need to worry about a bathroom, or where to sleep. Paul received a confirmation code for his fare and explained to the nice woman at the customer service window at the Amtrak station that he'd left his Visa card at home, but fortunately had the number. He'd just lost his mother and was going to her funeral. He was afraid to fly. He had tears in his eyes. That part wasn't hard. He was just aggressive enough to be intimidating, but not threatening enough to be a red flag.

By the time he reached Sacramento, he had formulated a plan for where to start his life: Salt Lake City. They had tech there, but it was an outsource hub centered primarily on video gaming, not a bubbling epicenter of new companies where someone might have known him in the past. He would find work that could be done virtually. No one had to see him to get their money's worth.

As soon as he arrived in the clean, buttoned-up city, he went to an AA meeting on West Louise Street. He stayed after, not just for the cookies and coffee, but also to begin making connections. He introduced himself as Jeff Ross to Sara, the woman leading the group. He had a shaved head, a scruffy beard that needed grooming, and reading glasses that magnified his eyes in a potentially unsettling way. He looked deeply wounded but sympathetic. He was in need of a shower but didn't have the leathery skin of the chronically homeless or the tremble or twitch of a hard-core drinker or druggie. He asked if she knew of any work for someone with computer skills. Sara was employed by a real estate company that had been trying to update its website. Maybe he could take a look? That afternoon he was sitting behind a desk installing a new operating system to fix the problem. Had he believed in such things, and he didn't, he would have said there was an angel watching over him.

Every action fake Jeff Ross took was an exercise in humility. He could be good at freelance computer work, but never flashy, inspired, or really great. He needed to be efficient, but not stand out. He had to appear to struggle, to take time, even if an assignment came easily. That turned out to be doable because every other aspect of living was so damn hard.

He missed his family. He wanted them. He understood that he'd never truly appreciated what mattered most in his life. But at least the decisions that had led him to this place were all his own. If he hadn't been the one in charge, he believed, none of what he was now doing would be possible. He likened it to the ability to tolerate a smelly bathroom if you were the one who made the stink. If the odor came from someone else, he would have headed for the door in disgust. People were so judgmental, except when it came to their own behavior. Then they could stomach all manner of savagery.

Paul Hill had been a loner before Lindsey, but after he met her, he embraced being part of a couple. The circle of friends mostly flowed from her and the children to him. He didn't keep in touch with the people he knew from high school or college. He was an innocent bystander in the social structure Lindsey built, which wasn't to say he didn't enjoy it—but it wasn't his doing until he started his business. After that, everyone they saw was somehow connected to the company, and all activities were part of his new, vaunted social position as a tech entrepreneur.

In Salt Lake City he retreated back to the original Paul: the guy who read non-fiction books or scientific articles until he fell asleep, usually still wearing his clothes; who was permanently wearing earphones, addicted to podcasts; who woke up grumpy and unaccommodating. He was the guy he would have always been if he hadn't married his wife. In Utah he was living the Paul Hill story without love.

His strategy for survival centered on keeping all children and families out of his immediate world. He bought groceries online or shopped at midnight when there wouldn't be kids in the supermarket aisles. He went out of his way to avoid driving by public parks, schools, or any kind of kid-friendly attraction. He was particularly triggered by anyone who was Olivia's, Carlos's, or Sena's age when he'd left. The kids would never grow older to him.

Paul acknowledged no holidays and found the birthdays of his family members the worst days of the year. He got drunk on Christmas and stayed soaked in alcohol through New Year's Eve, when people began taking down outdoor twinkle lights and finally stopped blasting sentimental holiday songs.

He could tolerate endless hours in a cramped room in front of a computer screen. He worked until one in the morning, fell asleep, then woke up at 3 A.M. and worked again till 5 A.M. He ate a candy bar, didn't brush his teeth, and went back to sleep. He lived in a motel that charged by the week, filled with undocumented workers who bought meals from the vending machine positioned under the bright bluish light next to the parking lot. He was polite but made no friends. He didn't look like anyone worth knowing, and that was a truth he could accept.

He bought a new Social Security number on the dark web and upgraded to an identity that was real in the eyes of the state of Utah. He was becoming more legitimate, and the prize was a driver's license, which was the key to the adult kingdom. He didn't get a passport to travel abroad because he wouldn't risk entering his fingerprints into any governmental system. It was a shame because he knew there were all kinds of opportunities for him in other countries. But the driver's license made him real enough.

He came up with a new narrative. He had once been an assistant computer science instructor in Florida, having relocated to make a fresh start in the West. He claimed that, with the help of the church, he'd straightened out his life. Paul crafted a few fake online sites that showed a quiet life lived in Panama City, with a bogus bio for Jeff, who had taught at Gulf Coast State College. The internet had no police. There was no one to challenge his stream of well-crafted lies. He briefly considered domestic work in a Russian or Iranian disinformation pod. He knew he could spin convincing stories, copying real graphics from actual institutions, as he created linkable options that led to more faux websites, all of it untrue, but looking so real, so professional, so accurate as to seem legitimate. Paul's favorite obscure movie had always been *F Is for Fake*, a docudrama made by Orson Welles. It was a messy treatise on authenticity and authorship. "Welcome to the digital world, Mr. Welles," Paul mumbled out loud one day as he carefully photoshopped a picture of his new self into a college classroom. "You were always ahead of your time."

Nine weeks into his residency in Utah, he had a full-time job earning decent money working for a video gaming company headquartered in Los Angeles. They had an office in downtown Salt Lake right off West Temple Street. He was the oldest person on the team, ancient by their standards. But from what he observed, the young weren't interested in the old, and they didn't ask Paul a lot of questions.

He tapered off his attendance at AA meetings, and three months from the day he arrived in Salt Lake City, he checked out of the cheap motel and moved into a studio apartment. He delivered the deposit as a cashier's check and explained his lack of credit history with a story about having done missionary work overseas in Latin America, where the Church of Latter-Day Saints covered his expenses. He bought everything he needed for the new place on Craigslist or at the Salvation Army, and he always paid cash. Back before EnGenStor, Lindsey had found thrift stores alluring. To Paul they were just picked-over garage sales dumped into shabby rooms. Plus, he figured most of the stuff for sale came from dead people, which was probably not even true. But now that he was a dead person, the creepiness factor of another departed guy's old shirts was gone. He felt strangely comfortable in someone else's worn jeans, even if they didn't fit that well. His weight was returning and his headaches weren't as persistent. He was building a new life for a new person, a non-communicative loner who ate a lot of peanut butter.

His discipline was shocking. He allowed himself to check his past life only once a week. Every Sunday he logged into Lindsey's email account. He read enough to get an idea of her mental state. The sent file was better than the incoming messages. The messages she wrote to her mother were the most revealing. It was the first time the two women shared secrets, and they were all centered on heartbreak, loss, and grief. He found himself taking screenshots of many of the most moving passages. He was both comforted and ashamed that he was so passionately mourned.

After Lindsey's email he went to Facebook to check on Olivia's page, even though kids didn't use the platform much anymore. Olivia's Instagram account was more revealing. The shocker was how quickly Olivia's friends moved on. In the first few weeks there was a lot of support on his daughter's account, but it soon disappeared. He found online culture utterly lacking in humility, and it was a cruel irony that he'd once had no problem with that. Jeff Ross was becoming a bitter man, but maybe, he thought, a better one.

When he gained access to Lindsey's banking account, he suffered the most deeply. The insurance money hadn't come through, and his wife had almost nothing. Once he saw a negative balance of $452.03 and had to stop himself from making an electronic deposit to bail her out. He felt helpless knowing his family had so little. He spent endless hours considering ways to get them money, but everything was too risky. He knew the address of the two-bedroom apartment where they lived, but sending cash anonymously would never work. He tried to concoct schemes for Lindsey to win a prize or stumble upon a grant, but the logistics were impossible. He needed to get the damn insurance company to pay up. He had to concentrate his efforts in that direction.

25

On the surface, Salt Lake City seemed to Paul completely wrong for gambling. The state of Utah had made all forms of betting illegal, one of only two states in the entire country to do so, the other being Hawai'i. So no poker clubs or casinos for miles. No scratch-and-win. Not even bingo night in church. But when he was dropping off a newly repaired computer late one night, a rush job on one of his side hustles that paid double, the man had a card game going. They were down a player. The guy asked if he'd sit in for a few hands. Paul won big.

That night ushered him into the underground world of Salt Lake City poker. As it turned out, there were all kinds of weekly games being played around town. Doors opened, and before long he graduated from the low-stakes circuit to honing his skills in deeper water. It was dangerous. Sitting at a poker table meant people could stare him down, so he wore tinted glasses that he explained were medically necessary, designed for people with mild color-blindness. He went about the game with the fanaticism of a man who had no social life, no family, and no obligations. When he took a break from work, he played online poker, five hands at a time, fine-tuning the mathematics of his game. It was not about instinct or emotion. It was only about the odds.

As the weeks turned into months, Jeff Ross ended up playing poker against prominent judges and dentists, even bishops from the church. He found himself shuffling up to deal in a group with a man who said he was a bounty hunter. That got his teeth grinding.

Jeff Ross counted cards and used probability theory. He won a lot more than he lost. The card table got him quicker to his next goal. He bought a five-year-old Toyota, which had been in a bad accident but repaired with mostly factory parts. The vehicle was not something that would turn any heads. But then again, neither was he.

Paul added substantially to his bank account, and felt a new measure of stability. He was in essence doing three jobs: the video game company, computer repair work, and gambling. He longed to go to Las Vegas to see what he could really accomplish, but that was off-limits. Casinos had "eyes in the sky," and the cameras housed in dark domes were forever watching, recording, and reporting.

But then Salt Lake got too small on the day a man said hello in a 7-Eleven, someone Paul didn't recognize and yet who knew his name. "You're Jeff Ross!" Paul wasn't wearing his tinted glasses and didn't have on his omnipresent baseball cap, but the guy still recognized him and followed at his heels as he headed to the cash register. "You really know what you're doing in a poker game—am I right?"

He was right.

Paul was becoming somebody.

And that was a problem. If a building contractor in a 7-Eleven wanted to know how hard to go in on a pair of jacks, it was time to move on.

His car was crammed full as he merged onto I-15 south. Since the introduction of suitcases with wheels, it would take decades to get rid of all the containers previously designed for travel. Paul had purchased secondhand an assortment of expensive luggage, even ones made from leather and monogrammed with gold initials at the handle—not his, sadly, but a reminder of a life of privilege.

He tried to reassure himself that most of his possessions were books. In an age when the words on all of the pages weighing down the backseat of the car could have been stored on the small screen that he had shoved in his jacket pocket, he accepted the fact that the printed page gave him comfort. And that was in short supply. Looking at the spines of the non-fiction hardcovers, with the many different colors, typefaces, and graphic designs, provided a small measure of happiness. The books contained adventure off-limits to someone living in a shadow world. The people in those pages weren't in permanent hiding; they could embrace life.

Paul drove away from Salt Lake, contemplating whether the urge to hoard was hardwired into humanity. The need to collect things— the desire, the basic impulse—had an explanation in evolutionary psychology. He figured a toddler demanded a favorite blanket for comfort because comfort translated to *this thing is mine.*

Paul picked San Diego because he wanted better weather. He'd spent years being wet in the Pacific Northwest. Salt Lake had a lot less rain than Oregon but a lot more snow. The smart money said he should go east. To really hide, he would be better served by getting away from the western states, with as much distance as possible from the tech world he once knew. But fake Jeff Ross still believed in his own ability to control situations. San Diego had more than fifteen universities and colleges, along with the US military. People coming and going was part of the DNA of the place.

He arrived in California with a slight degree of optimism. Paul checked into a motel that had weekly rates but was primarily for people on business. He hoped the days of tiny rooms with showers that dribbled water were forever behind him. A year after he had presumably died in the icy surf, he had more available resources than his wife, who was still waiting on the insurance claim. When he left the business motel in downtown San Diego, he chose a place in Mira Mesa, just north of the Marine Corps base. He rented a converted garage apartment in a neighborhood with a lot of active military, people mostly too young to have families. The owner of the property wasn't around much but appreciated the fact that his tenant never had a single friend over, paid in cash in an envelope placed on the porch on the first day of every month, and didn't complain about the difficulty finding street parking.

Life in San Diego was comfortable but boring. Paul took two different coding jobs, saved as much money as possible, and watched his favorite television series over and over again. He loved Walter White, an anti-hero with reasons for his evil behavior. The sixty-two episodes of *Breaking Bad* were each forty-nine minutes, for fifty total hours of storytelling, and while he knew the narrative well, he still viewed each episode wide-eyed with anticipation. He also did a deep dive into *The Sopranos*, wishing he had been more like Tony Soprano in the way he had handled adversity. The final episode of the epic show, titled "Made in America," spoke to Paul. He would fast-forward to the last scene of season six, episode sixty-two, and allow himself to weep as the soundtrack played Journey's "Don't Stop Believin'." Tony Soprano, in that final scene, was in a diner with his wife and two kids. He looked like a good husband and a father. That's what Paul Hill clung to, most especially because up north in Portland there were problems.

The state of Oregon had placed Paul Hill in legal limbo. Absent a body, the protocol for issuing a death certificate took seven years. Paul's surfboard and wetsuit booties had been recovered, but the insurance company, American Security, hard at work protecting corporate cash, was following the letter of the law. Paul hated these people fiercely, except on the rare occasion when he admitted to himself the reality—that his dying was a scam. Then he conveniently moved from loathing to rage, which felt different. He knew all shades of anger.

Lindsey's bank account showed the depth of the problem. He had to find a way to help her; he would need a surrogate to lend a hand. Paul resorted to what he considered to be a juvenile tactic. He wrote a letter to the editor of *Wired* magazine.

TO THE EDITOR:

I've been following the rise and fall of the start-up EnGenStor from a distance. The story has all the ingredients of a good drama. Recently at an industry event I ran into someone who told me that Paul Hill (who drowned while surfing) is officially in limbo in the eyes of the state of Oregon and that his widow and kids are unable to collect his life insurance. Is this true? Here in the Swedish tech community, we take care of our own. Do you know if any kind of group has formed to assist these people?

Most sincerely,
Lars Kallenberg
Stockholm

Lars Kallenberg was a real person. But he died of a massive heart attack the day Paul wrote the message. Paul's letter, sent via an email account he set up from a Swedish server—LarsKallenberg1 @TjohooMail—seemed authentic because Paul changed the time stamp so that it appeared Lars wrote it the morning he died. If an editor at *Wired* googled Lars Kallenberg, it was easy to see the man was impressive. He was known, but not so known that the tech blogosphere was buzzing with "Let's talk about Lars Kallenberg."

Paul had a feeling a magazine wasn't going to do much to authenticate the email. When he did hear back, in the form of a message from an intern saying the letter was being considered for publication, he responded that he was Lars Kallenberg's former assistant, Lise Sorensson. She detailed the fact that Lars had died suddenly, leaving the world a smaller place. Swedish people, in Paul's observation, were cold and reserved, but at the same time alarmingly forthright and even dramatic. It was a unique combination. After hearing from the fake assistant, the magazine wrote back that they were publishing Kallenberg's letter immediately.

Paul never knew the specifics of what followed. But what mattered was that a week from the day the letter appeared in *Wired*, he logged into Lindsey's email to see that Josh Lichtenstein, his former boss before EnGenStor, was now corresponding with his wife. He was going to help Lindsey get a death certificate.

Knowing that with Josh working on the problem, Lindsey had a fighting chance to get the seven-year waiting period reduced, Paul returned to making websites for small business owners. It felt better taking money from a woman who wanted to expand her coffee shop than from a divorced father of five kids who had a poker problem. It helped that San Diego was a sunny place. It had infrastructure problems and appeared to be in a perpetual water crisis, but blue skies out the windows gave Paul hope that Lindsey and the kids would be able to collect the two million (tax-free!) soon.

Then there was what felt like an earthquake. Not a real one, although Paul would have sworn the ground beneath him moved. He was coming up on two years gone when, on one of his Sunday online snoop sessions, he saw an email to Lindsey verifying that the state of Oregon was going to issue a death certificate for Paul Hill. He didn't jump for joy, or even pump his fist to celebrate. He felt relief, while at the same time deep sadness, to know he was finally, legally, in the past tense. His kids didn't have a father. As crazy as he knew it was, the loss overwhelmed him.

But Lindsey could move on now. His family had money; they would be able to get a house and, if she invested correctly, spin off yearly income. She would, he knew in his heart, work. If she stayed on a budget, his wife and kids were going to be okay. Paul had a lot of ideas about how she should proceed. He wanted to see one portion of the money set aside for college expenses. Olivia was going to be there in the blink of an eye. He envisioned money market accounts. Bonds. Single stocks only if they were in an area that made sense.

What he failed to consider was how damn impulsive Lindsey could be. She certainly had always seemed levelheaded. But there it was on a Sunday, only five weeks later, as he read through her email correspondence:

> From: Old Republic Title Company
> To: Lindsey Sisley
> RE: Property Close Settlement Papers—Mau Loa
>
> Lindsey—
> Mahalo! This is to let you know that the Mau Loa is officially yours as of 12:00 P.M. today. Wire transfer went through the day before yesterday and all docu-

ments have been recorded. Please give me a call when
you come to the island. I'd like to take you out for a
drink to celebrate the purchase of your new property.

Jiti Tanga
Title Officer—Old Republic Title
Honolulu Office, Hawai'i

Paul read the email three times. *Her "new property"?* Lindsey had
sunk money into a house in Hawai'i? He realized he had been neg-
ligent. Once she had received the insurance payout, he'd stopped the
frequency of his cyberstalking. He'd gone several Sundays without
reading her email once the death certificate had arrived. His pain
had been overwhelming.

But it hadn't been *that* long.

He quickly scrolled down further to read the real shocker.

From: Maddie Lau
To: Lindsey Sisley
RE: Mau Loa Motel

The Kalamas are accepting your offer for their motel.
Attached are escrow forms. Please notarize and return immediately with a wire transfer to the account
listed below. I look forward to meeting you and your
children. Yours was not the highest bid, but your legal
commitment to keep the structures in place and operate the business was the deciding factor.

Most sincerely,
Maddie Lau
Koko Properties, O'ahu

Lindsey *bought a motel?*

His wife had never shown any interest in being a small business owner. She hadn't even shown interest in *his* business when he

started one. Now here she was, taking so much of the money he'd died for and being reckless with it. In the emails he'd read over the past two years from her to her friends, her mother, even passing acquaintances, there had never been a word about a desire to be an innkeeper. Had she lost her mind?

Paul did his best to research the Mau Loa Motel and found next to nothing. The property was a parcel of land on the ocean just windward of the North Shore on O'ahu, away from the big waves. He hoped that was a good thing. The motel was near a town named Lā'ie, which had historically been a place where warriors took refuge, planting white flags attached to spears in the soil. He imagined Lindsey with a spear and white flag. It would have been funny if he had the ability to laugh.

He didn't; that had died with Paul Hill.

The only photo he found of the motel was from a blog written by a man calling himself TravelingSeaFanStan, promising everything you needed to know about places off the beaten track. The picture showed eight rundown structures, with a beautiful surf break as the backdrop. But Lindsey didn't surf, and Carlos was the only one who had shown any interest. His children had lost their father to the sea! Looking out at crashing waves didn't seem very healthy.

He and Lindsey had traveled to Hawai'i after they were married. Maybe that was why she was going back. She was so heartsick that she was returning to a place where they had been truly happy together. He had been able in the past to separate from her, to hold back his emotions. That was over.

He couldn't sleep.

The demons were returning.

The next day, he couldn't concentrate enough to work.

He tried to play online poker, something he hadn't done since Utah, and he lost more hands than he won. For two years he had thought he was going crazy from guilt, loneliness, anger, and poor judgment, but this was so much worse. For the next month he could barely eat. The weight loss returned. He was awake at all hours;

doubling up on over-the-counter sleep aids made no difference. The only thing that knocked him out was a bottle of wine, a scalding hot shower, and two Tylenol PMs.

And then the worst possible thing happened: He got new neighbors. A family with three kids moved in next door, and while the wooden fence that divided the property was so high he couldn't see over it, these people changed his life. A basketball hoop went up, and the sound of the bouncing ball every afternoon was accompanied by squeals, shouts, and bickering. The family owned a dog, and the kids ran around the yard every night for at least twenty minutes while the animal barked as if it were being paid to. Paul smelled their barbeque grill and the artificial but sweet scent that came from their dryer vent. They seemed to burn a lot of toast and brew a lot of coffee. They ate bacon almost every morning and pulled their TV outside to watch family movies every Saturday night as if they were at a drive-in. The younger girl bellowed along with the heroine of *Frozen* and her brothers joined her. They had pogo sticks and baseball bats and plastic swords. They threw Frisbees and jumped rope, tried to fly kites and played dodgeball. The kids fought like crazy. Their windows were almost always open and he could hear their toilets flush.

Because he was listening.

He hated these people.

And he was addicted to them.

The new neighbors put him through hell. They made him miss his kids in the most visceral of ways. His heart broke anew every time they opened the back door.

It was clear that the only thing to do was move.

But he couldn't leave them.

Then an idea formed. Not a brilliant idea. Not even a good idea. A notion that lodged in his mind and couldn't be pried from the jelly-like mass of his possibly leaky brain.

He would go to Hawai'i.

He would get a glimpse of his own children.

He would look at the Mau Loa Motel from a distance, in the dark, unseen, undetected. Maybe he could drive by their school. He might be able to get a glimpse of his kids outside on a playground, or leaving at the end of the day. Once he'd done that, he believed, it was possible that the cycle of obsessive thought would be broken. He would understand that Lindsey had done something smart, not foolish. And he would undertake this mission in such a way that no one would ever know.

He bought a round-trip ticket to Honolulu.

He would stay four days.

26

C hris helped clean up after dinner and lingered to have a second glass of wine. It was only after he said good-night, kissing Lindsey too hard on the lips, with too much urgency, that he understood he was coming undone. It was raining hard outside, and the waves sounded like a series of explosions as he paced in his cottage.

Something was going on with Olivia.

She had asked about his secrets.

He knew he was in trouble.

The world was unraveling.

The easiest way to deceive was to tell the truth about everything but the necessary lie. All other details needed to be real so they could be supported by personal memory. His first name *was* Chris. During his summers growing up, he *had* in fact worked for his uncle doing electrical work. He *had* been stung by a man o' war and he *did* hate the ocean. He *had* made an attempt at a career as a professional writer. He and Cassie *had* traveled to Europe before they were married, and they *had* been trying to have children. She *had* tragically died of cancer, and that *had* changed everything in his life.

Chris Bright was an English literature major at Howard University who sold a novel when he was just twenty-six years old. There was an agent. An established publishing company. He was considered to be a rising star. But the book underperformed, gaining no traction in a marketplace loaded with material that might have felt too familiar, or maybe not familiar enough. That was never clear. The expectations, both personal and professional, were set too high.

He couldn't help but soak in his disappointment. His book advance had been respectable, but it didn't take him long to burn through the money. When he talked to other writers, one thing became clear: It was unreasonable to expect to make a good living staring at his computer screen for hours every day hoping to spin ideas into stories. The most obvious answer was to find work as a teacher. That's what most writers did, even successful ones. They taught other people to follow their trail of broken dreams.

He couldn't do it. He went in the other direction, looking for a day job that would be meaningless, where he wouldn't give a shit, because his real work would always be telling stories. His father had wanted him to be a doctor. His mother just wanted him to be happy. He was failing on both counts. He vowed to dedicate his heart and soul to the early hours of every day, when he woke up to outline and write and rewrite. His next novel would be the book that made him known, appreciated, and respected. Because it would sell more than 3,017 copies. He would write for as long as it took, and he wouldn't turn it in until he'd finally got it right. His work would be unimpeachable. He'd fire a shot and hit a bull's-eye.

But the target kept moving. At first he had writer's block. Then he lost confidence in the merit of the story he was trying to tell. He abandoned three different outlines. He had the drive, but he couldn't find his voice. He started and stopped and started over so many times that his computer had dozens of different files with different titles, and even he had trouble finding the right one to work on.

Then an unexpected thing happened: He was good at the damn day job that was paying the bills. He worked hard, despite not wanting to. He couldn't help doing his assignments with speed and attention. The company promoted him. At the insurance company he didn't have a chosen path or even an area of interest. He started in customer service and discovered he had a natural way with people. He had no enthusiasm for sales, which was where the rest of the herd migrated. He stayed in customer relations but was moved over to underwriting. He was a problem-solver. He liked to analyze risk. He had always been good with numbers.

It was pure chance that led him into fraud investigation. He uncovered a false claim and saved the company a boatload of money. The people in Bloomington, where the company had its headquarters, noticed. They made him a very generous offer, and he relocated for more money and an impressive title. Novelists didn't need to live in Brooklyn. Maybe getting away from so many people trying to follow the same dream would be the answer. It certainly made going to get coffee an easier morning ritual knowing that he wouldn't run into someone from the world of publishing.

He still thought of himself as a novelist, but the card in his wallet said he was a senior fraud investigator at American Security. His story wasn't following an outline, but it was unfolding even better than any narrative about himself he would have written. When he married a woman he loved, it all went to another level. They were going to start a family. But the power of Cassie's intelligence, beauty, and compassion was no match for her carcinoma.

He stopped writing when his wife got sick. The air was gone from his personal balloon of contentment, and since her death it hadn't filled back up. Not even halfway. Because, he had to admit, he didn't process his grief well. To make the ensuing days and nights longer, his father died suddenly of heart failure after years of smoking and countless promises to quit. His mother moved to North Carolina to be near her sisters. His brother, who was six years older, worked for an accounting firm and lived what Chris considered a boring life outside of Columbus. They had never been close. Chris was alone in a state of perpetual disappointment, and it seemed only right that his rescue dog, the only thing left from his shared life with Cassie, got a rare blood disorder and died a week after diagnosis.

He kept his job but ignored other married couples, and when he was invited to a social event he always came up with an excuse not to attend. He exercised every day to the point of exhaustion and still had to drink too much single-malt whiskey every night in order to fall asleep. He watched sporting events on ESPN, never rooting for a specific team. If he ever switched the channel, it was to go to Hallmark because the movies, the repetitive, bland, predominantly white world populated by people with straight teeth, flawless skin, and the most fixable of all problems, was mindless science fiction to a Black man living in a house with his dead wife's clothing still hanging in the closet.

Cassie had been gone two years and Chris was still in an emotional tailspin. Her family didn't check in with him as often as they once did, and it was a relief. Cassie's mother sounded like an older version of his wife, and just the way she paused when she spoke made him angry. No one told him anymore to try online dating, and friends didn't suggest a fix-up with a cute cousin who'd just never met the right guy.

He went to work.

He did the job.

But people stopped thinking of him as someone destined for big things at the company.

Senior management questioned his value in his most recent review, which was a shock, but there was a difference between showing up and trying. His direct superior, the head of the division, suggested he take a leave of absence. Chris resisted. Then a case for what should have been a routine review came across his desk. Suicides didn't pay out if they were within two years of the policy being issued. The only other reason a claim could be denied was in the event of a natural disaster. Get caught in an earthquake and have the roof cave in? Not covered. Find yourself struck by lightning? Not paying. Fall victim to a bad winter storm on the Oregon Coast? Unclear.

The claim in question had issues. The policyholder had lived an expansive public life before his new company started to falter. The insurance policy he purchased had been in effect for only weeks when he died. Chris reviewed the file, snooped around, and discovered that the company had followed the law, waiting for a death certificate before paying. Its stated reason was that the body of the deceased had never been recovered. When they did pay, the widow immediately bought a motel in Hawai'i. There was nothing against the law about doing that, but it intrigued him. The woman had three kids. He admired her before he'd even met her.

Maybe after losing his wife he should have packed up and started over somewhere.

But what was the point of his flying to Hawai'i? What could he possibly learn from the trip?

After he got there, he would discover he was broken, but maybe capable of being fixed. Because the widow, the person he was spying on, lying to, hoping to manipulate into revealing something that might change the status of her claim, thus allowing the company to claw back the money, had some kind of hold on him from the start.

In the beginning, he studied Lindsey from every angle as if she were a file that he needed to analyze. She had muddy blue eyes that often looked gray, a high forehead, and a pointy chin. Her feet were on the small side, but her toes were long. She looked like she must have once been a runner because her hips were narrow and her calf muscles were well defined. Her forearms were splattered with a coating of freckles and her nose wasn't too large or too small. It was, he thought, a perfect fit for her heart-shaped face. She was so determined, yet so completely lacking in an organized business plan. This woman, with her tangle of light brown hair that seemed to resist control, made him laugh in large part because she was so often laughing at herself, as if to say, *I dare you to take any of this life seriously.* She was originally from Wales, and her accent was non-rhotic—the sound of the letter *r* disappeared from words in a way that was puzzling until he understood the logic and decided it was something he could listen to all day.

She was nothing like his wife.

It made it easier to care about her.

He couldn't replace Cassie. There was no version of Cassie who could be anything but lesser than the real thing. He'd never been with a white woman. He'd never had the interest. But there was another part of this equation that outweighed everything: Lindsey needed his help. Chris had been responsible for his wife up until the end, shopping, cooking, cleaning, doling out medicine in an endless cycle. If he couldn't make her better, he could damn well make sure things stayed on track.

What he didn't know he would miss, maybe as much as anything about being married, was being necessary.

That's why he went to buy groceries when Lindsey picked up the kids at school and why he ordered additional textbooks for Carlos and Olivia. He spent time looking for insects with Sena on the days when she would allow it, and early in the morning, when they were all still asleep, he set about pulling up the long-thorn kiawe, the rambling, dangerous invasive weed that grew around the property. He worried about these people.

Living in the little cottage with the ocean almost at his feet, he stopped being an insurance investigator looking into a bad-faith claim and went back to what he'd always wanted to be, a dreamer. He pretended that he'd spoken to his agent and a publisher when he hadn't in years. He felt so bad about lying that he ended up leaving his onetime agent a message, assuming she would never get back to him.

He was wrong. She sounded happy to hear his voice. He told her he'd been blocked, and then broke down and admitted that he'd given up. Twice. First on his talent. And a second time after having his heart broken. He couldn't believe he'd said those words to anyone, much less a person who after a dozen years wasn't much more than a stranger. But just admitting his problems was another step. He hung up both embarrassed and energized.

His agent said she would read anything he wrote. Anytime. Always. And that she had been waiting for the day that he would make the call.

He started to wonder if maybe it wasn't too late to pursue the original dream. Living with always-warm air, a constant gentle breeze, and the song of the sea caused the pain of his past to shift. The sharp detail of loss morphed to a blurry collage of better memories, not all focused on the end of Cassie's life and her torture of dying young. There were so many good times to remember. He had let the happier experiences be pushed out by those last, ugly frames.

Then he started writing at night. It made him less of a deceiver.

He poured himself into a rambling narrative as he imagined Lindsey's childhood in the United Kingdom. He used small reminiscences she revealed to build a character destined for a great love story with a mysterious man who lived a double life. The central question for his character was how he would tell the heroine that he was a liar. That he was a spy there to find fraud when he was the only fraud in the equation.

He came to suspect the kids were onto him. Maybe not Carlos, but the girls could run hot and cold. He wanted to tell them the truth. But he had no idea how to explain his deception. He really, truly tried to not become physical with Lindsey. If the romance raged on only in his head and on his computer screen when he wrote at night, it couldn't hurt anyone but him.

He should have left before it got intimate.

He asked for and was given all of his back vacation days, even though he'd used most of them when Cassie was sick. But he kept finding more things to do at the motel. After he finished rewiring all the cottages, he watched YouTube videos on how to fix plumbing and repair water damage. He experienced a mix of euphoria at being able to feel again and frustration at not being able to satisfy what was bottled up inside his mind and body.

He heard a knock on the door and knew it wasn't Lindsey; that's how connected he was to her every motion. He had his shirt off, and he called out "Just a minute!" as he grabbed a windbreaker off the back of a chair. The pounding sounded again. He opened the door to see Olivia in the shadows. Her hair was wet from the downpour; her face was set in fury.

"Olivia . . ." He had to hold the door tight to keep it open. "Is everything all right?" The wind was blowing rain on an angle. She was on the porch but still getting pelted. "Come in. It's terrible out there."

She didn't move. Her eyes flashed. "I know who you are, Mr. American Security."

He opened his mouth. Nothing came out.

"I want you gone. Off the property."

"I can explain—"

"That you're a liar? That you've tricked my mother? Just leave *now*."

"Olivia, I'm sorry. Please. Let me try to—"

"Get out of here!" She was shrieking. He stepped back. Her words came out like bullets. "After everything my family's been through, I won't let you be the one to take down my mother!"

He didn't dare speak. She was right. He nodded, but she wasn't finished.

"You're not leaving tomorrow. You're leaving *now*. Tonight! In a fucking windstorm!"

As if on cue, the wind kicked up a notch. The palm trees between the cottages bent like vacuum cleaner hoses at angles that didn't seem possible.

"Okay."

"Pack up. And get out. Don't leave her a note. Because there's nothing you can say that will make it better."

Before he even had the door closed, Olivia was down the steps and crossing the wet grass, which was soaked with so much water that the exposed blade tips looked like teeth.

27

Olivia didn't have to be quiet when she opened the front door. The howling wind covered up all other sound. She turned the deadbolt on the lock and started up the wooden stairs. Her heart raced; her arms and legs were shaky from the surge of adrenaline. She grabbed a towel from the bathroom and dried off her hair, then slipped into her bedroom and stripped off her wet clothing, tossing it on the floor as she grabbed a nightshirt.

Olivia felt a clarity she had never experienced before. There was power in her actions. She had used honesty against deception. She slid into bed, conscious of her little sister's light snoring on the other side of the room.

Olivia shut her eyes and saw the motel's old sign: IF YOU AREN'T SUPPOSED TO BE HERE, DON'T BE HERE! KAPU!

The traitor in the red cottage sure as hell wasn't supposed to be here.

Lindsey had fallen asleep but was woken by the wind. It was always breezy at the motel, but tonight the entire office building rattled, the old windows and doors shaking as air whistled through the gaps in the metal roof like a distorted ambulance siren. Before she had come upstairs to bed, Lindsey listened to a woman on satellite radio from the Central Pacific Hurricane Center explain: "We're really lucky this storm has stayed on a southern trajectory. We've had direct hits in the past by hurricanes, and we will again in the future. But this time we dodged another major bullet. Remember we need to always be prepared, folks. Mahalo!"

Lindsey hated being lumped into a category known as "folks." She couldn't stand it when a politician used the term, even if she liked them otherwise. Instead of absorbing the content of the broadcast, she had fixated on the language. Now she wished she'd listened more closely. She wondered if it was okay that the wind seemed to be getting stronger.

She remembered something she had read: Hawai'i is the only US state surrounded entirely by water, and the only state completely in the tropical trade wind belt. Apparently, this is what makes the weather so unpredictable. Lindsey wondered why it was called a belt. She really needed to get to sleep. She rolled over, and then after a few moments flipped back to the other side. Again. Left. Right. Knees up. Legs scissored. Hands against her cheek. Hands outstretched. She hoped they didn't lose electricity. The internet had gone out earlier. It was raining so hard outside. And it wasn't letting up. A real downpour.

Normally she loved how it could rain hard in Hawai'i and an hour later the warm air would dry up the moisture—it was so different from Oregon rain. But tonight it was just too damn loud to sleep. Her mind raced with conflicting impulses. Go see Chris. Stay in bed and try to fall asleep. Worry about the kids. Worry about Chris leaving. Worry about a storm. Don't worry about a storm. Worry about how to run a motel. Worry that the first guests were just days away. Worry about sleep deprivation, which was known to be the cause of serious health problems. Worry about the effects of too much worrying.

She needed to fall asleep or the next day would be ruined.

Lindsey looked around her room, which was where most of the supplies for the motel were being stored. There were dozens of new pillows wrapped in plastic stacked with cartons of unopened sheets and thin cotton blankets. New trash bins. Four dozen sets of blue-and-white-striped towels were piled next to boxes of Kleenex and toilet paper. Bathmats were wedged between coffee machines, coat hangers, shower caps, and new drinking mugs. She had purchased a year's supply of sugar packets, postcards, pencils, and envelopes. Less appealing was the mountain of cleaning and disinfecting supplies she would need. In the daylight it looked hopeful. But in the shadows the sheer volume of stuff illustrated the enormousness of the task of operating a motel. She had only seven days before it would all begin, and while she'd only accepted bookings in two cottages for that first week, the calendar was filling up quickly. It was both encouraging and terrifying. She wondered if all small business owners became insomniacs.

Lindsey got up and went to the bathroom. She had a few sleeping pills left from a prescription that was written for her after Paul died. There were pink ones and white ones. She couldn't remember which was stronger. She checked the date on the bottles and saw they were expired. But only by a few months. Lindsey popped two white pills into her mouth, washing them down with a gulp of coconut water that Carlos had left by the sink. As she headed back to bed she looked in on the kids; thankfully, they were all sound asleep, which was a miracle considering the pounding rain and the roaring wind. She turned to look down the hallway, and the small nightlight in the bathroom went off. Lindsey reached over and tried the bedroom switch. Nothing. So now the electricity was out.

She went to the window to check on the red cottage. No lights on in there either. There was ice cream in the freezer. She wondered how long it could last before melting. There was milk, cheese, and what about mayonnaise? Couldn't that kill you if it went bad? She wondered about the time frame for food poisoning. She would look it up, but there was no internet, so no asking Professor Google.

The wind outside was brutal. But soon the storm would pass.

Yes.

That's what the weatherperson had said.

Then tomorrow it would be halcyon. She loved that word. She wished people would use it more. *Halcyon* might make a nice first name. But maybe it was too pretentious. A quote from Shakespeare, remembered from childhood, came to mind: "If after every tempest come such calms / May the winds blow till they have waken'd death!"

People could go on about *Hamlet* or *Macbeth*, but she liked *Othello*. She repeated the line: "May the winds blow till they have waken'd death." What a thought.

Lindsey returned to her bed and shut her eyes. The sleeping pills worked on the GABA receptors in her brain, which controlled her level of alertness. She wished she didn't know so much about science. There was no reason to be alert now. She issued a command: *Give it a rest, systema nervosum.* She would concentrate on one thing to make the whole process easier. She repeated over and over again, "May the winds blow till they have waken'd death!"

Soon she couldn't put the words in the right order.

The wind was shaking the windows more violently, but the rattle was no longer frightening; it was turning musical. Her thoughts jumbling together were becoming nonsensical.

She moved from Shakespeare to Sinatra. She heard him. Was he outside? On the radio?

She had always been told that her grandfather had liked Sinatra. Her father had loved the Beatles. So did Paul. He used to say he wished he'd been alive in the 1960s. He felt like he'd missed out.

But that was part of who he was, she realized. He had the fear of missing out way before it was a trendy term. And by dying young, he'd missed out on everything that mattered.

Her mum had played a lot of Sinatra after her dad died.

She knew all the words.

Words without meaning and with meaning.

All or nothing at all.

Words swirling like leaves on a windy night.

Don't you know I would be caught in the undertow.

What were the words?

All or nothing at all.

28

The internet was out, and the broadband network on his phone wasn't working, either. There was no way to book a flight to Chicago, but he could get to the other side of the island, check into a hotel near the airport, and wait for morning. There was a tropical storm moving south, but if the forecasters were right, it would only mean strong wind and heavy rain.

Chris packed up, tossing his clothing into his suitcase, moving quickly but with the same precision with which he did everything in life. The electricity was off, so he used the flashlight on his iPhone to see, working to stay focused on the task at hand. He tried to convince himself that things would be okay. Not for him, but for Lindsey. For her kids.

Disregarding Olivia's instructions, he wrote a note explaining that a sudden family emergency had called him back to the mainland. He said he'd be in touch. He took way too long to write four simple sentences, agonizing over each word.

At 12:33 A.M. Chris Bright walked through the pounding rain to his Jeep. He couldn't remember ever being in wind this strong, or hearing surf this loud. The noise of the flexing palm trees, the thrashing 'akoko and Indian pluchea shrubs, all covered up the sound of the Jeep's engine as he pulled away from the motel. There was no one on Kam Highway as he headed north. Water fell from the black sky in swirling sheets. He put on the brakes and slowed to a stop. This looked to be a much bigger storm than had been forecast. His cellphone was dead because he'd spent too long with the flashlight app on, and the charging cord was packed in his bag. He'd only been out of touch with the world for two hours, but everything felt different. He questioned his judgment, but pressed his foot on the gas and kept going, very slowly, through the pounding rain.

He didn't think to turn on the radio until he'd battled the elements for twenty minutes in the darkness, inching through the deluge, dodging palm fronds, branches, even a wooden lawn chair that came flying out of nowhere eight feet up in the air, just missing his windshield. He was on a doomed mission, and as misguided as it all felt, it wasn't until his radio began making a rhythmic, pulsing sound that he realized the rain and wind were something truly ominous.

Chris pulled over to the side of the road to listen to the emergency storm alert. An abrupt change of direction had sent Hurricane Neville due north. It was expected to make landfall now on Oʻahu. Residents were being instructed to move inland immediately. This was a full-on weather emergency. The Central Pacific tropical cyclone was being compared to Hurricane Iniki in 1992. Chris worked in insurance. He knew the damage from Iniki had been catastrophic. He stared through the windshield. This was what could happen to specks of land in the middle of the world's biggest ocean. The Central Pacific Hurricane Center had failed to issue cyclone warnings in the twenty-four hours before Iniki hit, and now it was happening all over again. There was no way he would leave Lindsey and the kids alone at the motel. He put the Jeep in drive and swung around in a wide arc through a river of water across the roadway. He was going back.

Olivia had turned off her ringer. She received four text messages and slept through the pings. But her eyes opened when her phone, resting on the nightstand only inches from her head, started making a sound she'd never heard before. It was an insistent, pulsing honk. She reached for the device and read the lit screen:

THIS IS A MESSAGE FROM THE EMERGENCY ALERT SYSTEM. THIS IS AN EXTREME WIND ALERT, A COASTAL

FLOODING ALERT, AND AN EVACUATION ORDER. THE
NATIONAL WEATHER SERVICE HAS ISSUED EMERGENCY
STORM CONDITIONS FOR THE HAWAIIAN ISLANDS,
WHICH, FOLLOWING A DIRECTIONAL CHANGE, ARE
NOW IN THE DIRECT PATH OF HURRICANE NEVILLE, RE-
CENTLY UPGRADED TO A CATEGORY 5 STORM. NEVILLE
IS EXPECTED TO MAKE LANDFALL ON O'AHU WITHIN
THE NEXT TWO TO SIX HOURS.

Olivia sat up. Her phone again made the honking noise. Outside
it was the dead of night, but the wind was roaring. The windows
were shaking and she could hear the sound of the palm trees slamming into the side of the house. Her phone showed it was 2:17 A.M.

Across the room, Sena sat up. "What's going on?"

Olivia sprang from the bed. "Get up! Go wake Carlos. And
Mom! We gotta get out of here!"

"Where are we going?"

Olivia didn't answer. She pulled her jeans on over her pajama
shorts and grabbed the shirt that was on the floor. It was partly wet.
Water was dripping down from different areas of the ceiling. "Sena!
Go!"

Her little sister took off across the hallway to Carlos's room as
Olivia slid into her flip-flops. Then she had second thoughts and
grabbed her running shoes from under the bed, hitting the light
switch. Nothing. The electricity was out. She bent down and shoved
her shoes onto her feet as Sena came back into the room with Carlos. He had a leather cord around his neck with what looked to
Olivia like a tooth dangling from it.

"What's going on?"

Olivia shouted, "Get dressed! *Now!* There's a hurricane!" She
turned to Sena. "Did you wake Mom?"

Sena, still in her pajamas, shouted over the noise. "I tried! But
I don't know if she's really awake. The lights don't work. I couldn't
see!"

Olivia tucked her cellphone into her back pocket and ran to her mother's room. Unbelievably, she was still asleep. "Wake up, Mom!"

Her mother didn't stir.

Olivia grabbed Lindsey's shoulders and shook her till her eyes opened. She was groggy and confused. "What's going on, Olivia?"

"Get up, dammit! We're supposed to evacuate!"

Lindsey propped herself up on her elbows. It sounded like someone outside had turned on a garbage disposal. Or a wood chipper. The din of moving objects was everywhere. She shouted, "Wake the kids!"

"We are all awake!" Olivia yelled back.

Lindsey looked at the doorway to see Carlos dressed in shorts and his University of Oregon raincoat. Sena appeared at his side wearing her Hello Kitty pink pajamas and red rain boots.

Carlos shouted, "Mom! We gotta get out of here!"

No sooner were the words out of his mouth than they heard the sound of breaking glass from the floor below. Olivia screamed. Sena ran to her mother. Lindsey, her head thick with sleeping pills, got up, shouting, "Okay, stay calm!" She knew she sounded anything but calm. She wedged her feet into her shoes and then started for the doorway.

"Mom, you're in your underwear!" Olivia found a pair of shorts on top of the bureau and flung them in her direction. "Put these on! What's wrong with you?"

Lindsey didn't take off her shoes and had to struggle with her shorts. Then they all heard it. A person was bounding up the staircase. Heavy footsteps hit hard on the wooden treads. They all turned.

And then there he was.

In total shadow.

Thin. Angular. Bald. Wearing glasses. Soaking wet. But with features and posture they all recognized immediately. Lindsey felt the room start to spin. Her blood pressure dropped precipitously and sparks of light edged her vision. "Paul?"

Her knees buckled and she collapsed, falling into the stacks of sheets and blankets, out cold. Lindsey's last thought was *May the winds blow till they have waken'd death.*

The crush of seeing his family broke Paul Hill. The realization of all he had lost, of all the changes that had happened in his absence, was catastrophic. His children were his children, yet they were strangers moving in bodies he didn't know. Only Lindsey, crumpled on the floor in the darkness, looked the same.

Carlos backed up into the corner, believing he was in the presence of a living, breathing ghost. But Sena went to her father and put her hand on his shoulder as he dropped to his knees, sobbing. He managed to speak through his uncontrollable tears, though the storm drowned out most of his words. "I'm sorry. I'm so sorry" was all that could be understood. Olivia, trembling, knelt over her mother, cradling her head as her eyes opened.

Outside, the fury of the wind was rapidly increasing. The sound of ripping metal caused everyone, even Lindsey, to look up as the ceiling of the office building tore apart and the tin roof peeled back like the top of a sardine can. Directly exposed to the storm, all of the new motel supplies, along with the clothing, beds, books, and chairs, were lifted into the air. Everything swirled like dead leaves as rain poured down into the room. The blasting wind sounded as mechanical as an oncoming train.

Paul forced himself to his feet and scooped up Sena. With their arms covering their faces, they struggled to the stairs. Carlos was the first to descend, and he was pelted on all sides by rain and household objects. He was followed by Olivia, who was helping her mother. The combination of the shock of seeing Paul and the sleeping pills made Lindsey's legs nearly useless. She managed her way down the top three stairs and then her rubbery limbs lost control. She fell, tumbling like a rag doll until she hit the bottom step and her right leg snapped. No one could hear the bone break, but even in the darkness they could make out that her foot was pointing at the wrong angle.

Paul entrusted Sena to Olivia and went to his wife—according to a court decree, his widow. She was surrounded by the glass shards of shattered windowpanes. The Kalamas' decorative netting that had once been affixed to the ceiling was flapping around the room like a stingray. Paul lifted Lindsey into his arms as the front door, slamming open and shut, had enough and the rusty hinges ripped out of the frame, giving the howling wind another avenue of entry. It blew through the opening with the power of a turbine engine. The Kalamas' old mahogany desk was directly in the path of the new airstream. It flipped up on its side and skidded across the floor as if it were on wheels.

The desk hit Olivia in the back. She dropped Sena, and the moving furniture plowed forward, pinning the little girl against the wall. Carlos fought his way into the gap, pushing his younger sister out the side just before she was crushed.

It was now him against the desk and the wind.

Olivia and Sena, both screaming, tried desperately to help. Paul set Lindsey in the alcove under the staircase and grabbed one side of the desk.

Carlos felt his ribs give way. He tried to scream, but his lungs weren't working right. He struggled to keep his right arm up to his face to protect his neck. He could only inhale the smallest of breaths. It felt as if he was filming on his iPhone in the slow-motion setting. Sound was distorted. Reality was elongated into excruciating moments of terror. He shut his eyes. His fingers touched his necklace. The leather cord with the *makau*.

He was no match for the wind.

He was going to die.

His chest continued to flatten.

His fingers dug further into the *makau* as his jaw and throat were pushed back into the wall.

Then the pressure of the crippling desk lessened. The vise-like grip against his body eased. Carlos opened his eyes and was able to inhale. The desk was inching away. In the space that opened up between the wall and the furniture he saw not just his father's ghost but Chris. He was next to his dad, and they were both pulling the mahogany monster. Carlos heard Chris bellow: *"Move! Now!"*

Carlos worked his way out just in time because the two men couldn't hold on any longer. They released their grip and the desk drove straight through the wall to the outside, tumbling onto the wet ground. Carlos could only hear isolated syllables. Chris was yelling. So was his father, or his ghost. Olivia gripped his shoulder, pushing him. His side hurt. His neck and throat were on fire. He heard Chris shout, "The car! The Crown Victoria weighs over four thousand pounds."

Through the chaos and pain, Carlos wondered, *Who knows how much a car weighs?*

The storm came off the ocean at a speed that made walking upright impossible. Rain attacked from all directions, as if a fire hose had broken loose. Chris could see that all the cottages except his had no roofs. The pink cottage had been lifted straight up off its stilt supports and was gone, having disappeared entirely into the dark void. Lindsey's white Crown Victoria sat just twenty yards away. One of the front windows was down.

They crawled on hands and knees through the muddy gravel toward the car. Chris was thankful that the bald man had Sena. Her arms were wrapped around his neck and her face was buried in his soaking shirt. Olivia and Carlos followed behind. Chris helped Lindsey. She was in agony because of her leg.

The bald man made it to the passenger side of the Crown Victoria first. Olivia and Carlos were behind him. But he couldn't get the door open. Chris left Lindsey only three yards from the car and went to the driver's-side door. He pried it open only to find the car filled with feral chickens huddled on the floorboards and seats. The sound that came out of their feathered bodies was unlike anything he'd ever heard from a bird. They were screaming.

Chris tried to clear them away, but the terrorized creatures chose to defend the wet car interior. The birds pecked at his arms, and two chickens took a swipe at his face with their feet, drawing blood. Chris beat them back until, still shrieking, they wedged themselves under the front seats and against the windshield. Chris then pulled Sena up through the open window, onto the seat. Once she was inside he used his feet to hold open the door. Olivia and Carlos crawled in and went up and over into the backseat. The bald man went to help Lindsey. The wind was fierce, and a mix of flying sand, grit, and water made it nearly impossible to see. Chris struggled with the door as the bald man returned, dragging Lindsey. The two men worked together to get her into the car. Then the wind shifted abruptly, and two dozen chickens huddled against the windshield were instantly swept out the car's open window. Sena, screaming, reached out for the birds. Chris grabbed the little girl, afraid she might try to get out. The door slammed shut behind him.

The moving wall of water and mud began when, over a mile inland from the motel, a mountainside broke free. The rainfall came down so unrelentingly, in such a short period of time, that the nearly always wet earth reached capacity. What was once solid turned liquid. An enormous slab of volcano ridge cracked open and gravity did the rest. Forty-foot rocket-shaped Cook pine trees toppled and joined the river of mud, boulders, and vegetation barreling down the slopes toward the ocean. The steep terrain flattened out before Kamehameha Highway, but the surging mass had enough velocity to split off into channels, muddy veins of destruction that took down everything in their path. The mudslide washed away the asphalt in five different places as it crossed the two-lane road.

One branch of the destructive force headed straight for the Mau Loa.

The wooden KEEP OUT sign disappeared, a toothpick joining the liquid avalanche, which next hit the rusty old panel truck. It no longer mattered that it didn't have tires. It moved like a tiny toy. But most of the flow didn't turn at the curve in the drive. Instead, it kept going straight, crushing everything in its path. If the storm sounded like a freight train, the mudslide was a bomb. Boulders knocked together; trees and branches cracked and splintered. This was an unstoppable, thirty-mile-an-hour flow of natural chaos.

In the Crown Victoria, Lindsey, Carlos, and Olivia were on top of each other, faces pressed into the floorboard with screaming chickens wedged around them at all angles. Chris held Sena.

Lindsey lifted her head. She was on one side of the back window of the Crown Victoria, and Paul was outside on the other. He held on to the door handle as the rain and wind pummeled his body. A flash of lightning lit up the sky for a single snapshot. Paul's face was illuminated; his dark eyes looked as if they were on fire. Lindsey couldn't hear what he said, but she understood as he mouthed the words "Forgive me."

Paul Hill was outside the car.

And then in an instant he was gone.

Everything was moving. Lindsey felt an arm reach out and grab her. It was Carlos. He had her by the neck as more than four thousand pounds of metal, carried by the river of mud, rocks, trees, and plants, was pushed forward toward the Pacific Ocean. The car hit the Kalamas' wooden desk, which spun around and slammed into palm trees as if it were in an arcade game. The Crown Victoria became part of the debris flow, everything in motion at different speeds, objects ricocheting off each other, as it all surged across the parking area, down the embankment, and onto what had once been the sandy beach. Mud, water, and rocks came in the single open car window, cascading over their bodies. Sena, crying against Chris's chest, whimpered over and over again, "Help me."

In the backseat, Lindsey decided nothing was real. She was in a nightmare brought on by the sleeping pills. Her broken leg throbbed in pain with her exploding heartbeat. She tried to wake up, but there was nothing but the savage sound of the storm as they moved on a monstrous carnival ride. She reached out and found her oldest daughter's hand. She held it tight and shut her eyes.

29

There was a rusty tinge on the far horizon of the purple-gray sky. It was beginning to be light outside. Lindsey could hear rain and wind but not the roar of the storm. There was another sound. So familiar. Was she in a boat? She recognized the rocking motion of the sea. She lifted her head and saw the ocean out the car window. It was all froth and foam, surging silver ridges that crashed in all directions. It took time to understand she was in the backseat of the Crown Victoria, which was now half submerged in a very dark Pacific Ocean, being pushed forward and backward, half a dozen inches at a time, with each cycle of waves. She tried to move and felt only searing pain.

The last thing she remembered with any clarity was being in the bathroom washing down sleeping pills with Carlos's coconut water. She wasn't sure how she'd ended up in the car in the ocean. But more confusing than anything was the memory that Paul had appeared in the middle of the storm.

At her side, Olivia, motionless, her body covered in muddy water, had her head against Lindsey's back. Carlos was hanging half over the front seat. Lindsey could see Chris wedged up against the steering wheel. He had Sena, her eyes closed, held across his shoulder like a baby. Dark water came up to his armpits.

Lindsey pulled her arm out of the muck and touched Olivia's face. Her daughter muttered in a surly, teenage way, "What the fuck?"

Carlos stirred, wincing in pain.

Up front, Chris's head turned as Sena's eyes opened and she looked at her mother, repeating Olivia's words, "What the fuck?"

Lindsey reflexively mumbled, "Language."

Everyone shivered from exposure in seventy-nine-degree water. They tried to get out of the car but couldn't pry open any of the doors. The front window was the only avenue of escape. Olivia was the first to make it through, and she helped Carlos, who had fractured ribs and severely bruised shoulders and arms. Chris was able to pass Sena to her siblings. He then helped Lindsey, whose broken leg made any movement excruciating.

Once free from the Crown Victoria, they had to navigate the foamy surf, thick with debris. They moved as a knot, clinging to each other. Olivia had Sena on her back; Chris carried Lindsey, while Carlos gripped his shoulder to keep from falling. Pieces of the motel walls and floor bobbed in chunks around them. Lindsey spotted her kitchen toaster stuck in the mud-covered sand. There was a broken toilet seat swinging in a leafless tree.

They worked their way slowly up the sludge embankment to find that the red cottage was the only structure still intact. Everything else was gone, blown apart as if by dynamite. The back windows of Chris's cottage had shattered and the front door was split in two, but half of the roof was still on and inside the main room the metal ceiling fan hung in rigid defiance from the center beam. The old beds were up against the wall with a portion of one bedspread amazingly still dry.

Chris set Lindsey down on the mattress. Her right leg tilted inward at an angle and below her knee her calf was swollen to twice its normal size, as purple as if she were wearing a lavender stocking. In the tiny closet next to the bathroom Chris found a stack of towels, perfectly in place, all still dry. He brought them to Lindsey. Her whole body was beginning to shake. The enormity of the catastrophic storm was taking hold.

She tried not to cry. "Everything is gone. Every photograph. Identification. Piece of clothing. Everything I bought for the motel."

Olivia, standing in the doorway, whispered, "I guess I can get a new cellphone now."

Sena headed for the bathroom. Moments later they all heard, "Hey! There's no toilet paper in here."

Chris checked that the downed power lines posed no threat, and the kids were all allowed out of the cottage to investigate the ruins. Water, no longer violent, was flowing everywhere, running in a thousand streams and rivers into the ocean. Carlos, moving painfully with his damaged rib cage, took small, tentative steps on the available islands of mud. Olivia stopped to pick up pieces of their broken life. Sena crouched low to get a view under the cottage and saw in the shadows three chickens pulling worms and bugs from the soaked ground. She got down on all fours and soon was back on the cottage porch, mud clods falling off her knees and elbows. She held her favorite red chicken as she whispered through tears, "Tink made it!"

Carlos headed to where the office had once stood. Plumbing pipes stuck up out of the ground connected to only air. The shed was gone. His dirt pile and hole had washed away. There was no sign of a single tool. Trees and bushes were all bare, stripped of leaves. Carlos stared at what he thought was part of the office but then realized was the refrigerator. It had no door and was on its side, covered with mud. Smashed plates and kitchen pots were part of the debris, which included Olivia's orange shorts and one of Sena's bug books. Carlos spotted something in a piece of smashed cabinetry and went to investigate. He was rewarded with the discovery of a full, unopened jar of peanut butter. Armed with his prize, he headed back to the red cottage.

"We can take turns." Carlos wiped the dirt from the lid with his wet shirt and held out the container. They sat on the bed, sharing the jar, even Tink getting a portion, until it was all gone. The wind outside was blowing in gusts, no longer a continuous howl, as Chris said,

"You guys need to know I'm not a writer. I mean, I am a writer, but that's not my job. I work for American Security. I'm an insurance investigator. That's why I'm here in Hawai'i."

Lindsey's mouth opened, but no sound came out. She hadn't realized there was more pain left in the world.

Olivia had the superior tone of someone hearing old news. "Yeah. He didn't come because of a dead wife. He was sent to spy on us."

Sena, still holding Tink, looked from Olivia to Chris. "A spy like for the government?"

Olivia answered, "No. For business. Because of Dad's insurance policy."

Lindsey stared straight through him.

"I lied about who I was. But the things about my life—they were true. My wife did die from cancer. And I did publish a novel. I know electrical work because that was my summer job for my uncle. And I did grow up on the East Coast. I—"

Carlos interrupted. "Do you like the ocean? Yes or no."

Chris shook his head. "Not really. It's true I'm afraid." He reached out and touched Lindsey's arm. She flinched. "Lindsey, I was only supposed to be on the island for a few days. I wasn't ever going to move onto your property. That just happened. It wasn't some kind of evil plan. I stayed to help . . . because I wanted to be with you. With the kids."

Lindsey turned away. She couldn't even look at him.

Olivia joined her brother on the prosecution team. "So you knew Dad was alive?"

Another shock wave hit the room. Tink clucked. Chris looked confused. "That man last night . . . that was your *father*?"

They had all pushed that part of the night out of their minds. Carlos whispered, "I thought he was a ghost." He stared out the open doorway at the thousand muddy streams still dumping their water into the brown ocean. "What happened to him?"

Olivia held tight to the empty peanut butter jar. "I knew he was on the island. Sena saw him yesterday in Hale'iwa."

Lindsey stared at Sena.

"Mama, I was going to tell you," Sena said, "but you were too busy yelling at me about getting lost. He was across the road. I knew it was Daddy. But he got in a car and drove away."

Lindsey started to cry. "Why would he do this to us? What kind of person would abandon us like that?"

The room fell silent.

Finally Sena said, "Daddy came back to save us from the storm." She looked over at Chris. "And you did, too. But you're not from the spirit world."

"I told you to leave. I saw your Jeep drive away," Olivia whispered.

"I turned around once I realized how bad the storm was. I couldn't get through. I walked back."

Carlos put his hand to his chest. His ribs ached with every inhalation. "It's a good thing you did because that desk would have crushed me."

Sena took her brother's hand. "You saved me, Carl."

She didn't call him Carlos. It caused another shift as Lindsey began to tremble again. She stared down at her twisted leg, then out in the direction of the ocean, as she whispered, "Is Paul out there somewhere?" She had nothing in her stomach but the peanut butter. She turned away and vomited a swirl of yellow bile onto the floor. Carlos took one of the pillowcases and cleaned it up, tossing the soiled piece of cloth out a windowless opening.

No one spoke for a long time. All the horrors of the longest night of their lives came rushing back. The sky outside brightened, but rain continued to fall. Carlos shut his eyes, his hand gripping the *makau* still on the cord around his neck. Sena, curled into a compact ball, holding Tink, finally broke the silence. "Guys—what matters is that we survived." A new expression took hold on her face. It seemed hopeful. "I wonder if all the mongooses got washed away."

In the half-light of the still-stormy sky, a pueo—a short-eared owl—soared overhead. The wings of its mottled body flared wide,

and the bird's talons extended as it landed at a distance on an over-
turned tree. The roots reached up to the sky like branches. Lindsey
leaned down and kissed the top of her daughter's head. Sena's hair
left a salty taste on her lips.

30

Haku's father, Freeman Kahale, worked for the Hawai'i Emergency Management Agency. The island had been left with no electricity, broken gas pipes, a contaminated water system, dozens of fatalities, and thousands of injuries. The roads were impassable because of downed power lines, washed-out bridges, and huge sections of swept-away blacktop. An aerial shot from a search-and-rescue helicopter showed that the Mau Loa Motel was gone, and Haku begged his father to go check on Olivia and her family. By that afternoon, Freeman, with Haku and Koa at his side, was aboard a Coast Guard cutter that made its way up the windward side of the island.

Through his binoculars, Haku saw the tip of the hood of the Crown Victoria poking up out of the water on the mud-covered beach in front of all the Mau Loa cottages. The rest of the car was totally submerged.

"Oh shit."

Koa grabbed the binoculars. "There's one cottage left." He then spotted something. "I see them!"

"You see Olivia?" There was a tremble in Haku's voice.

"Yeah, bro. I see her."

At the same time, Haku and Freeman Kahale said: "Mahalo ke Akua."

They were taken to Dillingham Field, where the Red Cross had set up one of many disaster shelters on the island. Carlos was no longer having as much trouble breathing. The treatment for broken ribs was pain medicine and rest, but Lindsey needed immediate care for her broken leg and would be flown by helicopter with six other injured people to the Queen's Medical Center in Honolulu. Before they were separated, Lindsey, Chris, and Olivia were given Red Cross phones to stay in contact.

All three of her children wrapped their arms around their mother's neck, anxious about separating, but Sena broke the tension when she said, "Hey, guess what? Today is Pajama Day at school." She was still in her Hello Kitty sleepwear.

Carlos took his little sister's hand as Lindsey was carried off on a stretcher. Once she was inside the helicopter, Lindsey lifted her head to look out the window. Chris was standing under an awning next to the airstrip with her three children. He held a rust-colored chicken in the crook of his arm.

The Red Cross Family Shelter Box contained a tent, mosquito netting, four gallons of water, a solar light, four blankets and mats, and a cooking set with packets of freeze-dried food. There was also a plastic tub with four pairs of sweatpants (two child-sized, two adult-sized), and four long-sleeve T-shirts. They all still had their own wet shoes except for Sena, who had lost her red rubber boots. A line formed to get a toiletry kit, and then another longer line to take showers. By the end of the day Chris and the kids were exhausted but clean, dry, and dressed alike in clothes that didn't fit. It was still raining, and people who had arrived earlier had claimed all of the indoor space. Chris had the tent, but the prospect of using it in an open marsh of a soaked field was daunting. As the sun got lower, rainbows lit the sky.

Haku and Koa again came to the rescue. Olivia sent a text from the Red Cross phone to Haku's father, and as darkness fell the boys arrived in Haku's pickup truck to take them home. They had been able to navigate a route on back roads, avoiding the worst flood damage and the closed sections of Kam Highway.

The Kahales' house was positioned on the corner of a cul-de-sac just eight miles from the Mau Loa. A generator was running in the driveway. It made a rumble that Olivia would have found annoying, but when Haku explained it meant they had electricity, the thing sounded like a symphony.

The house was small, and it was difficult for Olivia to imagine what the living room looked like without so many people. Three other displaced families were also staying with the Kahales, along with five dogs, a cat, and a cage of lime-green parakeets. The furniture had all been moved into the garage and only the TV remained on a low table. The floor was covered with mats and towels. The two front windows had blown out in the storm and there was plywood where the glass would have been. Olivia was introduced to more people than she would ever be able to remember.

In the kitchen, Koa's mom stirred some kind of brothy stew in an enormous pot. Whatever it was smelled delicious. Steam rose up from four rice cookers plugged into a power strip on the counter. On the other side of the open screen door, an older woman stood in the backyard under a blue tarp grilling pork chops and chicken legs. Strands of dark hair streaked with silver poked out of a scarf that was wrapped around her head. It looked as if she were wearing a crown.

People kept coming and going. The front screen door slapped open and shut as visitors dropped off food or picked up supplies. Haku and Koa left with Haku's father and a neighbor to help capture two horses running along the flooded highway. Chris was on a satellite phone to his office on the mainland, gathering information about emergency services. It seemed as if everyone in the room except Olivia, Carlos, and Sena was talking. The three kids sat on outdoor cushions in a far corner of the room with Tink in a crate at their side. Sena and Carlos, slumped against Olivia's body, both fell asleep despite all the commotion.

And then at last dinner was ready. Everyone got in a line that started in the kitchen with rice and stew and then moved out the back door to where Tutu, Koa's grandma, served grilled meat. Olivia held Sena's hand, whispering, "Be polite, just say 'no thank you' when they offer stuff you don't want to eat."

Carlos, standing behind her, said, "Or just take a portion and I'll have it."

Chris helped the kids get served before joining the line. As people ate, silence fell on what had been a very noisy room. Carlos looked up at Tutu and said, "This is the best dinner I ever had in my whole life. And not just because I didn't eat anything today except some peanut butter and three PowerBars."

Everyone helped clean up once the meal was done, and then people staked out spots to sleep on the living room floor. Haku and Koa finally returned with Haku's father. Olivia wanted to ask about the horses, but they went into the kitchen to get food and she stayed with her brother and sister. Chris took the blankets and water from their Red Cross box and got the kids settled. He tried to reach Lindsey, but the call didn't go through after a recording announced all the circuits were busy. He sent a text message explaining they were at the Kahales' house and that the children were okay.

Everyone was exhausted but at the same time still fueled by adrenaline. Outside in the driveway the diesel-powered generator sounded as loud as city traffic. Olivia tried to imagine it was a vacuum cleaner, but that didn't make it less noisy. Koa's mom put on a DVD of *The Wizard of Oz*, with the volume on high, and the distraction worked. Soon Olivia couldn't hear the roaring machine, and the whole room, even Koa and Haku, who stood in the corner, both looking over at her every few minutes, started singing "Follow the Yellow Brick Road."

Just before Sena fell asleep, she murmured to her big sister, "I didn't realize that *The Wizard of Oz* was a storm movie."

From her hospital bed, Lindsey watched as a TV newscaster, looking windblown and sleep-deprived, spoke to the camera. "Hurricane Neville made landfall on Oʻahu as the strongest hurricane on record, with one-minute sustained winds of 148 miles per hour. Entire parts of the island are buried in rock and mud. Tens of thousands are now in evacuation centers. The abrupt change in the hurricane's path left the islands unprepared and in great jeopardy. More than half a million people were directly in the storm's path, with a trail of destruction never before seen in the Hawaiian Islands. The current count of casualties stands at forty-eight. More are expected as the cleanup continues."

Lindsey shared a hospital room with two other women who also had injuries from the hurricane. One had been hit by a fallen tree and was heavily sedated; the other, Iris, had fractured her pelvis in a car accident when her truck skidded off the road near Makapuʻu Point. Lindsey felt bad to be taking up a bed when the hallways were filled with injured people on gurneys. But she was repeatedly assured she needed to be there until her surgery could be scheduled.

Late in the day the rain stopped and the sun burst through the clouds, hot and unapologetic. The island had no electricity and only emergency generators were in use. The health department's statement advised people to boil their water before drinking. Lindsey explained to Iris that her children were staying with people she'd never met, who had sons her daughter knew from school. "They generously opened up their home."

Iris nodded. "Hawaiian hospitality. Aloha spirit. It's one of the most important things in our culture."

"I can see that."

"The islands have been through many storms. We've survived. We got through Pearl Harbor. Missionaries. Hurricane Iniki. So much change. But aloha spirit always lives on. If you have something, you must share. If you don't, you dishonor your family."

Lindsey nodded. She closed her eyes, and when she opened them again, several hours had passed and she had no idea where she was or why she was there.

It took several long moments to remember that everything her family owned had been lost.

A powerful storm rearranges the world. Along the shoreline, enormous quantities of sand move as ocean levels rise and fall, sometimes by as much as twenty or thirty feet. When the winds die down and the water recedes, there can be discoveries. Hawaiian petroglyphs had been found before on Oʻahu, and experts date them back over four hundred years, to a time before any European contact with the Hawaiian islands.

After Hurricane Neville, a stretch of soft rock was revealed at low tide in front of the Mau Loa Motel. Carved into the delicate sandstone were large petroglyphs, nearly five feet in length, representing two human figures. At their side were four smaller etchings, which appeared to represent a turtle, a bird, a dog, and a fish.

A man walking his dog four days after the storm was the first to see the petroglyphs. He used his phone to take pictures, which was important because the carvings were only visible for a very short time. Lindsey and the kids never got to see them, but Mia Manu was able to bring a team to the spot and document the etchings. Archaeologists in the islands and around the world were thrilled by the discovery, which was considered culturally significant.

When Carlos heard about the petroglyphs, he decided to give Mia the *makau* that he'd found. It was going to the Bishop Museum in Honolulu.

A heat wave followed the storm, adding yet more evidence that the world's climate variations were calling the shots. The hot sun turned the mud into a rock-like crust that made the recovery and cleanup even more difficult. Chris and the kids stayed with the Kahale family for four days. Olivia was in charge of her brother and sister, and they volunteered at the Red Cross center, while Haku and Koa were assigned to a crew alongside Haku's father. There was heavy equipment everywhere, and the armed forces from the eleven military bases on the islands worked with the National Guard to assist in the effort. Almost all of the roads on the island would end up needing to be rebuilt or resurfaced. Miraculously, Chris's rental car was still parked where he had left it, but the Jeep had too much water and mud damage to be salvageable. The Crown Victoria sank to the ocean floor and was pulled out by the tide over a hundred yards where, over time, it become part of a reef.

Assured that Olivia was okay looking after her siblings, Chris toiled around the clock for American Security, crisscrossing Oʻahu, navigating closed highways and washed-out bridges to assess property damage and help people begin filing insurance claims. He had never felt so needed.

Other patients with greater medical issues delayed Lindsey's surgery. There were only so many doctors and so much surgical space, which meant she ended up spending a week at the Honolulu hospital. Every night Chris called, and all of their discussions were about the practical realities of day-to-day life. They never talked about how they felt, or what had happened between them. The combination of the storm alongside the trauma of Paul's return caused Lindsey to experience intense anxiety. Nighttime was the hardest. The storm had struck in the dark, and while the nurses gave her sedatives to sleep, the medication didn't stop dreams so vivid she woke up convinced that her husband was in the room. She saw him as the shadow in the open doorway. He became the motion behind the hospital's privacy curtain, which she knew logically was only a flutter caused by the building's cooling vent. It was Paul's footsteps she heard when anyone approached her bed. The person she saw in her nightmares didn't look like the Paul from the night of the storm. The man in her manic visions was Paul from before he disappeared. In her overly alert, frantic state, she believed he was coming to hurt her. He had deceived her. His children. His community. His appearance was synonymous with the storm that tore their world apart.

There were several practical things that Chris had helped Lindsey do during the time he lived in the red cottage, and at the top of that list was purchasing comprehensive property insurance, with a supplemental policy for wind-related storm damage. Since there was no bank loan on the motel, it hadn't been a requirement when she closed on the property. Lindsey had been in no hurry to write another check, but he'd kept after her, doing the paperwork and presenting her with a plan he claimed he found online from American Security. She argued that she wanted to use another company, explaining it hadn't been easy for her with American Security. But Chris persisted, and she finally gave in.

For a second time, American Security came to her rescue: When it was determined that the damage to the Mau Loa Motel was primarily from wind, not from the runaway mountainside flooding, Lindsey's policy covered the cost to rebuild the cottages and even contained a provision to pay her for the interruption of the motel's business. Another part of the policy called for interim housing, and Chris arranged for her family to be put up temporarily in hotel rooms at the Turtle Bay Resort, where one wing out of the three had survived with only minimal storm damage.

Lindsey and the kids were given vouchers to live as guests at the hotel until a rental house could be secured. But as soon as they arrived, Lindsey wanted to leave. This was the place she had kept her children from ever seeing, the posh resort with a swimming pool perched next to the ocean, three restaurants, and two golf courses. This was the life of their EnGenStor days, and even the kids felt uncomfortable and didn't want their school friends to know where they were staying.

But Olivia had to tell Haku and Koa, who were too much a part of her life now to be excluded from anything. After the storm, Haku's mother had stopped fighting her custody battle. She claimed she was just grateful he survived. He could make his own choices now. He had one more reason to want to stay at Kahuku High School.

Inexplicably, there were people arriving at the resort from the mainland daily on vacation: honeymooners with glazed looks, and even a convention of loud dentists. Anxious to sit in the sun and relax, they weren't unkind; they were simply reminders that life went on uninterrupted for some people, even when so many were suffering close by.

Chris took a hotel room in Honolulu near the airport, which was in the neighborhood where American Security had its main office. He was a senior-level company executive, and his ability to make decisions was invaluable to the overburdened local team. He lessened his shame over his deception of Lindsey by working around the clock. After two weeks filing damage reports and authorizing financial aid claims, he announced his plan to go home to Illinois. He was leaving on Saturday.

31

Lindsey's leg was in a cast and there was no car to drive to the airport even if she had been able to step on a gas pedal. It was a relief, since she didn't want to be an emotional wreck standing curbside in front of the United Airlines terminal. Chris had a late-afternoon flight but called to say he was coming out to Kahuku to say good-bye before he left. Despite their many phone conversations, they had seen each other only twice since the storm. She couldn't straighten out her feelings of anger, self-doubt, gratitude, and humiliation.

The restaurants at the resort felt too formal, so they ate lunch at Giovanni's Shrimp Truck, which until it could be rebuilt was now an actual truck, not a permanent roadside attraction on cinder blocks. The business had relocated to a spot near the entrance of Turtle Bay Resort, which was a hub for the cleanup effort in the area. One of the workers from the hotel ferried them out in a golf cart to the highway, where they sat together at a picnic table. Carl ordered a garlic hot dog, which came drenched in spicy sauce. Sena got scoops of white rice and macaroni salad. Lindsey, Chris, and Olivia ordered the lemon butter version of shrimp scampi. It was supposed to be a celebration, but as Carl noted, "Most going-away parties are just plain sad."

They spoke about the petroglyphs. They were all upset that they hadn't been able to see them in person. Sena made a drawing of the images, which she brought with her to show Chris. She told him, "These kinds of carvings of people have been seen in Hawai'i before.

But not many have been of animals. The turtle. And the dog and the bird and the fish. I like the bird best."

"I like the sea turtle," said Carl.

"I like the dog," Olivia added.

"I think the fish is great," Lindsey answered.

Sena nodded. "You did cross an ocean to come to America. And an ocean to bring us to Hawai'i."

Carl pointed to the human figures. "Chris, which one do you like?"

Chris appeared to concentrate on moving the rice on his plate around with his fork. He took a long sip from his drink, then adjusted his napkin. "I like them all."

It was Olivia who got up the nerve to ask the unspoken question. "So when do you think you'll be coming back to Hawai'i?"

He didn't answer. His eyes met Lindsey's and gave away nothing. Sena, using a plastic knife to mix her remaining rice and macaroni, let him know, "Mrs. Palakiko told us that a goal without a plan is just a wish."

"My wish is that you come back soon," added Carl.

Chris managed, after finally eating one of the pink shrimp dripping with yellowy sauce, to say only, "We'll see."

The wind was blowing hard from the north when it was time for Chris to leave to catch his flight. The kids stood with their mother in the enormous open-air lobby of the resort as Chris popped the trunk of his rental car, revealing a single piece of new luggage. He removed a dive mask and snorkel from a plastic bag, which he handed to Carl. Olivia was given a new iPad, and Sena a thick book featuring photographs of the wildlife of Hawai'i. He turned apologetically to Lindsey. "I couldn't find anything right to give you—"

She interrupted, "I don't need anything."

Olivia put her arm around Sena. "Come on, we said good-bye." She shot Carl a look, and he turned to walk away with his sisters, giving his mother and Chris the last moments alone together.

Lindsey leaned forward on her crutches, working hard to keep her balance. Chris watched as the kids disappeared from view, then he reached up and touched Lindsey's cheek. "So . . ."

Lindsey kept her eyes on her hands, holding the bars of her crutches. She had promised herself to keep her emotions in check, which was hard to do since the storm. But she couldn't stop herself from asking. "So what do we do about us?"

"We take some time to figure out our lives."

He leaned forward and kissed her, and her lips parted. They both pulled back at the same time and looked into each other's eyes in silence. The moment was interrupted by Sena, who had broken free from Olivia and sprinted back to the curb. She did what her mother couldn't do, or wouldn't. She pleaded, "Don't go. Don't leave us. We want you here."

It was impossible for Lindsey, on crutches, to pull Sena back. "Sena, please—"

Chris picked up the seven-year-old. "Sweetheart, I need to go home."

"Why can't this be home?" Sena was crying now. He'd only seen her cry during the storm. It brought back part of the longest night of his life.

He managed to answer, "I need to be by myself for now," as he set her down on the curb. He then moved to the driver's-side door.

Lindsey's voice cut through the noise of the lobby. "Aloha, Chris."

He looked back. "Aloha . . ."

Lindsey and Sena watched as his rental car pulled away. A gust of wind twirled the golden-yellow ribbon in Sena's hair as she whispered, "*Aloha* means both hello and good-bye."

Sitting in a beach chair with her leg propped up, Lindsey heard an old Beatles song, "Tomorrow Never Knows." When she and Paul had first met, he sang this same tune, his voice filled with energy and promise. Lindsey looked up into the luminous blue sky dotted with dozens and dozens of billowy cotton-ball clouds.

She wasn't a motel operator. She had trained in science. She liked teaching. She was good at it. With the insurance money, Lindsey didn't want to rebuild the motel. The Mau Loa was gone, and it would forever be only a memory.

She had other things to do with her life.

32

It took the storm of the century to give Olivia, Sena, and Carl (known by everyone, even his family, by that name now) a sense of belonging. Survivors have a bond, and the Hill kids were on the inside after Hurricane Neville. Sena mounted a campaign to have the school district adopt a chicken as a mascot. It was an absolute fact that many fowl had successfully weathered the catastrophic storm and were again thriving in the islands. Most of the students signed her petition, but a high school coach who believed his teams would suffer being named after chickens blocked her effort.

In the days and weeks and months of cleanup and construction, the whole community came together to rebuild. There was an endless roundelay of fundraiser breakfasts, car washes, walkathons, bake sales, and auctions. Every event was an opportunity to make new friends. Lindsey was a part of it all. She had on a Red Raiders T-shirt and was working in a food booth at the middle school fair when a rental sedan pulled into the parking lot. Lindsey's new best friend, Mia Manu, looked down at her phone to read a text message, and then left abruptly to get more paper towels.

Lindsey put two dozen hot dogs in the warmer and was setting buns into a row of fluted paper trays when she saw a man coming through the crowd. He'd given her no warning, but even with his face obscured from view, she knew, just by the way he walked.

Her first words to him were "So you came back."

"I did."

"You don't want to be all by yourself anymore?"

"No. I want to be all by myself with you."

"I come with three kids."

"That's the best part. You're a package deal."

"I've changed since you've been gone."

"So have I."

She came around the hot dog table and moved into his arms. He pulled her close and whispered in her hair, "Aloha."

After living in a temporary rental, Lindsey signed a settlement with American Security. But instead of rebuilding the cottages at the Mau Loa, she took that money and instead bought an older house on the hillside near Kahuku, on the other side of Kam Highway. It was a simple place with three small bedrooms and uneven tile floors but a wraparound veranda with magenta bougainvillea growing around the supports. The house needed work, but it had a partial view of the ocean, and pieces of blue could be seen through the greenery. Lindsey picked the property because it came with a guest cottage, which Chris used as his writing office.

Lindsey donated the six acres of land off Kamehameha Highway, near Malaekahana Valley Road, to the Hawai'i Land Trust. Their mission was 'āina protection, and the property was slated to become a state park. A commemoration was held to honor what would one day be a campground where any resident of the state of Hawai'i would always have camping fees waived. The governor arrived to be part of the ceremony, and Lindsey and Chris stood with the three Hill kids and Pearl and Rangi Kalama, back from their time in Nevada, to honor the land.

A rental car with a contract issued to Jeff Ross had been found submerged in water less than a mile from the Mau Loa property. It was towed back to Honolulu seventeen days after the storm. In the statements Lindsey and Chris made to the authorities immediately after the hurricane, they reported seeing an unknown man on the beach that night. They believed he had been swept away into the ocean with the debris from the mudslide.

Cadaver dogs were brought in that week, but they detected nothing in the area. For eight days the water was too murky, too filled with mud and debris, for divers to search the ocean. When they finally did, they weren't able to locate anyone.

No body was ever found.

ACKNOWLEDGMENTS

I owe gratitude and deepest thanks to my editor, Caroline Bleeke. She took my original manuscript and, in her supportive but firm way, got the best out of me. Every writer should have someone as perceptive and gracious as a collaborator.

I also want to acknowledge the whole team at Macmillan. Thank you to Bob Miller, Megan Lynch, Malati Chavali, Sydney Jeon, Christopher Smith, Erin Kibby, Emily Walters, Frances Sayers, Eva Diaz, Sue Warga, Donna Noetzel, Keith Hayes, Katy Robitzski, Emily Dyer, and Drew Kilman.

Thank you to Crystal Watanabe and Jovanna Brinck for helping me try to get the specifics of Hawai'i right.

Amy Berkower is a dream agent and a close friend, and without her I wouldn't have attempted to move from children's literature to a novel for adults. I'm thankful every day that she is in my life.

Genevieve Gagne-Hawes read multiple early drafts of this book and provided great insight and guidance, along with Cecilia de la Campa and Celeste Montaño, who also work at Writers House.

Thanks to my Tuesday Zoom book group—we started during Covid with *To the Lighthouse*, and almost three years later we are still going strong, analyzing novels. Thank you, Barbara, Christopher, Crystal, Ed, Gigi, Julia, Leta, Maria, Maya, Melissa, and Teddy. "Who wants to go first?"

To my early readers—Katie Kleinsasser, Ava Shamban, Anne Herlihy, Teri Mason, Naomi Kasa, Alisa Allen, Kimberly Clark, and

Calvin Sloan—I appreciate your help and willingness to read unfinished work.

Neal Allen shared his stories of his mother's quest so many years ago to buy a motel in Hawai'i, and Laura Saccio helped me with specifics of current hotel ownership.

I need to say thank you to Don Weisberg for believing in me and my writing.

And all love to Gary A. Rosen, husband, best friend, writer, artist, basketball fan, and lover of dogs, the Beatles, cheeseburgers, and grandchildren.

In the 1960's, my father was a field selection officer for the Peace Corps. For four years this work took him once a month from Oregon, where my family lived, to Hawai'i. My dad would return with fragrant flowers (bought at the airport in Hilo) in a box for my mother, and a new roll of film containing magical photos. As often is the case, a parent's attachment to a place is imprinted on a child. I loved the islands before I'd ever set foot there.

I owe much gratitude to the people we have gotten to know over the years in Hawai'i for their kindness.

ABOUT THE AUTHOR

Holly Goldberg Sloan is the author of seven books for young readers, which have been translated into twenty-seven languages. Her novel *Counting by 7s* was an E. B. White Read-Aloud Honor Award book and has sold more than a million copies. Also a noted feature film writer, Sloan wrote the Disney blockbuster *Angels in the Outfield* and was the first woman to direct a live-action film for Disney with *The Big Green*. The mother of two sons, Sloan lives with her husband in Santa Monica, California. *Pieces of Blue* is her debut novel for adults.

Recommend *Pieces of Blue* for your next book club!

Reading Group Guide available at

flatironbooks.com/reading-group-guides

Glossary of Boating & Nautical Terms

"I like good strong words that mean something . . ."

— Louisa May Alcott, Writer

s with any discipline, study, process, or way of life, each has its own special language made up of words and phrases particular to that specific area.

Speak with a mathematician and you'll get axioms, theorems, graphical notation, variables, and probability. Those who study the grammar of language will often converse about syntax, discuss preposition stranding, linguistic prescriptions, affixes, and inflections.

But those of us who have chosen this watery way, well, we have a rich, varied, and somewhat skewed special language for us to communicate with, one that often very few outside the boating lifestyle, can either fathom—pun very intended—or relate to. Good, makes us even more special.

Therefore, in order to get you kind of up to speed on some nautical terminology that will have you getting a bit of salt under you as you start out, here is a short list containing some of the more familiar definitions as well as other, rather esoteric interpretations, many from long gone days. Enjoy.

Aft: defined as being near or at the stern end of a boat or ship. For you married couples having a bit of a spat while underway—as inevitable as the sun rising in the east; and guys, take some good advice from someone who has been there, done that: swallow your pride and ask for directions when you need to—it's where you will go to get some distance between you and your offending mate.

Abaft: do not get this one mixed up with aft. Abaft means behind or going towards the stern end. It does get muddled sometimes but hang in there.

Abeam: when something is to one side, either port (left) or starboard (right) of the vessel. Running in a sea that is abeam means the waves are coming from one side and can be, unless you have a Seakeeper Gyrostabilization unit engaged, rather uncomfortable for those on board. This situation has been known to create very sudden and quite upsetting projectile vomiting. If so engaged in this activity, make sure you or the poor suffering person is poised with the wind at his or her back lest it really get nasty. You might want to have someone holding on to them as well while they finish trying to empty the contents of their stomachs. And that green or ashen tint to their faces will return as soon as they step back onto terra firma. The sooner the better. Guaranteed.

Arghh: while the spelling is questionable and has been seen in several iterations, this guttural utterance by pirates, while closing one eye if not already patched and lifting a tankard of grog high into the air, has most likely come into being from old Hollywood movies such as *Treasure Island* (the 1934 black and white version, starring Wallace Beery and a very young Jackie Cooper, or the 1950s version starring Robert Newton, the former of which, in my opinion, is far superior) and most recently, *The Pirates of The Caribbean* franchise. It can also be heard in bars from Down East to Down Home to Down Under on September 19 of each year, for that is the designated Talk Like A Pirate Day.

Aground: I guess you have this one figured out. To be avoided at all costs as you can incur lots of damage to your running gear if so equipped, the bottom of your boat, and either outboard or I/O lower units. A soft, controlled landing on a sandy beach is okay as long as you lift your outdrive or outboard engine up and out of the water previous to making contact. Inboard boaters, and those with pods, should not do this and instead, anchor out in deeper water and swim into the beach.

Amidship: Kind of what it looks like; in the middle of the ship or boat. Can be referred to as amidships, midship, or midships. Some of these are fairly intuitive. Arghh.

Astern: As well, don't get this one mixed up with either aft or abaft. This one means in the direction of the back, or stern, of the boat—aft, yes?—and can also be used to indicate something beyond the aft end of the boat—astern, yes?; as in "Why is that boat following astern of us? My wake wasn't that bad."

Athwart: The first known use of this word was sometime in the 1500s. As a preposition, it is defined as that position from side to side of; across. As an adverb, across from side to side. Clear now? Anyway, I always thought a thwart was a seat or plank that ran from one side to another in a rowboat. Of course when you go to stop, prevent, conspire against, impede, hinder, or obstruct someone from doing something, you "thwart" them? I mean, what does that have to do with a rowboat seat? And athwartships, making its debut in the mid-1700s, is defined as going across a ship, from side to side. Are we having fun yet?

Bar: Besides a sand or mud shoal as that found in some harbors, channels, and lakes, it is generally a place where, sooner or later, all of us mariners wind up. Bars can be found in all parts of the world whether at, near, or very far away from the water. Like hitting a bar with your boat, it's best to use good judgment sometimes when walking into one as well.

Beam: One of the important measurements by which boats are designed and built, it refers to the width as well as that direction lying at a right angle from the boat's centerline. When connected to the indefinite article "a," it turns into abeam. (See ABEAM, above)

Bearing: This is an important one because it denotes the visual direction one sees to an object whether it is another boat, a shore point, buoy, or anything else that may be important to your present and future position, track, route, or course. That's it. No quip here.

Bight: Take a long length of line—never call line on a boat, rope; it's not cool—and holding one end in your right hand and the other end in your left, let it hang between the two. That belly in the line is a bight. It's also a notch—notice the shape—in a shoreline as that found in the Norman Island Bight, in the British Virgin Islands for example. Here you will find the Pirates Bight Bar (See BAR, above) ashore, and for the far more adventurous, the legendary *William Thornton* floating bar and restaurant—known affectionately as the *Willy T* by those who have been so anointed—where many a brave soul, after imbibing well into the night, have stripped naked and jumped into the water off the old ship's decks. The reward? You get a special T-shirt that is known throughout the world. I break mine out every once and a while on birthdays and holidays.

Bilge: Surely, the one place on your boat where cleanliness is not only an issue, but can be an ongoing battle between the forces of good and evil. Being the lowest part of the boat within the hull, water, oil, spare change, screws, washers, bits of wire, old dirty rags, the keys and the LED flashlight you have been looking for, various tools such as pliers and vice grips, and a host of other objects and things that have gone missing can often accumulate here. Make this area a constant prime time endeavor to keep clean and debris free. Your bilge pump is located here and should it be unable to do its job, you could have some problems. Bilge water, usually described as an oily, smelly mix, is a good invective for you politically correct mariners who do not want to use a more familiar and saltier epithet when discussing whether or not someone is telling the truth.

Bitter End: The place where the anchor rode connects to the boat. When you are at the end of your line, you're said to be at the bitter end. It's up to you to plug that into any situation you can imagine where your back is up against the wall or between the proverbial rock and a hard place. And besides being one of New York City's oldest rock clubs, it is also yet another great British Virgin Islands destination. The Bitter End Yacht Club on Virgin Gorda is a favorite stop when island hopping in them thar parts.

Bow: The forward, pointy end of a boat. But what about catamarans, whose design can sometimes, take on a flatter appearance? Or a pontoon boat? Bow rider? Come on now. Let's move this along.

Bowline: Pronounced not as the pointy, forward end of a boat (See BOW, above) but more as in bo—like losing the second "o" in boo—and not line—but dropping the e, and winding up with something pronounced as lin—kind of a short, affectionate name for Linda—so in the end, it's "bo lin" or, if you like, a lazy way of saying bowling; bowlin' by dropping the g. Anyway, known as the "king of knots," it's a handy dandy one to know and show off your marlinspike seamanship skills with; that particular expertise where old time sailors mastered the art of knot tying and splicing among other handy chores while facing starvation, infection, disease, extreme boredom, whippings, vicious officers, unreasonable rules and regulations, storms, being attacked by war ships, and other pleasantries associated with being at sea in the days of wooden ships and iron men. It is a secure, strong knot that does not slip or bind. You tie it by reciting a rather well-known verse that goes something like this: here's the rabbit hole, and now the rabbit gets out of the hole where it then runs around a tree and then goes back into the hole, and voila! You've got yourself a bowline knot. Go to www.animatedknots.com to see how you can get this one done along with several others.

Bristol Fashion: It's what we boaters always strive for: having things aboard, as well as that about our person, always in shipshape condition, neat, clean, in the best working order, and always conforming to the high ideals of proper seamanship. Some think that includes wearing coral colored pants or shorts and a lime green, button-down, oxford shirt along with a pair of bummy, well worn boat shoes. Fashion indeed.

Bulkhead: Sometimes known as a wall in nautical terminology, they can define the shape and layout of compartments, living accommodations, engine rooms, and the like. Often, they can be watertight compartments as well. I've heard the term used interchangeably with knucklehead, when referring to someone who comes on your boat and just can't get the seafaring thing going.

Cast off: This is the moment of truth for many a new boater. The engine is running, everyone is aboard, and now you watch as each line attaching you to your dock is undone. Okay, you're ready to go. It's time.

Chafe: A rather familiar term denoting some abrasion is taking place. This can most readily be seen with dock lines and if yours begin to show signs of wear and tear, it may be time to replace them and get some protective chafe gear at your marina store. You also might want to watch out for those aboard who "chafe" you the wrong way. Trust me, this is far worse than minor wearing and can result in unnecessary confrontations while at sea. The outcome of this is never a good one.

Channel: That portion of a navigable seaway that is designated as a safe and proper passage. It is marked with buoys and should always be used paying careful attention to the known depth. Watch out for the careless, ignorant, slapdash, unaware mariner who drops the hook in the middle of a channel for a family outing including cooking on board and putting the rafts, floats, and snorkeling equipment to use. A dolt to be sure.

Course: The direction in which you are going. Of course.

Current: This is the horizontal movement of the water due to the rise and fall of the tide. For you river boaters, it is the normal flow of the water. Either way, this can be an important factor to consider when docking in areas where there is considerable current. You will quickly discover this when trying to back into your slip and you suddenly wind up t-boning a piling.

Dead ahead/Dead astern: Absolutely, well as close as can be, to being right ahead or right behind your boat. With some older boaters who have been around since the 1960s, it can be misconstrued as referring to a certain rock band of that era having a rather fervent following. These mariners will strain their eyes in that particular direction in hopes of perhaps sighting any member of the long gone group. Riding that train.

Dead reckoning: As long as we're on this "dead" track, this means of navigation relies on several factors including present course and speed to determine where you are and how long it's going to be to the next stop or place along the way—kind of, "I reckon we're about here." It's a bit more complicated than that, but you can get a fairly accurate read on your present position by referring to your GPS/chartplotter.

Deadrise: Last one. Promise. This is the distance from the bottom of the boat measured to the point of its widest beam. Usually expressed as an angle, it determines how "soft" a boat will ride and is a rather complex set of equations used by marine architects and designers involving the beam and other construction factors. And no, sorry to disappoint but those long gone band members are not coming back as zombie rock and rollers.

Ebb: Clear and simple; the outgoing tide.

Fathom: The nautical equivalent of six feet of depth. So when Jules Verne wrote *20,000 Leagues Under The Sea*, and one league is equal to 3.452 miles, where 5,280 feet is the measurement for one mile, and if a fathom is six feet—I was going to try to convert fathoms to leagues in some way but, getting a headache just thinking about it, decided not to bother—the story took place, at times, 69,040 miles beneath the sea? No it didn't. I just can't fathom it.

Fore/Aft: Going from the front of the boat to the back. Bow to stern. Stem to stern.

Handsomely: Yes, this is a nautical term and it refers to something done very well, with panache, and in the proper manner whilst aboard a boat, vessel, ship, or any of means of conveyance that is connected with the water. And it is absolutely politically correct to refer to a female skipper as doing something "handsomely," as in, "She docked that boat handsomely."

Head Seas: When the waves are coming right at you in the direction in which you are heading. With little ones, there is no problem. With sizeable ones, well you should have stayed at home. Always check the weather situation in your area before setting out. Trust me, you can always go boating another day and on days with big head seas, you will have wished you did.

Knot: If you must know: 1 knot (kt) = 1.15077945 miles per hour (mph).

LOA: Length Overall. An important measurement especially when you are checking into a marina that asks for it as they charge by the foot for your stay. It is supposed to be the distance from the tip of the bow (See BOW, above) to the end of the stern. But if you have an extension for your anchor, or a swim platform, you will most likely be engaged in a lively conversation as to the exact LOA of your particular vessel with the marina manager or dockmaster.

Nautical Mile: Again, if you must know: 6,076.12 feet. For you metrics, it's 1,852 meters.

PFD: The official terminology for a personal flotation device. Or, in the vernacular of everyday life, a life jacket.

Rafting Up: A common social event whereby two or more boats will tie up together, side by side and properly fended off at a calm anchorage, on a mooring ball, or even in a dock where there is enough space in order to hang out for the day or an afternoon. Usually involves a lot of eating and water sports.

Screw: Common term for a propeller. Can also be called a prop or a wheel. If you think this is bad, the Eskimo word for snow has some fifty different expressions.

Scuttlebutt: This is a good one and again, can be used when one wishes to be politically correct as it refers to gossip, dock talk, fish tales, rumors, idle chitchat, and other such hearsay and horse hockey that often travels between mariners. It takes its origin from days gone by when sailors would meet at the water cask, the so-named scuttlebutt, and shoot the breeze, perhaps to schedule the next failed mutiny.

Swell: These are long, rather large waves that do not crest but will roll along and are accompanied by many others. Depending on how big they are, this sea condition can be quite uncomfortable and will affect those aboard prone to motion sickness. Not swell at all.

V-hull: A hull shaped like a V? Yes? Well, what else would you call a hull shaped like a V? Certainly not a P.

Voyage: Refers to making a complete trip and not a passage, journey, tour, excursion, outing, jaunt, spree, or visit. And may all yours be safe ones.

▲ And may all yours be safe ones.

Index